Berkley Prime Crime titles by Melinda Wells

KILLER MOUSSE
DEATH TAKES THE CAKE
THE PROOF IS IN THE PUDDING

The Proof Is in the Pudding

Melinda Wells

BERKLEY PRIME CRIME, NEW YORK

THE BERKLEY PUBLISHING GROUP
Published by the Penguin Group
Penguin Group (USA) Inc.
375 Hudson Street, New York, New York 10014, USA

Penguin Group (Canada), 90 Eglinton Avenue East, Suite 700, Toronto, Ontario M4P 2Y3, Canada
(a division of Pearson Penguin Canada Inc.)
Penguin Books Ltd., 80 Strand, London WC2R 0RL, England
Penguin Group Ireland, 25 St. Stephen's Green, Dublin 2, Ireland (a division of Penguin Books Ltd.)
Penguin Group (Australia), 250 Camberwell Road, Camberwell, Victoria 3124, Australia
(a division of Pearson Australia Group Pty. Ltd.)
Penguin Books India Pvt. Ltd., 11 Community Centre, Panchsheel Park, New Delhi—110 017, India
Penguin Group (NZ), 67 Apollo Drive, Rosedale, North Shore 0632, New Zealand
(a division of Pearson New Zealand Ltd.)
Penguin Books (South Africa) (Pty.) Ltd., 24 Sturdee Avenue, Rosebank, Johannesburg 2196,
South Africa

Penguin Books Ltd., Registered Offices: 80 Strand, London WC2R 0RL, England

PUBLISHER'S NOTE: The recipes contained in this book are to be followed exactly as written.
The publisher is not responsible for your specific health or allergy needs that may require medical
supervision. The publisher is not responsible for any adverse reactions to the recipes contained in
this book.

THE PROOF IS IN THE PUDDING

A Berkley Prime Crime Book / published by arrangement with the author

PRINTING HISTORY
Berkley Prime Crime mass-market edition / February 2010

Copyright © 2010 by Melinda Wells.
Cover illustration by Ellen Weinstein.
Cover design by Lesley Worrell.
Interior text design by Laura K. Corless.

ISBN: 978-0-425-23311-5

BERKLEY® PRIME CRIME
Berkley Prime Crime Books are published by The Berkley Publishing Group,
a division of Penguin Group (USA) Inc.,
375 Hudson Street, New York, New York 10014.
BERKLEY® PRIME CRIME and the PRIME CRIME logo are trademarks of Penguin Group
(USA) Inc.

PRINTED IN THE UNITED STATES OF AMERICA

10 9 8 7 6 5 4 3 2 1

To Norman Knight

▪ Acknowledgments ▪

I am immensely grateful to the following:

Editor Kate Seaver, who inspired this series. Thank you for your suggestions, which made this a better book.

Priscilla Gilman and Morton Janklow. I'm so lucky to be represented by you! Thank you for your unwavering support, and for your guidance.

Claire Carmichael, a terrific novelist, and a brilliant instructor. Thanks to you, I'm a better writer than I would have been without your "athletic eyes."

D. Constantine Conte, mentor and treasured friend. I've learned so much from you.

Carole Moore Adams for creating the pudding in this book. (Her recipe is included.)

Penrose (Penny) Anderson, Fred Caruso, Penni Crenna, Seana Crenna, Linda Dano, Richard Fredricks, and Betty Pfouts for contributing some of their wonderful recipes. "Della" and I enjoyed making them!

To my "secret weapons," the test readers who see the early manuscripts and give me their invaluable reactions: Arthur

Abelson, Carole Moore Adams, Gina Anderson, Penrose Anderson, Christie Burton, Rosanne Kahil Bush, Jane Wylie Daley, Ira Fistell, Nancy Koppang, Judy Tathwell Hahn, Jaclyn Carmichael Palmer, and Anna Stramese.

Wayne Thompson of Colonial Heights, Virginia, who inspires me and makes me laugh.

Berry Gordy: Your place in my heart is, and always has been, unique.

1

"You're going to love what I've done to promote your show!" said Phil Logan, as soon as he finished gasping for air.

Phil, head of publicity for the Better Living Channel where I hosted *In the Kitchen with Della*, had spotted me walking with my black standard poodle, Tuffy, along the grassy area at the far end of the cable network's North Hollywood production facility. He'd waved wildly and burst into a sprint to join us.

Because the property was surrounded by a security fence, I'd let Tuffy off the leash. He had been sniffing happily at scented trails that no human could follow, but he stopped and looked up to watch Phil dashing toward us.

What with Phil's abundant mane of sandy hair and his unlined face, he looked a decade younger than his thirty-two years, but he wasn't in as good shape as his reedy frame suggested. By the time he covered the fifty yards that separated us he was red-faced with exertion and looked ready to collapse.

I reached out to steady him. "Lean forward, Phil. Put your hands on your knees and take deep breaths."

After a few gulps of cool air, his complexion lost its unnatural crimson shade and resumed its normal color, which was somewhere between parchment and the ivory keys on a piano. A workaholic, Phil Logan was definitely an indoor man.

He straightened up. "You're just what every guy needs—

a good-looking woman who's a nurturer. Unfortunately, my ex-wife was only good-looking." He shook off that rare moment of melancholy and aimed a triumphant grin at me. "Wait 'til you hear my news!"

I admired Phil's zeal for his job, but I had every reason to be wary when I saw that "I've got a great idea" expression on his face.

I said, "Your last stunt almost put a Los Angeles Dodger on the disabled list."

Two weeks ago, as a tie-in to the show I was preparing called "Cooking for the Ball Game," Phil convinced me to put on a Los Angeles Dodgers baseball uniform and be photographed "practicing" with the team.

I'd warned him that I wasn't even remotely athletic. "In school, the only team I was ever chosen for was Debating."

"You don't have to *play*," he'd said. "Just take a couple swings with the bat while my photographer gets some shots."

One of the new Dodger pitchers, a polite young man who told me that his mother loved my show, threw an easy one toward me. I swung. Miraculously, the bat connected with the ball, but cheers turned to gasps when the ball struck shortstop Tony Cuervo on the ankle. His yelp of pain brought the team's medic running. In addition to feeling awful that I'd hurt him, I had a horrible vision of the team's owner suing me for the player's astronomical salary.

Luckily, Cuervo wasn't injured. He claimed he just cried out because he was surprised "the girl" could hit a ball. The picture that landed on the sports page of the *Los Angeles Chronicle* showed me gaping in horror, like that Edvard Munch painting, *The Scream*.

Nicholas D'Martino, the man in my life, now calls me "Slugger."

The *Chronicle* headlined the story "Cook Conks Cuervo." Phil got it picked up by the wire services and published all over the country.

"National publicity," he said proudly.

"You mean national humiliation."

"They spelled your name right, *In the Kitchen with Della* got a bump up in the ratings, and people all over the country who only read the Sports section now know about you."

In a gesture of fondness, Tuffy leaned against Phil's thigh. Phil responded by reaching down to give him an ear scratch, but at that moment Tuffy spotted a squirrel a few yards away and took off after it. Tuffy was five years old, and try though he might, had never caught a squirrel. I presumed that by now he gave chase just for the exercise.

Watching Tuffy, Phil said, "Your big guy gets fan mail. My secretary answers it for him, on paw print stationery I had made."

"Isn't that going a little far? Too cutesy?"

"It's good public relations," Phil said. "Speaking of which, our crazy Dodgers story opened the door to this new opportunity, which I grabbed like a mongoose grabs . . . whatever they grab."

"Cobras," I said.

Phil's lips retracted in a grimace. "I hate snakes. Sorry I brought it up."

"I'm almost afraid to ask, but what opportunity are you talking about?"

The happy grin returned. "You've heard about the Celebrity Cook-Off Charity Gala at the Olympia Grand Hotel this Wednesday night."

"Of course. All the entertainment news reporters have talked about it. But the celebrities who'll be participating are major movie and TV stars. I'm not in that league."

"True," Phil said, "but what I got you is even better. There'll be twenty celebs, but you're going to be one of only three *judges*."

"How can that be? Wednesday is the day after tomorrow. The names of the judges were announced weeks ago."

"Ahhhh, but one of them had to withdraw this morning." Phil's tone was positively gleeful. "It's the retired chef who runs that wildlife sanctuary north of Santa Barbara. One of his endangered species bit him."

"That's terrible! Is he all right?"

Phil gave my question a dismissive shrug. "He just got a scratch on that big red drinker's nose of his, but he's acting like he'll need major plastic surgery before he can appear in public again. Frankly, I think he wants to use this as an excuse to have some work done. In a few weeks he'll emerge from seclusion looking—as they say—*rested*. Anyway, the point is that as soon as I heard he'd backed out of judging, I rushed over to the charity's PR office and offered you as a substitute. You're still hot from the Tony Cuervo story, so they said yes. I called my secretary, dictated the press release announcement over the phone, and had her do a blast e-mail to all the outlets."

I stared at Phil in astonishment. "You told everybody I'd do it before you asked me?"

"Well, yeah. The national story I sent out doesn't just mention your TV show, I also promoted that mail-order fudge business you started up—Della's Sweet Dreams. A second release went out to the local outlets that also mentions you teach cooking classes in Santa Monica."

Two vertical frown lines suddenly appeared between Phil's eyebrows. "Jeez, this came up so fast I forgot to check. You still teach cooking, don't you?"

"Yes, on weekends."

"That's a relief." Phil's face relaxed, but he didn't look happy. "Not making sure about the classes first—that was careless of me. I pride myself on the fact that anyone can take a Phil Logan press release right to the nearest bank."

Take a press release to the bank . . . Hearing another of

those semi-metaphors I'd come to think of as Logan-isms made me smile with affection for Phil.

Seven months ago Mickey Jordan, owner of the Better Living Channel, out of desperation, had hired me as a replacement host. The desperation was both his and mine. He'd fired the previous host and had to fill vacant time on his cable network, and I was on the verge of drowning in debt trying to keep my little cooking school going. Now I was probably on the second-lowest rung of the "celebrity ladder," but the fact that I was known to anyone at all beyond my immediate circle of family and friends was because of Phil Logan's passion for his work.

Phil pulled a folded sheet of paper from his inside jacket pocket and handed it to me. "Details about what criteria you're supposed to use for judging, and how many points you can give any particular dish. When you show up Wednesday night you'll each be given your judging cards and a clipboard. Hey, this'll be the easiest gig in the world. All you'll have to do is walk around in an evening gown and watch other people cook."

Perhaps remembering my notorious lack of interest in fashion, his eyes narrowed and he frowned at me. "Do you have an evening gown?"

"I used to . . . but it's been years since—"

"Never mind. I know some designers—I'll get you a loaner. Try not to spill anything on it."

Phil started to leave, but stopped after taking a single step. When he turned back to me I saw an expression on his face that I'd never seen before: embarrassment.

"Look," he said, glancing down at the ground, "you know by now that I don't get involved in other people's sex lives, but I think in this case a kind of warning is necessary."

Instantly on the alert against criticism of my relationship with Nicholas D'Martino, I bristled. "Hold it. We're not going to discuss my personal life—"

His head came up and he met my eyes. "Not *you*—it's your friend I'm worried about."

Nicholas? "Oh, Phil, what in the world do you think I could do to a grown man?"

That produced a sly little smile. "I'll bet you could do plenty, and I'm sure ol' Nick wouldn't mind a bit, but that's not what I mean."

"Then what are you talking about? Do I need a translator?"

I saw comprehension dawn in Phil's eyes. "You don't know, do you?"

"Apparently not."

"It's your fudge partner, Eileen O'Hara. I know she's kind of your unofficial daughter, but do you know who she's been having a *thing* with?"

"No."

"It's one of your fellow Celebrity Cook-Off judges, Keith Ingram. Della, when it comes to women—especially the kind that are young and haven't been around much like your Eileen—this is a bad dude."

I'd met Keith Ingram once, four months ago, when he interviewed Eileen and me in order to do a story in his syndicated food column about our just-launched mail-order sweets business. "I think you're mistaken, about her being involved with him," I said. "Since the day the article about us came out she's never mentioned him to me."

"Do you think she tells you everything?"

She used to, when I wasn't so busy . . .

"The piece he wrote was so over-the-top favorable, especially to Eileen—'the beautiful UCLA business major with a great idea'—I suspected he had the hots for her," Phil said, "but then I forgot about it."

"How do you know they're seeing each other?"

"I hear things . . . which leads me to the reason I brought this up. I know you're a mother figure to her. She's going to need you to be there for her when he dumps her."

"But if he and Eileen actually are involved, what makes you think—"

"When I was at the charity's PR office signing you up for the Cook-Off gig, I found out Ingram's getting it on with that flaky heiress who's the tabloids' flavor-of-the-month."

"Tina Long?"

"That's the one. A few years ago she couldn't make the grades to graduate from a fancy private high school, so her father bought it. Suddenly Tina's the co-valedictorian. Poppa Long hired a novelist to write her speech for her, but the guy forgot to tell her how to pronounce some of the words."

Photographs that I'd seen of Tina Long on gossip magazine covers flashed into my mind. She was a generically pretty girl with blonde hair arranged in a dizzying number of styles, but beneath each new coif there was always the same vapid expression on her face.

Phil's voice interrupted my thoughts. "Ingram's making money with his column and his TV guest shots, but he likes to live big. You know how I got him to do the column on your business?"

In a tone full of irony, I said, "Because we make *really* good fudge?"

He snorted. "I wish that's what it took. I had to arrange a free trip to New York for him on Warner Brothers's private jet."

"Phil, I know you mean well, but I'm not comfortable talking about Eileen behind her back." Sensing that it was getting late, I checked my watch. "It's four o'clock. In a few minutes I've got to start taping the last of today's three shows." I whistled for Tuffy. He looked up from his explorations and came trotting back toward me.

Phil escorted us to the door to the studio and opened it.

I said good-bye and was about to go inside, but the touch of his hand on my arm stopped me.

"What is it, Phil?"

"Publicity is a very *personal* job," he said. "And I usually love it. Seven-day weeks, twenty-hour days—I thrive
on building or enhancing careers. But we try to protect our
clients, too. The people I work with are family to me. Better, really, because we're close by choice, not an accident of
blood. I told you about Ingram because I feel an obligation
not to let you get blindsided. Eileen's going to be hurt, but
the facts are that her father is a cop. Tina Long's father is a
billionaire, and she's his only child. You do the math."

2

I tried to put worry about Eileen aside in order to concentrate on the show I was about to tape, but she had been entrusted to me for most of her life, and my maternal feelings for her were strong. I had never been blessed with a biological child, and thus Eileen O'Hara had been my only shot at motherhood. But there was nothing I could do for Eileen at this moment, and I had a professional obligation to fulfill.

After giving a quick touch-up to my TV makeup in the tiny backstage dressing room, I led Tuffy out onto the studio's TV kitchen set. He trotted over to his padded dog bed next to the refrigerator and settled down to watch me cook for the cameras.

We should have finished for the day an hour ago, but technical glitches during the first two shows had put us behind. Unless this one went off smoothly, we'd run into the time scheduled for taping the auto repair show, *Car Guy*.

The repair shop's standing set was next to mine at the west end of the cable network's no-frills broadcast studios. No one wanted to upset the temperamental mechanic who'd had his name changed legally to Car Guy. Car, as we called him, had turned a surly on-air disposition and a penchant for smashing things when agitated into the highest rated program on the BLC. Although no one mentioned it when Car was around, according to the latest figures, my show was now running a close second to his.

I looked around my kitchen set. Everything seemed to be ready. The lights had been reset and positioned according to the dishes I would be making in this episode. A quick survey of the pantry cabinet and the refrigerator showed me the stagehands had restocked them from the list of items I'd need for this show. All I had to do was not ruin the dishes.

In the glass-enclosed control booth above me, I saw director Quinn Tanner's knife-blade-thin body leaning over the shoulder of the board engineer. As she spoke to him, I saw him respond with an affirmative nod. She straightened, pushed a few strands of long black hair back from her pale face, and gazed down at me. Through my earpiece, I heard her British accent and her habitually frosty tone. "Take your position, Della."

Hoping a little humor would warm her up, I said, "When the police arrest bad guys they tell them 'assume the position' and they have to spread their arms and legs for a pat-down."

That got a chuckle out of Ernie Ramirez, operating Camera One, and a smile from Jada Powell, piloting Camera Two. There were a few seconds of heavy silence from the director's booth until Quinn said, "I don't think that will be necessary—unless, of course, you're carrying a concealed spatula."

It wasn't much of a joke, but it was the first I'd ever heard her make, so I laughed.

"Enough frivolity," she said. "Move one meter to the right, Della. Let's get through this taping before global warming kills us all."

I moved a step to the right. Through my earpiece, I heard Quinn recite her beginning-of-show routine. "Theme music up . . . Opening credits . . . Five seconds . . . four . . . three . . . two . . ."

I smiled at Camera One just as the red light came on above the lens. "Hi, everybody, I'm Della Carmichael. Welcome to *In the Kitchen with Della*. As anybody who's ever watched me knows, I'm not a trained chef, but I love to create in the kitchen. I make the kind of meals anybody can make with a little encouragement, and with ingredients you can find just about anywhere. I always do my own shopping because I never know when I'll spot something—preferably on sale—that inspires a new dish. It happened again yesterday. A fireman with a full shopping cart got into the checkout line behind me at the supermarket. I knew he was a fireman because he was wearing the shirt and boots and the heavy yellow pants, with a radiophone hooked to his belt. The only things missing were the coat and hat and the big red fire engine outside.

"I asked him if he was shopping for his firehouse, and he said yes, and that it was his turn to cook. I asked him what kind of things he prepared for his teammates, and he said, 'Whatever can be made in under forty-five minutes and can be reheated if we get a call out.' That conversation inspired the theme of today's show: 'Food That's Fast and Durable.'"

I moved around the set, describing what I was doing as I collected a box of pasta and jars of prepared sauce from the pantry, and a big bag of broccoli florets from the freezer. "First up is a main dish that has three ingredients and requires only four steps to make: Linguine Alfredo with Broccoli."

I filled a pasta pot with water and turned the flame up high to bring it to a boil quickly. "I'm making linguine today because sixteen-ounce boxes were on sale, four for three dollars. An irresistible price. There was also a special on jars of Bertolli Alfredo Sauce. If you watch the show regularly, you've probably seen me make my own Alfredo sauce, but frankly—and it's a little embarrassing to admit—this brand is even better than mine. In addition to Linguine Alfredo with Broccoli being delicious and inexpensive, you can make it in just eleven minutes: two minutes for the pasta water to come to a boil and nine minutes to cook the linguine and broccoli."

While waiting for the water to bubble, I opened the sauce, poured it into a pot, and turned the burner below it on low.

"My Grandma Nell taught me to cook. I call it going to the University of Nellie Campbell. She was one gutsy gal—came to America from Scotland all by herself when she was fourteen years old. A cousin in San Francisco sponsored her immigration, but she had to support herself. The only job she could get was as a kitchen maid in the home of a wealthy family. After a few years of watching and helping, she succeeded the old cook when the woman retired. When Grandma Nell herself retired, she came to live with us."

The pasta water was ready. I indicated the pot. "We've got a nice, roiling boil going here." I demonstrated as I talked. "In goes a toss of salt, and now the box of linguine." Picking up a slotted spoon, I said, "Give the pasta a couple of stirs to keep the strands from sticking together."

In my ear, Quinn started the countdown to the commercial break. I said to the camera, "I'll be back in a couple of minutes and then we'll start making a bright and tangy bread salad with fresh vegetables and an olive oil–based dressing that's both delicious and also good for your hair and complexion. Then we'll do the last two parts in our four-step main course. Don't worry if you can't write down the instructions. You'll find the recipes on the Web site: www.DellaCooks.com."

While the cameras were off, I rinsed out and refilled Tuffy's water bowl. Because it was hot under the TV lights, I added a few ice cubes to it. Tuffy fished one out and crunched on it happily.

When we were taping again, the overhead camera took a close-up of the pasta in the boiling water.

"The pasta's been cooking for almost five of the nine minutes it needs," I said. "Now I'm pouring the contents of a twenty-eight-ounce bag of frozen broccoli into the water with the linguine. In four more minutes, they'll be ready for the final step."

While the pasta and broccoli cooked together, I started on the bread salad by tearing a loaf of Italian bread into bite-size chunks. I told the camera, "Bread salad is called Panzanella by the Italians. I don't know if you realize it, but bread has been around for thousands of years. Loaves were found in ancient Egyptian tombs, along with jugs of wine. I guess the loyal subjects didn't want their Pharaoh du jour waking up and being hungry and thirsty. Or lonely. Some rulers had wives or girlfriends put into the tombs with them. That thought gives a whole new meaning to the poem that goes 'A loaf of bread, a jug of wine, and *thou*.' " I gave an exaggerated shudder. "Don't worry—I'm not going to tell you so much about the history of bread that you'll change the channel."

As though he'd been given a cue, Tuffy got up from his bed and came over to the preparation counter to watch me. Camera Two's light clicked on and Jada Powell moved in to catch Tuffy's cocked head and quizzical expression.

I looked down at Tuffy, acknowledged him with a "Hi, Tuff," and turned back to the camera to chat about food as I cut up tomatoes, and cucumbers, red onion, a clove of garlic, and made little confetti-like strips out of rolled up leaves of fresh basil.

As soon as the linguine and broccoli finished boiling, I ladled out one cup of the liquid and put it into an empty jar of Alfredo sauce before I drained the linguine.

Pouring the pasta and broccoli into the pot of warm Alfredo sauce, I said, "As you saw, I saved a cup of the nice starchy pasta water. If you need to reheat this dish, or heat the leftovers next day, you'll want to add a little of this water to thin out the sauce.

"By the way, you don't have to be a vegetarian to enjoy vegetarian meals. I like meat and chicken and fish, but I enjoy pasta and veggies so much that I eat like this two or three times a week. Varying your meals—veg and non-veg—is healthy, and it stretches the food budget, too."

Quinn's voice in my ear told me it was time for another series of commercials.

I said to the camera, "I've got to take a little break, but I'll keep working on the salad, and when we come back we'll mix up the dressing. Then we'll finish off this meal by making the world's easiest dessert: a fresh fruit and store-bought sherbet parfait." I held up a tall crystal parfait glass. "Isn't this pretty? I bought a set of them for six dollars at a yard sale. Anyway, after you have a main dish with a creamy sauce like Alfredo, I don't think anything tastes better than fresh fruit sherbet. And it looks so pretty, too.

"Now if the phone rings and it's someone you can't get off the line for half an hour, or if the plumber finally shows up to fix that leak, don't worry about missing these instructions. If you're just tuning into the show today, this is a reminder that they're all on the Web site: www.DellaCooks .com."

■   ■   ■

The show went off without technical problems, and I didn't drop anything, or cut myself while chopping. In a new personal best, we finished ten minutes ahead of schedule.

As soon as Quinn called, "That's it," I thanked the crew and performed the usual ritual of setting out plates, paper napkins, and cutlery, and invited them to help themselves to what I'd made.

I didn't stay to eat with them this time because I was eager to get home to talk to Eileen.

3

During weekdays, six PM is rush hour. If I were coming from my home in Santa Monica across Beverly Glen Canyon and going into North Hollywood where the Better Living Channel's studio was located, it would have taken me at least an hour and a half—unless there'd been a car crash somewhere in the narrow cut in the mountain that separated Los Angeles and its west side suburbs from the San Fernando Valley. In that event, I'd be stuck in "gridlock hell" for anywhere from an extra half hour to the start of the next millennium.

But I was lucky this evening because I was going in the opposite direction from the seemingly endless line of cars inching their way into the valley. Traveling south from Ventura Boulevard toward Sunset Boulevard, I found my side of the road was virtually empty. I zipped along at a speed drivers on the other side of the road I imagined could only watch with longing.

Normally, I didn't speed through the canyon, but tonight I wanted to get home to see Eileen. We'd both been so busy lately that we hadn't spent much time together, even though she had lived in my house most of the time for the last fifteen of her twenty-one years. When my husband, Mack, was alive, we called her our "spiritual daughter." We'd not managed to have children of our own. Eileen called us by the honoraria "Aunt Del" and "Uncle Mack."

John O'Hara, Eileen's father, had been Mack's LAPD partner until Mack died. (I hated the phrase "passed away"; to me, it diminished the enormity of the loss.) John, who had risen to the rank of lieutenant, was still there, still dedicated, if increasingly disillusioned with the politicians and their meddling with the force.

Eileen's mother, Shannon, one of my two closest female friends, had struggled with paranoid schizophrenia for the past twenty years. She'd had to be hospitalized when medications stopped working, or when she'd ceased taking them because, she said, they made her gain weight. Her current psychiatrist had devised a combination of medications without that side effect and so she was taking them as scheduled. For the past few months Shannon had been more like the woman I first knew than she had been for years. That made all of us who loved her happy.

I was thinking about Shannon as I drove, because I wondered if Eileen had told her mother about her relationship with Keith Ingram. It seemed strange that my unofficial daughter hadn't told *me*. She'd confided when she lost her virginity during her freshman year at UCLA, and I'd held her hand through her various romantic ups and downs since then. But I didn't know anything about her involvement with Ingram—assuming that Phil had the right information. I had to admit that he usually did.

When I reached my little two-bedroom cottage in the 500 block of Ninth Street in Santa Monica and steered my Jeep into the driveway, I saw that Eileen's slightly battered, old red VW wasn't there.

I unhooked Tuffy from his safety harness, let him out of the vehicle, and took him for a short stroll before we went into the house. He'd had a major walk around the studio lot before we'd left North Hollywood and he'd relieved himself thoroughly. This little jaunt was just a stretch-of-the-legs for both of us.

My small gray and gold calico cat, Emma, met Tuffy and me at the front door. After the two four-footed friends touched noses, Emma looked up at me and meowed a greeting. Or perhaps it was a rebuke—I'd been away longer today than usual.

On the hall table, which was our traditional message center, I found a note from Eileen, telling me that she'd gone out to dinner with friends and not to wait up for her.

Friends? I wondered. *Or with one special friend?*

In the kitchen, as I fed Tuffy and Emma and washed out and refilled their water dishes, I thought about Eileen. I couldn't love her more if she really were my daughter, but did that give me the right to pry into her private life? She was twenty-one years old; in a few weeks she'd be graduating from UCLA. She had taken the fact that I used to make fudge to give as Christmas presents when I was in college and too poor to buy gifts and translated that into the concept for our mail-order and on-site fudge business. She was there at our Della's Sweet Dreams store and factory in Hollywood every day, overseeing the project that she'd talked Mickey Jordan, owner of the Better Living Channel, into financing for us. Eileen O'Hara was an intelligent, responsible grown-up.

But I still worried about her as though she were ten years old.

The ringing of the phone jarred me out of my thoughts. I picked up the receiver and heard the voice of Liddy Marshall, my other closest female friend.

She was speaking in a rush of excitement. "I bought five tickets!"

"Tickets to what?"

"To the Celebrity Cook-Off, of course! You're going to be a judge."

"Liddy, I just found out about that a couple of hours ago. How in the world did you know?"

"It was in the entertainment report on the four o'clock news. I phoned for the tickets right away. Thank heavens they still had some left."

"But they cost five hundred dollars *apiece*."

"It's deductible," she said. "And it's for a good cause. The Healthy Life Fund does research into children's diseases."

Liddy Marshall and her husband, Bill, a successful Beverly Hills dentist, were well-off financially, and very generous, but I couldn't understand why she'd buy five tickets to watch a bunch of celebrities cook their favorite dishes in the middle of a hotel ballroom. I asked her about that.

"I told you—it's because you're one of the judges. And it's black tie. People don't dress up enough anymore. If you look at those wonderful old movies on TV—everybody wore evening gowns and tuxedos just to go out to a nice restaurant for dinner. Oh, Shannon and John are going with us. Eileen, too. Won't this be fun?"

I wondered . . . But then I told myself I was being silly. Liddy and Bill Marshall were delightful company. So was Shannon, now that she was on the right medication. It probably would be an enjoyable evening.

But one thing surprised me. "Did John actually agree to put on black tie to watch celebrities cook?"

"He tried to refuse, but Shannon persuaded him." Liddy laughed. "He's probably hoping he'll get called into work on a murder case."

"I saw the list of celebrities—at least two of them I know John has arrested in the past."

Liddy giggled with amusement. "Maybe one of them will break a law Wednesday night. I've never seen Big John be a cop. This gala could be even more fun than I expect."

"It's going to be work for me, studying what's happening at all of the stoves and voting for a winner, but I'll enjoy having you all there."

We were about to say good night when Liddy had a new thought: "What are you going to wear?"

"Phil Logan is going to borrow something from a designer for me."

That impressed Liddy. "Ohhhh, just like the stars do! For a straight guy, Phil has really good taste."

In a joking tone, I said, "Meaning that I don't have good taste?"

"Of course you do—in food and friends. But when it comes to clothes . . . I mean, you look nice in those sweaters and skirts and jackets you like to wear, but you're not exactly on the cutting edge of fashion. Just put yourself in Phil's hands. That's settled. Now, what are you doing tonight? Are you seeing that gorgeous Italian?"

"Nicholas is Sicilian. No, he's up in northern California. What I'm going to do when we hang up is make myself some scrambled eggs for supper, organize the rest of my week, then take a warm, foamy bath and collapse into bed."

■ ■ ■

By the time I'd eaten, made out the marketing lists for the classes I would be teaching this weekend, and gone over the recipes I'd be making on camera for Thursday night's weekly live broadcast of *In the Kitchen with Della*—rehearsing the movements and timing them in my head—it was nearly eleven o'clock.

As soon as I put aside my pen and pad to stretch the kinks out of my shoulders, Tuffy got up from where he'd been dozing by the back door and came over to stand beside me. He looked at me with eager expectation in his bright black eyes and wagged his hindquarters vigorously.

I scratched him below his ears. "Oh, Tuff, I would recognize you if you were in the middle of a million black poodles. And yes, I know what time it is." I took his leash down from its peg on the wall and hooked it to his collar.

I gave Tuffy an especially long pre-bedtime walk through the neighborhood, both because I knew how much he enjoyed his explorations and because I needed a big dose of fresh, cool air. Now that I'd finished my work, my mind came back to concern about Eileen.

Tuffy and I had been strolling for more than half an

hour, and were almost back to the house, when the cell phone in my pocket rang. I fished it out. "Hello."

"Hi, Slugger." It was Nicholas D'Martino.

"Is this an obscene phone call?"

"Absolutely." And he proceeded to whisper a few sentences that started to make me jittery.

"Stop. That's enough, unless you're in your car on your way over here."

He sighed. "I wish. But I'm still up in Carmel on the Lopez murder story. Did you know that you're speaking to the world's most intrepid reporter?"

"*Lois Lane?* Gosh, your voice is deeper than I'd expected."

"Do you want to hear about my triumph or not?"

"Of course I do."

Nicholas was usually so cool when he talked about his work, but tonight I heard pride in his voice. "I broke the case. The local cops are mad as hell because I turned up evidence that they missed, but it enabled them to arrest the killer."

"Congratulations. That's wonderful. Tell me all."

"You'll read about it in tomorrow's *Chronicle*. Front page, above the fold. I've got a few days of follow-up here, but I'll be back Friday. You available that night for dinner and . . . whatever?"

I smiled, imagining the *whatever*. "I'm available. Your place or mine?"

"Mine. I'm going to make dinner for you. Actually, it'll be takeout, but I'll heat it up. Afterward, I'm planning to broaden your education."

"Hmmmm. Sounds interesting."

"Bring money," he said.

Money? That jolted me out of my erotic fantasy. "What are you talking about?"

"Coins: nickels, dimes, quarters. I'm going to teach you to play gin rummy."

"I already know how," I said. "But do we have to play for money?"

"What do you want to play for?"

"How about . . . the winner has to make passionate love to the loser? Or vice versa."

He laughed. "You make me want to come home right now, but I've got to be intrepid for a while longer."

We were about to say good night when I thought of something to ask him. "Keith Ingram, the food critic? His column runs in the *Chronicle*. Do you know him?"

"Sure. We're not close buddies, but we work out at the same gym. We've watched some fights together, and gone on a couple of the paper's Super Bowl trips."

"What kind of a person is Ingram?"

"He's an okay guy. Pays the check when it's his turn. Why?"

"It may be that Eileen has become involved with him."

"Whoa!" Nicholas's tone abruptly changed from casual to sharp. "No. Not good. Eileen's a sweet kid. When it comes to women, Ingram is bad news. If she's seeing him, talk her out of it before she gets hurt."

■ ■ ■

Eileen hadn't come home by the time I went to bed. I fell into a restless sleep, and a few minutes after two in the morning I woke up. The house was silent. I got out of bed and went down the hall to listen at Eileen's closed door. I leaned in close and strained to hear, but I couldn't detect any sound from within. Very gently, I turned the knob and peeked inside.

Her lights were off, but there was just enough illumination from the moonlight coming through the filmy curtains that I could see her bed had not been slept in.

Suddenly, the piercing trill of a ringing phone shattered the stillness in the house.

It was my bedroom phone.

I felt a lurch in my chest and my heart began to pound. Calls that come at two o'clock in the morning are not likely to bring good news. I hurried back down the hall to my own room and grabbed the receiver.

"Aunt Del?" It was Eileen. She was sobbing. "I tried to drive, but the car . . . Oh, Aunt Del, can you come and pick me up?"

I forced myself to sound calm. "Honey, are you all right? Have you been in an accident?"

It took a few choked-back sobs before she was able to speak. "No accident. But the car won't move, and I don't have my wallet—oh, I'm such an idiot!" She began to cry again.

"Eileen, let's calm down. Take some slow, deep breaths." When I heard her doing it, I said, "That's it. Good. Now tell me where you are."

She did. I was surprised because it wasn't an area of Los Angeles where any of her friends that I knew lived.

"Stay in the car with the doors locked," I said. "I'm on my way."

4

Eileen's twelve-year-old red Volkswagen with the UCLA sticker was parked about a mile north of the Sunset Strip, on the 2100 block of Laurel Canyon Boulevard.

Narrow, twisty Laurel Canyon is a rustic enclave of free spirits, many of them in the music business, but in recent years affluent professionals have joined the performing types by migrating to this woodsy oasis in the center of Los Angeles.

I was able to spot Eileen's car only because she'd told me to look to the right when I got to the sign on my left that said Kirkwood. She had pulled up parallel to a small dry cleaner and laundry establishment, which was just a few yards below the Canyon Country Store, a popular landmark at the corner of Laurel Canyon Boulevard and Kirkwood Drive.

As I turned right into a shallow parking area, my headlights swept Eileen's car. I saw the outline of her head, bent over the steering wheel. She looked up, blinked in the glare, and gave a weak little wave.

I steered the Jeep to a stop just ahead of her car and got out. Simultaneously, Eileen emerged from her little VW and came toward me. In the spill from the nearby streetlight I saw that her long blonde hair, usually so carefully brushed, was a disheveled mess. Her eyes were red and swollen, but she had stopped crying.

"Tell me what's happened."

"The car died," she said. "I don't know what the matter

is, and I couldn't call Triple A because I forgot my purse back at . . . I ran out so fast that—oh, Aunt Del, I've been such a stupid idiot!"

I put my arms around her in a comforting hug, then stepped back so she'd have to look at me. "Let's take care of the simple problem first," I said. "What's the matter with your car?"

"I don't know. It was fine, but then I stopped here for a few minutes—I was so upset I could barely see. After a little while, when I turned the key again, the car made a kind of *grrrrr* sound, but it wouldn't move."

"Maybe it's just flooded. Let me try to start it."

Eileen handed me her key, but I didn't have any better luck. The car wasn't going to move for either of us. In defeat, I climbed out of the VW and reached into the pocket of the jacket I'd thrown on over the Bruce Lee T-shirt I'd been sleeping in and my nearest pair of sweatpants. I removed my cell phone and my wallet, extracted my Auto Club card, and punched in the number for emergency roadside service.

When the dispatcher answered, I gave her my name and club card number, told her where I was. From memory, I recited the make, model, and plate number of Eileen's car.

"The car won't start," I said. "It might be a dead battery, but it could be something that requires a tow, so would you send a vehicle capable of towing?"

The voice on the other end agreed, took my cell phone number, and said that one of their trucks would be at my location within thirty minutes.

I thanked her, disconnected, and repeated the information to Eileen. "Now, we've got some time alone before road service arrives. Let's sit in the Jeep and you tell me what's upset you so."

We settled into the front seats. Eileen stared through the windshield into the darkness. The light from the streetlamp molded her features as artfully as though it was the work of a great cinematographer. I couldn't help marveling at her beauty. She had her mother's large eyes and nicely sculpted cheekbones, and her father's strong chin. She had a streak of John O'Hara's stubbornness, too, but she didn't have his toughness, and that left her as vulnerable as a chick just out of its shell.

"I thought he was so wonderful," Eileen said. "He's the most exciting man I've ever met."

Although I was sure I already knew, I asked, "Who?"

She expelled a breath. "Keith Ingram."

"Does he live near here? Is that why you're in Laurel Canyon?"

She turned partway around in the passenger seat and gestured toward a tiny road just behind us, rising into the hills.

"Rothdell Terrace. His house is about a hundred yards up there—a miniature Swiss chalet." In a tone full of irony, she said, "You can't see his place from here, but can you make out that brown house just above us? The one facing out toward Laurel Canyon Boulevard?"

Following her line of sight, I stared into the darkness. "Do you mean the one with the bell in the top window?"

She nodded. "Jim Morrison lived there. 8021 Rothdell Terrace. Keith's house is several above Morrison's. He has a framed article about the Doors in his den because in it one of them says that Rothdell Terrace is the 'Love Street' in their song, 'Love Street,' and that the Canyon Country Store over there is the 'store where the creatures meet.' When Keith told me he lived on 'Love Street' it was the first time we were . . . *together.*"

I knew I would never be able to listen to that song with enjoyment again.

"Aunt Del, I thought I was in love with him, but tonight I realized what an idiot I've been." She shuddered. "What I found out . . . Ewww, he disgusts me so much! But *I* disgust me, too. Oh, Lord."

She blew out another breath, and when she spoke again her tone was icy. "He said he loved me—before—but tonight he acted surprised that I'd believed him. He said 'I love you' is just something men say when they want to get somebody in bed. Then he told me he's getting married—said we'd have to stop seeing each other for a while. For a *while*! He said after a couple of months he'll call me and we'll get together, but we'd have to be *discreet*!"

"The miserable bastard." I was so angry I wanted to scream, but I controlled myself by gripping the steering wheel tight.

Eileen started to cry. "I told him I'd never let him touch me again, but he just laughed and said that we'd be together as often as he wanted me because . . . Oh, Aunt Del—there's something awful!"

"Ingram is scum. Worse than scum, but he can't make you see him again."

"You don't know what he's done!"

"Then tell me. It can't be so bad that—"

"It is! When I said I wasn't going to see him again, he opened the door to this armoire he has in his bedroom, across from his bed. He showed me a video camera in there. He's been taping us! He said if I didn't do everything he wanted me to do, whenever he wanted it, he'd put those tapes on the Internet so everyone . . ."

"Wait a minute. He couldn't do that without exposing himself, and that could damage *him*."

"I was so shocked I didn't think of that, but he did. He said he'd had his own face blurred out, so no one could tell who he was." She buried her face in her hands and leaned toward the console until her head nearly touched the surface. She moaned in despair. Her agony stabbed at me. I wanted to do anything possible to take her pain away.

I reached out to stroke her back, to comfort her as I had when she was a child, but she straightened abruptly. Trembling with fury, she whispered, "I hate him! I wish he were dead!"

Before I could reply I heard the sound of a vehicle approaching. Through the rearview mirror, I saw that the Auto Club truck had arrived.

"That was fast. I guess this time of the morning things are slow," I said.

I went through the usual ritual with the driver: explaining the problem and showing my Auto Club card.

A few minutes later he gave us bad news.

"It's not the battery," he said. "It might be a short in the electrical system."

"Oh, no. Can you fix it?" Eileen asked.

"Sorry. It'll have to go to a repair shop. The car can't stay here—you're in a yellow zone. Where do you want it towed?"

"Gosh, I don't know . . ."

"Car Guy," I said.

The tow truck driver's attitude went from polite indifference to interested. "That mechanic on TV?"

"Yes." I turned to Eileen. "You don't have a regular shop, and I know Car is honest. What do you say?"

Eileen nodded. "That's a good idea." She looked at her watch. "But it's three o'clock in the morning."

"Take her car to the Better Living Channel studio on Lankershim Boulevard in North Hollywood." I gave him the address, and my Auto Club membership number. "I'll call the security office to tell them you're coming. They'll let you in the gate and show you where to leave the car."

"You got it."

While the Auto Club man prepared to tow Eileen's car, I dialed the studio number. Guard Lew Parsons answered. His voice was deep and husky. Hearing him made me think of those animated bear family bathroom tissue commercials: Lew sounded like the big Poppa Bear looked.

"Hi, Lew. It's Della Carmichael."

"Hey, there, Mrs. C. Wha' chu cookin' up this late?"

I told him that the Auto Club tow truck was going to be arriving soon with a red VW and asked him to have it put in one of Car Guy's slots.

"Would you tell him that I'd like to know what's wrong with it, and if he'd be able to do the work? Ask him to call me at home tomorrow. You have the number."

"Will do."

"Thank you, Lew. Good night. Or, I guess I should say 'good morning.'"

"It's all the same to me," he said.

I disconnected the call as I watched the Auto Club truck pull away in the predawn darkness and head north up Laurel Canyon Boulevard with Eileen's little car behind it.

Eileen sighed, and I turned to see her staring up Rothdell Terrace, in the direction of what she'd called Keith Ingram's mini Swiss chateau.

"You said you left your purse at the creep's house. Why don't I go wake up that jerk and get it for you?"

"No," Eileen said. "I can't look at him."

"I understand that. Why don't I call him tomorrow and arrange to pick it up for you?"

She nodded. "Thank you." Her eyes were filling with tears. "This is so awful. What am I going to do?"

I put my arm around her shoulders and gave her an encouraging squeeze. "Don't think about it right now. I'll figure out something."

My voice sounded confident, but it was sheer bravado. The truth was that I didn't have even the beginning of an idea how I was going to get Eileen out of this awful situation.

5

Tired as I was, I still didn't sleep soundly. When my door-bell rang at seven o'clock on Tuesday morning, only three hours after I'd finally been able to go to bed, I was already more than half awake.

Tuffy, who had been sleeping at the foot of the bed, sat up, on full alert. I heard a low growl in his throat.

My first thought was that my visitor was Phil Logan, bringing the designer dresses he'd borrowed for me to wear to the Wednesday night gala, but this was a little early, even for Phil. And Tuffy never growled at Phil.

So who was at the door?

The bell rang again. Tuffy followed as I hurried, bare-footed, to the front door, struggling into a robe as I went.

A glance through the front window revealed a young man I'd never seen before. He was in his early twenties, wore jeans and a T-shirt that advertised some rock group. Its name was partially obscured by the young man's leather jacket. A bright green and yellow helmet was tucked beneath his right arm. A Barneys New York shopping bag dangled from his other hand.

With my seventy-pound black standard poodle—an intimidating sight to strangers—beside me, I opened the front door a few inches. "Yes?"

The young man raised the shopping bag. "Delivery."

"What is it?"

"It's a delivery," he said. "For Eileen O'Hara."

I opened the door wider. "I'll take it."

He handed it to me.

"If you'll wait just a moment—" I was going to say that I wanted to give him a tip, but he either didn't listen or didn't care because he was hurrying back down my front path to the street, where he'd parked a motorcycle.

The Barneys shopping bag wasn't fastened at the top. I saw that it contained a purse I recognized as Eileen's.

"Who was that?"

I turned to see Eileen. She didn't look as though she had slept much either.

I took the purse out of the bag. "I think this is yours."

She didn't reach for it, but instead stared at the closed front door. "Was that . . . ? Did . . . *he* bring it?"

"A messenger," I said.

Eileen took the purse from my hand, opened it, and fingered the contents. "No note. I guess he's too cautious to write something I might show to his fiancée."

"You wouldn't do it," I said.

"He doesn't know that. He doesn't know me at all." She clamped her lips together in an angry line.

"Ingram knew you well enough to realize you'd never agree to being taped." I folded the paper shopping bag into quarters.

Eileen indicated the Barneys bag. "What are you going to do with that?"

"Right into the trash. Keith Ingram touched it. This isn't something I want to use again."

"I'm glad to see your passion for recycling things has a limit," Eileen said.

"Honey, let's forget him for now. I'll make us some breakfast."

She shook her head. "No thanks. I haven't got any classes today so I'm going back to bed for a while." Mumbling that she'd see me later, she went down the hall to her room.

Going to bed sounded like a good idea to me, but when I turned around I discovered that Emma, my little calico cat, had joined Tuffy and that both of them were staring at me. The message in their eyes was unmistakable: They wanted breakfast.

"Okay, guys," I told them. "You win."

After letting Tuffy out for a quick trip to the backyard—the prelude to our usual long morning walk—I fed the two of them. I was now too thoroughly awake to return to bed, so I took a shower and put on a fresh T-shirt and pair of sweatpants.

Lack of enough sleep tends to make me hungry. I tell myself that it's my body compensating for loss of rest by craving food for energy. This morning I also told myself that cooking—working with my hands on an old, familiar dish like stuffed French toast—would clear my head to think about Eileen's problem. The only thing about the situation that gave me any comfort at all was the fact that we had some time to come up with a solution. By his own stated timetable, Ingram wouldn't be coming after Eileen for at least a month or two. Still, there was a huge threat hanging over Eileen's head, and I wasn't going to rest easy until it was removed.

As the coffee brewed and I was whipping up the milk, vanilla extract, and egg mixture, I thought about Ingram. I didn't know enough about him yet to devise some counterthreat.

I was using my paring knife to carve one-inch-long openings in the bottom crust of French bread slices and scoop out a little of the insides when the doorbell rang again.

What now?

I turned off the heat under the pan in which two pats of butter were melting and hurried to the door.

This time when I glanced through the front window I saw Phil Logan pressing the bell. Over his other arm, he carried three long garment bags.

When I opened the door, Phil greeted me with a pleased expression and indicated the garment bags. "It's hard to get sample gowns for somebody who isn't a size two, but fortunately there's this new Spanish designer who appreciates women with curves, so I got you a couple of . . ." He lifted his chin, and wrinkled his nose. "What's that wonderful aroma—and do you have enough for me?"

"There's plenty."

I led Phil to my bedroom, where he hung the garment bags on the bathroom door, and followed me into the kitchen. Briefly, I considered asking Phil for information about Ingram, but I decided against that. Phil would want to know why, and I couldn't tell him.

Unaware that I was worried about anything, Phil set the table for breakfast. He had eaten here many times over the months, and knew where the plates, napkins, and cutlery were. As soon as he'd completed that task, he joined me at the counter beside the stove.

"What are you making?"

"Stuffed French toast."

"Stuffed? How can you stuff toast?"

"You can't use an ordinary presliced loaf, but if you use French bread, it's simple," I said, demonstrating. "I just insert a spoonful of fruit preserves into the pockets I've cut in the bread slices, spread the filling around inside, and put the little rectangle of bottom crust I opened up back into place. That seals the preserves inside the bread. Then I dredge the bread in the egg and milk mixture, and put it into the heated skillet."

As soon as I dropped the egg-coated bread slices into the pan, they began to sizzle in the butter. The heat released the delicious scent of vanilla extract and fruit preserves into the air.

"It only takes a few seconds on each side."

I gently lifted the corner of one slice with my wide Mario Batali spatula to check the underside. When it was just the right shade of golden brown, I said, "Perfect." I turned the slices over to brown the other side.

Phil, unable to be inactive for more than a few seconds at a time, poured mugs of coffee for us and brought our plates over to the stove. I scooped the slices of French toast out of the skillet and transferred them to the plates.

"Just one more thing." I picked up the little sifter I kept especially for powdered sugar and gave the slices a light dusting.

At the table with our plates and coffee, I watched Phil cut into his toast and smile with delight as the preserves oozed out. When he began to eat, his expression turned ecstatic, and he began making satisfied "Hmmm" noises. His reaction reminded me of that famous fake orgasm scene in *When Harry Met Sally*.

In a wry tone, I said, "I guess it's as good for you as it is for me."

He touched the napkin to his lips. "If I ever decide to get married again, I might give Nick D'Martino some competition."

"Phil, I'm fifteen years older than you."

"When a woman cooks this good, it doesn't matter," he said. "Besides, since you won't lie about your age, I'm promoting the idea that forty-seven is the new thirty-five. I got an article about that coming out in next month's *Vanity Fair*. One of the dozen photos is a still from your show."

Phil finished that first piece of toast, and the three more that I made for him. When he was full at last, he thanked me and got up from the table. "Let's get to work. I have to see how you look in those dresses."

Eileen came into my room while I was modeling them for Phil. She was a little pale, but her hair was brushed and she was dressed in a clean blue tracksuit.

"Hi, you two. What's going on?" To someone who didn't know her well, Eileen sounded normal, but I knew it was an act of will.

I said, "Phil borrowed three designer gowns for me to choose one to wear for . . ." I stopped, feeling awkward.

Eileen faked a smile. Her lips curved up, but the expression didn't make it all the way to her eyes. "That's okay," she said. "I know it's for the big gala tomorrow night."

She studied the peach chiffon gown with the empire waist that I was wearing, and then the black silk and the blue jersey dresses on hangers.

"The one you're wearing looks great," she said. "But the asymmetrical neckline on the black dress isn't going to be flattering. The blue jersey matches your eyes, but it's going to cling in the wrong places."

Phil made a circle with his right thumb and forefinger. "You've got a good eye. The peach chiffon gets my vote, too."

The sudden ringing of the phone caused Eileen to flinch. Her composure slipped for just a moment. I wanted to whisper a word of comfort to her, but I couldn't do that in front of Phil.

When I answered, I heard Car Guy's voice. He got right to the point.

"The red VW—it belongs to the cutie who lives with you, right?"

"Yes, it's Eileen O'Hara's. Do you know what's wrong with it?"

"Just a loose wire to the distributor cap. No big deal. It's ready to go. If she picks it up herself, I'll give her the company discount."

"Careful. Her father's with the LAPD."

"Don't worry—I did my time. If she threw herself at me, I wouldn't catch her. Seriously, I'm not going to charge for a loose wire. I found the problem in about five seconds."

"You're a nice man, Car."

"Yeah, well, keep that to yourself," he said gruffly.

I relayed the repair information to Eileen.

She took the receiver and thanked Car warmly, then looked at me and asked, "Can you drive me over there?"

"I'll take you," Phil said. He was putting the two rejected gowns back into their garment bags. "I've got to go out to the studio anyway."

"That's great," Eileen said. "Thanks."

While I was in the bathroom, carefully stepping out of the borrowed designer gown, Eileen knocked on the door. "Aunt Del?"

"You can come in."

She opened the door only enough to say, "After I get my car, I'm going to our store to do the inventory."

"How are you feeling this morning?"

"Not great, but I'll keep busy." She paused, looked at the floor, and then looked up at me. "Have you thought of some way to stop Keith?"

"Not yet, but there *is* a solution and we'll find it. Please believe that."

"I'll try." There was a note of childlike disappointment in her voice; one of her three parent figures—me—had just let her down. I felt terrible.

Changing the subject, I asked, "Will you be home for dinner?"

She shook her head. "Daddy's working, and Mother was going to be alone, so I'm meeting her for an early bite."

Dressed in my own clothes again, I came out of the bathroom. "Where's Phil?"

"Waiting for me in his car."

"Eileen, we *are* going to solve your problem. In the meantime, promise me you're not going to do anything foolish."

"You mean more foolish than what I've already done?" Her voice had a bitter edge. "I don't think I could."

We heard the discordant *bleep-bleep* we recognized as the horn in Phil Logan's Mercedes.

"The Publicity Man Honk-eth. I gotta run." She gave my hand a quick grasp, and then she was gone.

I was left alone to worry about her, and to wonder how in the world I was going to protect her from Keith Ingram.

If the girl in this fix had been anyone except his own daughter, I would go to John O'Hara for help. But John was the last person on earth in whom I dared confide now. As controlled as he was professionally, Mack had described him to me once as a sleeping volcano.

Years ago, John had broken both the arms of a hospital orderly when he'd caught the man trying to molest Shannon, during one of the times she'd been confined to a psychiatric facility. I couldn't predict what he might do in defense of his daughter.

I decided that I had to confide in Nicholas D'Martino and ask him for help. As a crime reporter, he was a skilled investigator. Maybe he could discover something Ingram was hiding—a powerful counterthreat that would force him to give us the video of Eileen.

If there wasn't anything to use against Ingram, perhaps Nicholas and I could come up with another plan. But he wouldn't be back in Los Angeles until Friday, and I didn't know how long I could keep Eileen from doing something reckless.

Friday seemed a long way off.

6

Eileen came home Tuesday night some time after I'd gone to bed. Wednesday morning she was gone before I got up, but she left a note saying that she was going to Della's Sweet Dreams, our retail fudge and brownie business on Hollywood Boulevard.

She called at ten thirty to give me a positive report about our on-site sales.

"The walk-in business has doubled in the last two weeks," she said. "I think we should stay open two hours longer, for the people who want to pick up dessert on their way home from work. And I think we should hire a second counter clerk."

"Go ahead. You and Walter interview the applicants."

Walter Hovey was our factory manager, a retired actor with the silver-haired looks and cultured bearing of an ambassador to the Court of St. James. We'd had the good luck to inherit him when Mickey Jordan bought the building and equipment of the bakery Walter had been working for.

Eileen asked, "Do you want to interview the ones we like best?"

"No. I trust your judgment. What about circulating the word at UCLA and USC? This might be a good job for a student."

"I'm on it. I'll see if I can find one who doesn't like sweets so he or she won't eat up our profits."

I laughed. She said good-bye and disconnected before I had a chance to wish her luck in finding the right person.

Her little joke told me that she hadn't lost her sense of humor. That was a good sign, but I was a little worried about her emotional state. Someone who didn't know Eileen as well as I did would have thought that she just sounded excited, but I could tell that the level was a little too high to be normal. It concerned me, but I told myself to be glad that she was keeping busy.

■ ■ ■

The plan for Wednesday evening was that Liddy and Bill Marshall would pick me up and that we would drive in their car to the Olympia Grand Hotel. Shannon had called earlier to say that she and John would meet us at the gala.

When I opened the door to Liddy's ring, I was astonished to see neither her ivory Range Rover nor Bill's bronze Cadillac in front of my house. Instead, parked parallel to my front lawn, there was a black vehicle almost as long as a bus. Beside it stood a heavily built man in a boxy black suit, the jacket's buttons straining against his girth. He wore his black chauffeur's cap pulled down to a scant inch above his thick eyebrows.

"You hired a limousine?" I asked.

"It's so we don't have to stand in line at valet parking for an hour at the end of the night," Bill said.

Long-limbed, lean, and energetic, Bill Marshall, Beverly Hills DDS, looked comfortable in his dinner jacket. At age forty-eight, he played basketball on Saturdays, and sometimes Liddy went to cheer him on. Afterwards, they'd have a "date night." Liddy told me that since last September, when their twin sons went off to college in the east, she and Bill were living like newlyweds again. "It's the first time in eighteen years that we can run around the house naked," she'd said. "Thank God I haven't deteriorated too much."

And she hadn't. Twenty-five years ago, Liddy had been crowned "Miss Nebraska." Like so many blonde and blue-eyed American beauties before and since, Liddy packed her crown and sash and headed for Hollywood with dreams of stardom.

It only took a few months of her being pawed by casting directors and propositioned by agents and producers before Liddy realized that the life of an actress was not for her. The night she set eyes on a young man with shaggy blondish hair and what Liddy called an "adorable nose-and-a-half" she knew what kind of life she really wanted. Twenty-three years later, she was still happy about the choice she'd made.

As soon as Liddy came through the door, she instructed me take a few steps backward and do a full, slow turn in front of her.

Liddy clapped her hands enthusiastically. "You look gorgeous in that dress. It's Jorge Allesandro, isn't it?"

"How did you know?"

"I saw his trunk show at Neiman last month."

"I wouldn't have known Jorge Allesandro from Taco Bell if Phil Logan hadn't drilled me on his name. In case someone in the media asks *who* I'm wearing."

As usual, Liddy looked stunning. Her square-neck black silk gown with long sleeves was the perfect frame for her light hair and the teardrop diamond pendant that had been a twentieth-anniversary present from Bill.

"Where's Eileen?" Liddy asked.

That startled me. "Is she still going with us?"

"Of course I am."

I turned to see Eileen coming into the living room from the hallway. Her hair had been professionally arranged and her makeup was subtle but perfect.

"Why shouldn't I go?" Her direct gaze at me communicated the request that I not answer that question.

Bill stared at Eileen. "Wow. When did funny-looking little Gigi grow up?"

Eileen laughed. "Several years ago, Uncle Bill. You just

never see me in makeup, or wearing anything but running clothes."

"I'm glad I'm not twenty anymore, Eileen," Liddy said. "I wouldn't want to compete with you for a man. And you're wearing Jorge Allesandro, too. It's gorgeous." Liddy turned to me with a teasing twinkle in her eyes. "That fudge business of yours must be doing very well."

"This dress is on loan." Eileen glanced at me. She looked embarrassed, and I guessed that it was because she was wearing the blue jersey gown that she'd said would cling in all the wrong places on me. "Phil suggested I wear it," she said. "I hope you don't mind."

"Of course I don't. It looks perfect on you," I said, meaning it.

Turning to the Marshalls, but including Eileen, I said, "I have to be at the hotel half an hour before the doors to the ballroom open, to check in at the manager's office and get my judging gear. I hate the thought of you three just standing around in the lobby, waiting."

Bill draped one arm each around Liddy and Eileen. "Don't worry about us. I'll take the girls into the cocktail lounge for a drink and let all the other men envy me for being with two such beautiful women." He nodded toward the front door. "You gals ready?"

"Just a minute." I took Eileen's hand. "Honey, come help me look for my evening bag. We'll be right back."

As soon as we were out of sight and beyond the hearing of Liddy and Bill, I said, "Are you sure you want to come tonight? Are you up to being in the same room with that rotten jerk?"

Eileen's eyes glittered with anger. "I want him to see what he's missing," she said.

■　■　■

The Olympia Grand Hotel was located on Wilshire Boulevard, a few blocks east of Westwood Boulevard, at the western edge of a swath of elegant high-rise buildings that contained some of the most expensive condominiums in the world. Platinum Row, some called it. For the residents, those condos were mansions with a concierge, on-site plumbers, electricians, and maid service, and without the need of gardeners. Several of the buildings also included private chefs among the amenities.

The limousine Bill hired—I couldn't bring myself to call it *our* limousine—turned into the lane leading to the hotel's entrance. We were behind two other identical black vehicles.

The driver stopped and came around to open the rear door and to help us out. I saw that two more limousines had made the turn from Wilshire to the hotel's entrance and were slowing to a stop behind us.

I asked Bill, "How are we going to find the car when the evening's over?"

The driver gave a little salute with the fingers of one meaty hand. "I'll find you. My name is Rudy."

Bill thanked him, then steered his three female companions toward the entrance to the Olympia Grand Hotel and through the heavy glass and brass revolving doors. Exceptionally handsome doors, the entwined initials O and G were etched onto the glass panels in ornamental calligraphy.

Inside, the crowded lobby replicated a Hollywood set decorator's idea of a pagan temple: high ceilings, soaring sconces wired for electricity but miming candlelight, and walls covered by vivid frescoes featuring Greek gods at play.

"This is very flattering lighting," Liddy said. "I haven't been here since Gene Long bought the hotel and redecorated it."

I reached out for Liddy's hand and pulled her beside me. "Do you mean Eugene Long, who has a fleet of oil tankers and an airline? Tina Long's father owns this place?"

Liddy nodded. "The hotel is his hobby. I don't know how he can pay attention to his businesses with the time he has to spend getting that dippy *celebutante* daughter of his out of trouble. I'm not surprised he's got a reputation for getting plastered as soon as the sun goes down. If she were my daughter, I'd drink, too. Why are you interested in them?"

I was saved from having to think of an answer. Bill and Eileen had nearly reached the entrance to the lounge when he seemed to realize that Liddy wasn't with them. He turned around and gestured for her to catch up.

"See you later," I said, gently shooing her toward Bill and Eileen. I watched them disappear through the archway into the cocktail lounge, where a pianist was playing melodies from Broadway musicals.

Peering through the humanity parading across the lobby, I saw a notice board on an easel announcing that the Celebrity Cook-Off was going to be held in the Elysian Ballroom at seven PM. A few yards from where I stood there was a door with a brass sign identifying it as the "Manager's Office." According to Phil, that was where I was supposed to present myself to collect my judging cards and clipboard.

The only negative about this event was that I would have to see Keith Ingram. I didn't want him to suspect that I knew what he had done to Eileen, so I would have to be polite to him. It was a revolting thought, but necessary until I figured out what to do.

Straightening my posture, I headed toward my destination through the crowd of strangers. Several of them glanced at me with that "Do I know you?" look in their eyes. I smiled back. Perhaps they'd seen the show, but didn't recognize me all glammed up.

Reaching the entrance to the manager's office, I was about to knock when the door opened and a man emerged. Slightly taller than medium height, slender but muscular, wavy hair the color of milk chocolate. Handsome. He looked like a combination of an athlete and a poet: Michelangelo's *David* in a dinner jacket.

But the sight of him made me want to retch––because I had nearly collided with Keith Ingram.

7

Staring at Ingram, I was furious at myself for thinking he was charming when I'd met him several months ago. It had been only a passing thought on my part, but Eileen must have found him fascinating. While he was interviewing us about our fudge business, I was too intent on trying to give him good material for his column to notice her reaction to him. Even if I had been that observant, I couldn't have guessed how corrupt he was.

When I looked at Keith Ingram now, the image that flashed into my mind was the ugly, concealed picture of the "real" Dorian Gray. And I remembered the warning from *The Merchant of Venice*: "All that glisters is not gold . . . gilded tombs do *worms* infold."

The worm said, "Hello, Della Carmichael." Ingram's voice was as smooth as maple syrup. "I hear we're going to be judges together."

"Hello." My tone was blandly polite.

If he noticed my lack of warmth, he gave no sign of it. Instead, he smiled like a lying politician, and extended his hand in greeting. I pretended that I didn't see it.

I was fighting the powerful urge to grab the clipboard he had tucked under one arm and bash him over the head with it. But I restrained myself. During twenty years as a policeman's wife I'd perfected the art of hiding my feelings when it was necessary. Although Mack must have known how afraid I was every time he left the house to go on duty, I never let him see my fear. It remained unspoken between us, but each time he came home, I greeted him as happily as though he'd been gone for a year.

Ingram's lips were moving. I realized he was talking to me and tuned back in to hear him ask, "Have you met our fellow judge yet? Yvette Dupree?"

"No."

In a tone of contempt, he said, "The so-called Global Gourmet."

"So-called?"

"Perhaps I should have said *self-styled.*" Ingram inclined his head toward me and lowered his voice. "Don't let her accent fool you. She's about as French Moroccan as Colonel Sanders was. My guess is she does most of her traveling on the Google Express."

"I like her books. When my husband and I went to Italy, we found every restaurant she recommended exactly as she'd described it, even in the smallest towns."

"Have you traveled much in Europe? Other than Italy? Through Asia? Or South America? India?"

"No."

Ingram shrugged. "Ah, well, that explains it." He lost interest in me and began scanning faces in the lobby.

Before I could think of a riposte—it was one of those frustrating moments with a boor when you think of some brilliant squelch only much later—he said, "See you inside."

I watched Ingram swagger off in the direction of a sudden flurry of photographers' lights flashing and shutters clicking. Through the entrance strolled the subjects of their frantic interest: California's glamorous governor and his equally glamorous wife. I felt a wave of revulsion when the governor and his wife and Ingram greeted each other like old friends and posed together for the cameras, but then I gave the state's First Couple the benefit of the doubt. Elected officials seldom knew everything about the people with whom they appeared in photos.

A short time later, equipped with my clipboard, a pen, and a packet of twenty judging cards each with a contestant's name on it, I was in the main ballroom—called the Elysian Room—of the Olympia Grand Hotel. It had been decorated like Hollywood's version of a scene out of *The Arabian Nights*. The ceiling was tented with lengths of silk, anchored by and billowing out from a dozen sparkling crystal chandeliers. At least twenty-four artificial palm trees were spaced against the outside perimeter, their green fronds casting shadows that resembled bony fingers against the ballroom's cream-colored walls.

There were no dinner tables in the Elysian Room this night because three-quarters of the space was filled with twenty working stoves, each manned by movie and TV celebrities in black tie or evening gowns. Members of the public who had paid five hundred dollars apiece for the privilege could wander throughout, watching stars cook and bake in the competition. Money collected for tickets would be donated to the Healthy Life Fund. The hundred-thousand-dollar prize for the best culinary creation would go to the winning star's favorite charity.

Famous travel and food writer Yvette Dupree, author of a dozen *Global Gourmet Goes to . . .* books that covered the sights and cuisines of at least half the known world, came toward me through the crowd and introduced herself.

"You are Del-la," she said. Her accent—a lilting mixture of French and something exotic—made my name sound almost like a dessert.

Yvette Dupree was a petite woman, and her great mane of tawny hair might have accounted for a quarter of her total weight. Heavily tanned, with the toned arms of the champion golfer that I'd read she had once been, she wore a strapless metallic gold mermaid dress so tight from torso to knees that she walked with the tiny steps that reminded me of a documentary I'd seen about Chinese women who had had their feet bound.

"I'm delighted to meet you," I said.

" 'Ow do you do, *cherie*. I mus' tell you 'ow I enjoy your show."

"Thank you. That's very kind. Your book on Italy gave me a great experience of the country."

"Ahhhh, *Italia*. Zee men . . . superb lovers . . . but"—she shook her head—"zay do not give *grande* jewels."

Because she was wearing an impressive collection of large gems around her neck, encircling both wrists, and decorating several fingers, I guessed that none of these big-carat baubles were from Italian men.

"That's useful to know," I said.

Yvette peered at me through thick false eyelashes: first at my unadorned neck, then at my naked wrists, and finally my ringless fingers. She nodded to herself, as though she had come to some personal conclusion. "You do not need diamonds to wear," she said. "Keep zem in your bank."

That would be good advice, if I had any diamonds to put in a bank.

Moving to another subject, she said, "Do you know there are *pas de*—pardon, I mean *no* psychiatrists *en Italia*?"

I admitted that I hadn't heard that, but I added that I thought the actress Audrey Hepburn had been married to an Italian who was a psychiatrist.

"No psychiatrists," she insisted. "*En Italia*, when peoples have zee problem zee men go to zee mamas and womens go to zee priests. America, *c'est merveilleux*, but too many psychiatrists, all wanting to know about one's sentimental life."

I had no idea what to say to that, but a response wasn't necessary because now her gaze had passed me and had focused on the sea of glamorous—and glamorized—people who thronged the ballroom.

"All zis for zee charity. *Bon*." Twirling one perfectly manicured index finger in the direction of the cluster of stoves, she said, "We must be judging, *oui*?"

"*Oui.*" It was one of the few French words I knew.

"*À bientôt.*" She smiled and moved away on tiny little steps toward the first line of gas stoves.

I had only that one brief conversation with Yvette Dupree, but I liked her. She was a little gaudy, and had some odd opinions, but she seemed unpretentious, and she exuded warmth that made her pleasant to be around.

Surveying the ballroom, I saw Keith Ingram in the middle aisle, jotting something on his clipboard. With Yvette going along the far left row of celebrities, and Ingram in the middle path, I decided to begin my study of the activities along the right side of the room.

I'd reached my fourth stove when out of the corner of my eye I glimpsed a familiar figure: a man who towered over most of the men around him. Because he'd been my husband's partner and our friend, I'd seen those broad shoulders and that military-short hair at least a thousand times over the course of twenty-two years. Almost simultaneously, another moving body caught my attention: Shannon O'Hara, looking voluptuous in a sea foam green evening gown. Several yards behind her husband, Shannon's halo of red curls bounced as she tried to get through the crowd to catch up with him.

I was wondering why John O'Hara was moving so rapidly, leaving Shannon to struggle in his wake, when I felt the *click* of comprehension in my brain: John was speeding like a locked-on missile right toward Keith Ingram. The food critic's back was to him, but John's left hand grabbed Ingram's right shoulder, yanking Ingram around to face him.

Ingram grunted in surprise and jerked out of John's grasp, but before he could utter a protest, John's right fist shot out. With a heavy *thud*, John's knuckles connected with Ingram's jaw. It sounded like Rocky Balboa thumping that side of beef.

Propelled by John's blow, Ingram reeled backward,

stumbling against a corpulent, white-haired spectator. The older man tottered, but he clutched at a nearby waiter and managed to keep his balance while Ingram tumbled to the floor on his rear end. Ingram's legs flailed in the air, like a huge turtle that had been flipped over onto its shell.

8

Instinct had sent me rushing toward the action just as John's fist started toward Ingram's face. Too late to stop the punch, I pushed in front of John just as Shannon, Liddy, and Bill reached him. Amid a babble of shocked voices, Ingram struggled to his feet, helped by the overweight man and the waiter.

Prodding John's chest hard with the end of my clipboard, I whispered, "What's the matter with you?"

John's dark eyes were almost black with fury. He clamped his mouth tight and backed away from me.

All around us, photographers' flashes were going off. Some gala attendees moved away from the combatants while others inched closer to get a better look. And two large uniformed security men pressed through the throng toward us.

Pointing at John, Ingram shouted to the security guards, "Arrest that maniac!"

The guards started toward John, but the fierce expression on his face stopped them. Her eyes wide with shock, Shannon clutched John's arm while he stood rigid.

"Now, now, let's not turn some little misunderstanding into World War Three."

It was a new voice on the scene, a man's, soothing, and smooth as softened butter, the voice of a midnight disk jockey who played Frank Sinatra songs until dawn. But it wasn't a disk jockey joining us. I'd heard that voice and seen his face in television interviews about the success of his multilayered financial empire. Tall and slender, with thick silver hair framing even features, he was as handsome as he was rich.

"There's no need to arrest anyone." Eugene Long's tone was genial. He held a glass with an amber-colored liquid in one hand, and with the other he gave the shoulder of the nearest of the two guards a friendly pat. "Why don't you boys go to the Palm Room down the hall and have a big steak dinner with all the trimmings. Just sign my name to the tab." He took a healthy swallow from the glass. I probably wouldn't have noticed except for Liddy's remark about Long being a heavy drinker. His eyes seemed exceptionally bright, but that might have been a trick of the lights; he didn't sound drunk.

The guards thanked their employer. One aimed a final frown at John, and the two of them headed toward the exit. As the crowd parted to let them through, I saw Eileen across the room. Her hands pressed against her lips as though suppressing a scream.

John leaned down to whisper something to Shannon, then took her hand from his arm and gently put it into Liddy's. After giving Bill a brief nod, John hurried out of the ballroom. With his eyes fixed on the exit, he couldn't see Eileen, who was standing frozen, out of his line of sight.

Eugene Long drew Ingram away from the crowd and was speaking quietly to him. I hurried past the rows of stoves that separated us and grasped Eileen around her wrists, lowering her hands from her mouth.

"Why did your father explode? Did you tell him what Ingram did to you?"

She shook her head. "Mother knew I was upset and was getting agitated because I wouldn't tell her why, so I gave in and said Keith was threatening to ruin my reputation. Right after that, Daddy came into the room. I didn't even know he'd come home. He didn't say anything, but now I realize he must have overheard us talking about Keith."

We were interrupted by an irritating electronic screech from the direction of the stage at the far end of the ball-room. Eugene Long took a sip from his glass, wiped his lips, and bent over the speaker's stand. He tapped the microphone and muttered, "Is this thing on?"

A technician popped up from beneath the pedestal and assured him that it was connected.

"Good boy," Long said. He straightened and raised his drink in salute to the prosperous audience under his vaulted roof. With the bonhomie of a politician, he said, "Cheers, everybody, and welcome to the Celebrity Cook-Off. Tonight, in this very room, there are more stars than we can see in the sky—at least not unless we get some of the Santa Ana winds to blow the smog away. Seriously, thank you all for being here. Now, people, hold your applause until I've introduced everybody."

As a spotlight hit each celebrity at his or her cooking station, that star responded with a wave, or a blown kiss, or a fist pumped in anticipation of victory. When Long pronounced the final name, he said, "Let's show our appreciation for these great talents with the big hearts who are giving their time tonight for the Healthy Life Fund."

Sustained applause from their fans.

"Now I'd like to introduce the three accomplished people who are going to pick the Celebrity Cook-Off winner. First, a beautiful world traveler, and my old and dear friend, the Global Gourmet, Yvette Dupree."

Yvette waved her hand that held the clipboard. Because she was short, the group nearest her had to step to one side for her to be seen by more of the crowd.

"Next is lovely Della Carmichael, hostess of *In the Kitchen with Della* on the Better Living Channel. Show us where you are, Della."

The spotlight found me. I gave a quick little wave with my free hand. While I was at ease teaching food preparation on television—I'd been a high school English teacher for twelve years before I started the cooking school—I was a little embarrassed to be introduced at an event full of famous people when I wasn't on the premises to cook. I was much more comfortable with a spatula in my hand than a clipboard.

"Now for a shot of testosterone, a man whose nationally syndicated food column influences what people eat from coast to coast. Here he is, the sworn enemy of fast food: Keith Ingram."

There was brief, polite applause for the judges. Seeming to relish the spotlight, Ingram waved with both hands thrust high. It was a gesture too large for the less-than-wild enthusiasm the gala attendees felt for the judges. We were not the luminaries that people in the ballroom had paid five hundred dollars apiece to watch.

From what I could see, it didn't seem as though John had done permanent damage to Ingram's face. I admit to being torn about that. On the one hand, I didn't like violence, but when it came to Keith Ingram and what he was threatening to do to Eileen, I would not have trusted myself if I had found him alone on a country road and I knew how to drive a backhoe.

"And now," Long said, "it's my pleasure to introduce the love of my life. I wake up every morning a happy man, just because I know she's going to do something that day to make me crazy—or make me smile. She's going to make one of you smile, too, because she's in charge of the one-hundred-thousand-dollar check that's going to be awarded tonight." He made a sweeping gesture toward the side of the stage. "My daughter, Tina. Come on out here, baby doll."

From behind the length of velvet curtain that framed the stage stepped Tina Long, carrying a two-feet-high-by-four-feet-long cardboard check. All that was visible of her behind the cardboard were the blandly pretty face above it that had graced so many tabloid gossip magazine covers in the past year, and two pipe-cleaner thin legs below. The hands that gripped the mock-up were pale and slender, their fingers bright with pink nail polish onto which pink glitter had been sprinkled.

Long enthusiastically led the applause for Tina as she took a bow.

When the clapping died down, Long said, "As you can see, the check has been partly made out. There's the bank, the date, and the amount: one hundred thousand dollars. All that has to be filled in is the name of the charity selected by the winning celebrity, and my signature. Then, thanks to one of the stars here, some good cause is going to get a fabulous surprise tonight."

Keith Ingram had moved next to me. "And what do we judges get? Nothing but indigestion from a bellyful of amateur cooking."

Turning away because I couldn't stand to look at him, I glanced across the ballroom to where Eileen was standing with her mother.

She was staring at Keith Ingram with a degree of hatred that I wouldn't have thought possible in this gentle girl who had lived with me for most of her life.

9

We were one hour into the ninety-minute cooking competition. Up to this point, according to the instructions we'd received in the hotel manager's office, we three judges had been free to move about as we liked, watching the progress being made at the twenty separate stoves in whatever order we wished.

The ballroom had been divided into five sections, with the stoves placed in groupings of four per sector, with the sectors numbered one through five. Paths six feet wide, marked by velvet ropes attached to brass stands, outlined the walkways through which the judges and members of the audience could stroll. The sectors were numbered to make it easier for the people attending to find their favorite celebrities. A program sheet with the locations diagrammed had been handed to each patron who entered the ballroom.

During the last half hour before time would be called and the celebrities—finished or not—had to present their dishes, all three judges were supposed to move along the quadrants of stoves together, carefully examining the dishes that were being prepared.

Sector One was at the end of the ballroom closest to the shallow stage. Sectors Two and Three formed the row on the west side of the room, with Sectors Four and Five comprising the row on the east side. If I described the layout to Nicholas on the phone later, I'd tell him to picture a torso with a head and two outstretched arms. Sector One would be the torso's head—just below the stage—with Two and Three being the extended right arm and Four and Five being the left extended arm. Those reaching arms pointed toward the wide, double-door entrance to the ballroom. A uniformed security guard—not one of the two who had come charging in to confront John—had been posted there to make sure that anyone who tried to enter the event had a ticket to it.

Ingram, Yvette, and I had worked our way through the crowd to stand beside Sector Four, on the left side of the ballroom, halfway between the stage at one end and Sector Five. Dozens of people swarmed about, which sometimes made it difficult for us judges to keep moving. I didn't mind, because having a lot of people around made it easier for me to avoid looking at Keith Ingram.

Wolf Wheeler, a comic movie actor in Sector One, was attracting attention to his workstation by tossing several eggs higher and higher and catching them to keep the airborne rotation going. At first his antics irritated me because I was sure he was going to drop the eggs and I hate to see food wasted, but then I realized he was a really skilled juggler performing an amazing routine. I watched him for a minute, and wished it could have been longer, but I was supposed to be concentrating on what the stars in Sector Four were creating. I pulled my attention away from him and went back to acting like a judge.

The celebrities in this quartet of stoves were three actors and an author. Francine Ames, whose dark-haired beauty had been compared to young Elizabeth Taylor's, had starred for nineteen years as an often-married vamp on TV's longest running daytime soap opera.

Oona Rogers and Vernon "Coupe" Deville were married-to-each-other action movie stars. As sinewy as gymnasts, approximately the same height, and with matching face-hugging caps of sleek bronze hair, they looked more like brother and sister than like a non-biological couple. According to the entertainment press, they had met a few years ago when they were cast as costars in an espionage thriller. They fell in love among the car chases and explosions. That first picture was such a box office success it had been followed by a series with the same two leading characters.

The last member of this cooking quartet was British author Roland Gray, whose international espionage thrillers had earned him the distinction of having had the most novels to reach number one on the *New York Times* best seller list during the first decade of the twenty-first century. Gray, whose hair was more salt than pepper, wasn't handsome by any conventional measurement, but with his easy smile and blue eyes that fastened like lasers onto the person to whom he was speaking, he was undeniably charismatic. I had started reading his novels during the months after Mack's death, when I was trying to adjust to sleeping alone in our bed. Classic movies on television, mystery novels, and Gray's breathtaking plots and his fascinating secret agent hero took my mind off my pain for hours at a time. I appreciated Gray having done that for me.

Ingram, Yvette, and I surveyed the cooking activities, assessing the individual dishes and checking the skill level of the various celebrity chefs.

Vernon "Coupe" Deville was sautéing onions for his Philly Cheese Steak. He had his burners on high, with the result that the combination of butter and olive oil he was using sent little dots of hot grease into the air.

Ingram addressed Yvette. "Step back. You don't want to get splattered." Since I hadn't been included in his warning, I guessed that he didn't care if grease hit me.

Oona Rogers, Deville's wife, wasn't endangering anyone. Her workspace was much neater than his, and she wasn't splashing the marinara sauce as she stirred it into her Chicken Parmesan.

Moving on, we watched Francine Ames take a partially baked strawberry-rhubarb pie from her oven and start to remove the aluminum collar she'd fastened around it to prevent the edges of the crust from becoming too brown. When a big hunk of piecrust came off with the collar of foil, her pretty face screwed up into a grimace.

"The pie will taste just as good," she told us as she put it back into the oven for its final fifteen minutes of baking.

At the last stove in Sector Four, author Roland Gray was stirring a pot on the stovetop. "I'm making Lemon Pudding Surprise, from an old recipe of my mother's. The 'surprise' will be little bits of candied fruit at the bottom." His cultured British accent conjured images in my head of Number 10 Downing Street and the Royal Shakespeare Company, and the audacious secret agent who was my favorite of his literary creations.

"I was quite inspired by the show you did on comfort foods," he said. "When I was growing up, this pudding was what my mother made to soften life's little blows."

"I look forward to tasting it," I said.

Ingram scowled at me. "You're not supposed to get chummy with the contestants. We can't show favoritism."

It took all of my self-control not to snap back at the odious creature, but there had been enough confrontations here tonight. I forced my thoughts away from how much I detested Keith Ingram. Instead, I surveyed the room full of enthusiastic amateur cooks.

The aromas that were coming at me from every corner of the Elysian Ballroom were making my mouth water. I was hungry. Knowing that I would have to taste twenty separate dishes this evening, I hadn't eaten anything that day except one piece of seven-grain toast and a slice of cheese with my morning coffee.

I was finding it easy to concentrate on what the celebrity cooks were doing, because the mobile audience was behaving respectfully. Even though they were drinking as they wandered through the room, they were as polite as spectators at a golf match. Their whispered comments to each other made a soft background rustle, like the sound of a breeze ruffling leaves.

High-pitched laughter from across the rows of kitchens startled me. I looked up to see a woman emitting "Oh! Oh! Ohhhh!" noises of excitement as she and others stared in awe at new antics of Wolf Wheeler. Other voices called out, "Higher. Higher!" and "That's impossible!" as Wheeler juggled wine glasses—tossing them high in the air, catching them in front of him and behind his back and then tossing them again.

All over the ballroom, people were turning to focus on Wolf Wheeler's amazing juggling act. The clamor level rose with shouted comments of encouragement, interspersed with sharp intakes of breath.

I was watching, too, when a drop of something very hot struck the back of my hand. I yelped in pain, but before I could find out what it was, suddenly my side of the room was enveloped in thick, acrid smoke.

A man's voice yelled, "Fire!" In that instant, the scene in the ballroom changed from convivial to chaos. People screamed and coughed, and shouted.

Someone's elbow struck a sharp blow to my diaphragm. It sent me reeling backward and against a stove. Suddenly feeling heat, the self-preservation instinct kicked in. I wrenched myself away from a stovetop flame just in time to avoid being burned. Turned around, disoriented, I had no idea which way to go toward safety.

Ceiling smoke detectors began to shriek.

Blinded by the smoke, I collided with a man. He grunted, then grabbed my arm and pulled us both down to our knees. I was too surprised to struggle as he pushed me under a preparation counter.

With my face forced close to the floor, I could breathe a little better because the smoke began to rise. The shelter of the counter kept us from being hit or trampled by the terrified crowd.

Heavy footsteps pounded into the ballroom. I recognized shouted orders from firemen, and heard the sound of powerful blowers being activated.

It didn't take more than two or three minutes for the smoke to dissipate. The smarting in my eyes eased. With a few blinks, my vision began to clear and I looked up. One mystery—how firemen had arrived on the scene so quickly—was solved when I saw that the men who'd come to our rescue weren't regular city firemen. Yellow patches on their green jackets identified them as the hotel's private fire safety officers.

I heard one of the officers swear. "Jesus H. P. Christ—it was just a smoke bomb!"

The man who had been sheltering me helped me to stand. It was Roland Gray.

"Thank you," I said.

"As I rule, I don't pounce on a woman until a month of dinners have been shared," he said in his charming British accent. "Ah, well. Ms. Carmichael, when you're calculating your decision about tonight's prize, I do hope you will take into consideration the fact that I *thought* I was trying to save your life."

Smiling, I indicated my clipboard. "Sorry, but saving my life isn't one of the judging criteria."

Suddenly, his nose wrinkled with distaste. "Oh, no!" He hurried toward his stove. I followed, and saw immediately what had happened. During the excitement the burner under his lemon pudding had been left on. The pudding had boiled over, sending a thick, yellow river erupting over the pot and flowing down the side of the stove.

Gray shook his head. "My delectable dessert is DOA."

Behind us, a woman screamed.

I whirled to see Yvette Dupree, eyes bulging, her arms crossed against the clipboard she pressed tight against her chest.

She was staring at the crumpled body of Keith Ingram, who lay facedown in a widening circle of blood.

10

Roland Gray was first to recover from the shock that had momentarily frozen the rest of us. He bounded forward, grabbed Ingram's shoulder to turn him over onto his back—and was hit in the chest by spurting blood.

The stench hit my nostrils and I nearly gagged. I hadn't known that fresh blood had such a sickeningly sweet, metallic smell.

Then I realized that blood pumping meant a heart still beating. I grabbed a roll of paper towels from the counter beside Roland Gray's stove and dropped to my knees, hoping to stem the bleeding, but rough hands wrenched me away. I dropped the roll as two of the safety officers took over, trying to save Ingram.

It was a hopeless task. I'd known it was, even as I'd tried to stop his bleeding. Keith Ingram had been stabbed in the throat, and the wound was a gaping well of flesh and muscle.

Ingram wasn't going to be able to blackmail Eileen, but I couldn't forget that the video he'd made was an unexploded bomb that would go off if the wrong person found it.

Roland Gray interrupted my thoughts. He had been trying to dry his shirt and jacket with another roll of paper towels, and offered a fat wad of the sheets to me.

I looked at him, puzzled.

"Your dress," he said.

Dress? I looked down and gasped. "Oh, Lord!" The front of my peach chiffon gown—my *borrowed* designer creation—was soaked with Ingram's blood.

Did I have enough money to pay for destroying an original Jorge Allesandro? If Phil Logan didn't kill me, that designer might.

Eugene Long claimed my attention by appearing with a portable microphone in his hand and taking control of the room.

"All right, everyone. Please, stay calm." The babble of whispering voices quieted as everyone focused on Long.

"Mike, call the police," Long said to the nearest security officer, who obeyed his boss. At Long's raised hand signal, the security man at the entrance to the ballroom moved swiftly to close the doors and stand in front of them.

Long said to his captive audience, "I'm afraid that we'll all have to remain here until the police arrive, but please move back toward the walls to keep this area around the . . . around this tragic *situation* clear. For those of you who are uncomfortable standing for some length of time, I'll have the waitstaff bring in chairs."

Before I could move away, Tina Long pushed her way through the crowd with such force that she almost fell over Ingram's body. Looking down at him, she started to shriek.

Shoving his microphone under one arm, Long embraced his daughter. With her face pressed against his chest, she stopped screaming, but I could see her shoulders shaking.

"Baby doll, calm down," Long said. "Everything's going to be all right."

How is everything going to be all right? I wondered where Long kept his crystal ball.

Tina babbled something unintelligible and started sobbing and gulping for air.

Yvette Dupree stepped forward, stretched her arms out, and said to the girl. "*Ma cherie*, come."

With a nod of assent, Eugene Long guided his hysterical daughter into Yvette's arms.

"Go through the kitchen and take her to my suite," he said. "Give her some brandy and make her lie down."

When Long had introduced Yvette, he'd referred to her as his "dear friend." Apparently, that wasn't just show business—speak. It was clear to me from the scene I was witnessing that Eugene Long and Yvette Dupree were, at the least, close friends. Tina must know her, too, because she allowed herself to be transferred from her father to the French woman without complaint. And I noticed Yvette didn't ask the location of Long's suite as she hurried Tina toward the kitchen doors.

Someone in the crowd yelled, "Hey! How come they can leave and we're stuck in here?" The voice came from a portly man whose red-veined face suggested that he drank too much port.

Long glared at him. "My daughter is ill." His tone, colder than a bucket full of ice, discouraged further protest. As though a personality switch had been flipped, he flashed a bright smile. "Hey, waiters—bring everybody here fresh drinks. Including me."

Seconds after Yvette and Tina disappeared, the ball-room doors opened and six uniformed LAPD officers streamed in.

Roland Gray moved up to stand next to me. "When the owner of the Olympia Grand reports a crime, the police respond more quickly and in greater numbers than they would to the cry of an ordinary citizen," he said in his clipped English accent.

I was torn between my automatic defense of the police and the realization that Gray was probably correct. In many circumstances, wealth and celebrity bought at least some degree of preferential treatment.

Eugene Long, who had remained next to Ingram's body like a sentry, waved the police over toward him. Two officers double-timed it in his direction and the other four fanned out around the perimeter of the room.

Long showed them Ingram's body. The two officers were careful not to go too close to it, and immediately positioned themselves so as to keep anyone else away.

New movement at the ballroom's entrance caught my eye and I saw another member of the law enforcement fraternity rush into the ballroom, but this one was dressed in black tie: John O'Hara.

John spotted Shannon, Eileen, Liddy, and Bill standing together near the entrance and joined them. Shannon's expression was stony, but I could see Eileen weeping. John hugged his wife and daughter and murmured a few words. He lifted his head, surveyed the room, and spotted me. He said something to the Marshalls, left Eileen and Shannon with them, and headed toward Long, and where Keith Ingram lay dead.

I stepped forward, preventing John from going closer to the body, and to the police. "I thought you'd gone home," I whispered.

He shook his head. Noticing the blood on my dress, he said, "Are you all right?"

"I'm fine. But—"

"That's the man, Officers!" Eugene Long's voice boomed. I turned to see him pointing at John O'Hara.

11

"That's the man who assaulted Mr. Ingram tonight. Arrest him," Long demanded.

I could see that the officers recognized John. Puzzled, one of them said, "But this is Lieutenant O'Hara."

"John?" It was a new voice, but I recognized it. I turned to face John's partner, LAPD detective Hugh Weaver.

The two partners were striking in their physical contrast: At the age of fifty, John O'Hara was six inches taller than Hugh Weaver, and two years older, but John looked younger. John still had the hardened physique of the football player he'd been in college. Weaver's body had probably been hard once, but too many burgers with fries, and much too many beers, had turned his beef to lard. I'd never seen Weaver without his clothes—and any circumstance in which that could happen was unimaginable to me—but I was pretty sure that his body would look like the Pillsbury Doughboy's.

Weaver said, "Hey, John—you didn't answer your phone. How'd you get here before me?"

"I was here already. And I took tonight off, remember?"

Weaver, careful not to step in Ingram's blood, leaned over, gave the body a cursory look, straightened again. Indicating the victim, he asked John, "Who's that?"

"Keith Ingram."

Long inserted himself between the partners and addressed Weaver. "Are you the detective in charge?"

"Yeah. Who are you?"

Long appeared startled, as though he couldn't believe Weaver hadn't recognized him. "I'm Eugene Long, owner of this hotel." I half expected Long to add that his taxes paid Weaver's salary, but he didn't.

"The dead man is Keith Ingram, a nationally syndicated food critic and one of the judges at our Celebrity Cook-Off." Long jabbed his forefinger toward John. "Earlier tonight this man physically attacked Mr. Ingram. I had him removed from the premises, but I think it's likely that he slipped back into the crowd and committed the murder."

"You do, huh?" Weaver lifted his shoulders in an exaggerated shrug and curved his lips into a false smile. "Well, since you solved the case, I guess we can all go home."

Long's posture stiffened. "I do not appreciate that brand of sarcasm."

"No? I got some others I can use."

A flush reddened Long's cheeks.

I wasn't fond of Hugh Weaver, but at that moment I could have hugged him for putting the arrogant billionaire in his place.

Weaver ignored Long and focused on John. "Did you 'assault' this Ingram guy?"

"I hit him. It was close to an hour ago."

"Was he injured? Did you knock him down?"

"Ingram got back up pretty quickly," I said. "And he carried right on with the judging, so I don't think John hurt him."

Weaver asked John, "What did you do after the altercation?"

"I left," John said.

"Where'd you go?"

"For a walk, to cool off. I stayed on the hotel grounds because my wife and daughter are here. I came back inside when I saw cops arriving."

"You're going to have to give a formal statement," Weaver said.

John nodded. "Of course. You'll have it in the morning."

Long's expression was set on *sneer*. "O'Hara said he went for a walk. That means he doesn't have an alibi."

Weaver sneered right back at Long. "You watch too many TV cop shows." He glanced around and wrinkled his nose in distaste. "What's that smell?"

"The last whiffs from the smoke bomb and burned food," I said. "Most of the cooks abandoned their stoves when the chaos started."

John's partner had registered my presence with a brief nod when he arrived, but now he focused his attention on me. "What are you doing here?"

"I'm one of the cook-off judges."

"Did you see who killed Ingram?"

"No. I was watching an actor who was juggling. Then somebody set off a smoke bomb—"

"Save it," Weaver said. He was looking at the entrance to the ballroom. I followed his gaze and saw the arrival of a man and a woman wearing Windbreakers that identified them as members of the police Scientific Investigation Division. I'd never seen those two before, but I recognized the woman who came in with them: Dr. Sidney Carver, LA's new medical examiner. Her nod at Weaver was perfunctory, but she smiled warmly at John.

In a wry tone, she said, "This better be worth my missing the *NCIS* marathon. So, what have you got for me, Big John?"

"He's not on the job tonight," Weaver said.

"John O'Hara is a suspect," Long announced.

Dr. Carver cocked her head and lifted one eyebrow. "This promises to be an interesting case."

I'd first met her a few months earlier, at the scene of another brutal murder, when I'd had the misfortune to be the person who discovered the victim. Dr. Carver's pewter gray hair was cut short and shaggy, she wore glasses with outsized red frames, her clothes reeked of cigarette smoke, and her manner with everyone except John was as stinging as peroxide on a fresh cut. It was clear that she liked John, but I'd yet to see her smile at anyone else. I knew John liked her, too, because he told me it was a pleasure to work with a medical examiner that was so good at what she did.

Not long after she was hired, Nicholas had interviewed her for an article in the *Chronicle*. He told me he'd commented that her gray hair was an anomaly with her younger-looking face, and asked her age. She'd replied that it was none of his "f***ing business," but if he insisted on printing something, then he could quote her as saying she was "somewhere between fifty and death." He'd followed that question by asking if she was married, or had a significant other. Nicholas said she'd looked at him as though deciding where to cut and replied, "When I meet a man of the appropriate age, education, and income, it's usually in my professional capacity."

Dr. Carver drew on a pair of latex gloves and knelt to examine Ingram's body as SID techs photographed the scene.

Weaver moved back a few steps. "John, go stand with Shannon and Eileen. Long, take a seat somewhere out of the way. I'll talk to you in a few minutes."

Without a word, John did as Weaver instructed.

Long grumbled. He, too, obeyed, but instead of finding a place in the crowd to await his turn for questioning, Long strode to the stage. He picked up the microphone and made that annoying *tap-tap-tap* noise to be sure it was live.

"Hello, everyone. I'm afraid that this hasn't turned out to be the event we signed up for. It's a very sad night with the loss of one of the titans of the world of food criticism, and now we must remain here for a while as the police do their work. To make your waiting time a little easier, I'm going to instruct our staff to bring you all anything you'd like to eat or drink—on the house. Anything our kitchen can make or pour."

Scattered applause greeted that announcement. Long smiled, but held up his hand for quiet. "That's not all. Tonight was supposed to bring the charity of our winning star's choice a check for one hundred thousand dollars. Obviously, the contest can't be completed, so I'm going to send to the charity chosen by each of our twenty competing celebrities a check for ten thousand dollars—"

Much louder applause interrupted him. Long smiled at that, but after a moment held up his hand to stop it.

"Thank you, but that's not all. Each of you who came to watch the cook-off donated five hundred dollars to the Healthy Life Fund to be here. Well, to show our appreciation for your patience, we're going to match every one of those five-hundred-dollar donations with my own personal check to that fund. We'll work from the guest list, and be sure that each donation will be in your individual names, so remember to deduct the additional five hundred when tax time comes around." Long's face assumed a somber expression. "There's been a tragic death in our midst tonight, but we're going to make sure some good comes out of it."

In a wry tone, Roland Gray said, "Did you notice that he's using the 'royal we'? '*We're* going to match' and '*we're* going to make sure' and so forth. My guess is that he's intending to run for public office in the next few years. Probably for governor."

"You could be right," I said.

Roland Gray's speculation made me think. If Eugene Long did intend to enter politics, I wondered what he thought about the prospect of having Keith Ingram as a son-in-law. I'd learned about Ingram's bad character easily. Surely Long must know the nature of the man his daughter had fallen for.

■ ■ ■

After Weaver instructed the uniforms on scene to collect names and contact information from everyone in the

ballroom, I watched the SID techs as they processed the
area. From where I stood I had a good view, and knew that
they hadn't—or hadn't yet—found the knife someone had
plunged into Keith Ingram's neck.

Weaver took my arm and steered me around to the end
of Roland Gray's stove until we were as alone as it was
possible to be in a room full of formally attired, bejeweled,
irritated people muttering their displeasure at not being allowed to leave the ballroom.

"When the brass find out John slugged the victim, he
won't be allowed anywhere near this case. As his partner
I'll likely be thrown off it, too. This may be my only chance
to talk to anybody here, so I'll start with you. Tell me what
you saw. *Exactly*."

I did, as quickly and as thoroughly as I could, while
Weaver took notes. When I got to the part about Yvette
Dupree screaming, Weaver said, "This Dupree woman saw
the body first? Where is she?"

"Eugene Long's daughter became hysterical. He asked
Yvette to take the girl to his suite."

"Nobody should'a left here! You know better than
that."

"What could I have done? I don't have any authority."

He calmed down. "Oh, yeah. For a minute I forgot
you're just a cop's wife—widow."

Hugh Weaver's tactlessness didn't bother me; I was
used to it. In conversation, he may have been as clumsy
as someone trying to dance while wearing snowshoes, but
according to John, he was a good detective. Weaver could
say any stupid thing he wanted to as long as he was trying
to save John. If John were arrested, the emotional trauma
might send Shannon into a relapse, and Eileen would be
devastated by guilt because of what her ill-fated romance
with Keith Ingram had done to her family.

Weaver and I saw that Sidney Carver had finished her
preliminary examination of Ingram's body and was strip-

ping off her latex gloves. That was Weaver's cue to join her. I couldn't hear what they were saying, but it was clear that she was leaving.

Weaver came back to me. "The SID techs will be working the area for quite a while yet, but soon the body's going to be removed to Carver's office for autopsy. I can't wait any longer." Weaver punched a number into his cell. When he reached his captain at the West Bureau Station on Butler Avenue, he reported the unusual situation: that John O'Hara had been in the vicinity of a homicide, and that he'd also had a hostile encounter with the deceased before the murder.

I liked that "hostile encounter" bit. It sounded a lot better than saying John had physically attacked Ingram.

Weaver scowled at whatever his captain was saying. When their brief conversation was over, he snapped his cell shut and nodded unhappily.

"Just like I thought. They're dispatching another detective to take over the case. But I'm here now, and I'll keep going until I'm eighty-sixed."

With me close behind him, Weaver began collecting information from the celebrities in Sector Four, and those attending the gala who had been in our area when the smoke bomb went off. No one saw—or at least no one *admitted* to seeing—anything helpful.

Weaver had filled a dozen pages in his notebook when I saw another man enter the ballroom. While I didn't know his name, from his sports jacket, slacks, and the stern expression on his face, I was certain he was a West Bureau detective.

Weaver muttered a curse. "Bad news just walked through the door. That's Manny Hatch. He hates John's guts as bad as I hate perverts."

"Why?"

"A few years ago—remember the murder of that big music guy in Bel Air?"

"Yes. John caught the killer."

"It started out as Hatch's case. From the get-go, Hatch figured it was the wife and wasn't looking at anybody else. John kept digging and found evidence that it was the victim's stepson. Hatch was embarrassed. Ever since, he's blamed John for his not getting the promotion he thinks he deserves. With Hatch on the job, John's chance of getting out of this clean just fell through the hole in the outhouse."

12

From the sour expression on his face, LAPD detective second grade Manfred (Manny) Hatch came into the Elysian Room with a chip on his shoulder so big I saw it half a ballroom away, just from observing his arrogant manner with the hotel's uniformed employees. He glowered at them as though he was the head of the INS and they—even the blond Norwegian waiter and the African American security guard—were illegal aliens he'd like to ship back across California's southern border.

Detective Hatch behaved only marginally better to the prosperous guests in the ballroom, but he had enough sense of self-preservation not to go too far in trying to intimidate them. Hatch's type was by far a minority in the LAPD, but I'd seen such behavior before. John called them "little Napoleons," even though, like Hatch, some of them were close to six feet tall.

Hatch's manner improved when Eugene Long approached him. Unlike Hugh Weaver, Hatch must have recognized Long, and realized that Long's immense wealth could be a more powerful cudgel than was Hatch's badge. Hatch's facial expression relaxed from a scowl into something approximating a collegial smile. But I imagined that secretly he'd be one happy detective if he found Long—or one of LA's other power brokers—standing over a murder victim with the weapon in his hand.

My attention was diverted to a man at the entrance to the ballroom, standing beside the police officer guarding the door. Dressed casually, in a brown tweed jacket over a moss green turtleneck sweater and tan slacks, he had a ruddy complexion and light, curly hair, cut short. I noticed him because he was waving in my direction, but he wasn't anyone I knew. Then I realized that the man was signaling to Roland Gray, who was standing next to me.

"A man at the door is trying to get your attention," I said.

Gray glanced toward the entrance and gave the stranger an answering wave.

"That's Will Parker," Gray said. "He drove me here tonight."

"Your chauffeur?"

"My assistant, actually. Helps with research, but he drives me occasionally. I'd better go tell him we'll be a while."

I watched Gray cross the room, speak first to the police officer and then to Parker. Gray's assistant was shorter than his employer, and seemed to be a few years younger. He reminded me of someone . . . As I was turning away, I realized who it was—the British actor, Trevor Howard, when he was about forty and starred in the classic ill-fated romance that played often on cable: *Brief Encounter*.

The "encounter" between Gray and Parker was brief, too. Parker turned away from the entrance and Gray started back in my direction.

"The officer at the door has no idea when we'll be released, so I told Will to go get himself some dinner and come back." Gesturing toward the police, Gray asked, "Anything happening?"

"It looks like Detective Hatch has finished talking to Eugene Long. Now he's heading toward Hugh Weaver."

As we watched, John joined Weaver and Hatch. The three detectives spoke quietly to each other. Even though I couldn't hear the words, it seemed from their body language that it wasn't a pleasant chat. John's posture stiffened and

I saw his jaw muscles tighten. Down at his side, Weaver's hands balled into fists. Weaver must have been told to turn over his notes, because one hand uncurled enough for him to reach into his jacket pocket to retrieve his investigator's notebook. Clearly fuming, he shoved it at Hatch.

■ ■ ■

Finally, the last of us present during the time of the murder were told we could go home, but admonished to keep ourselves available for further interviews.

Eileen left her mother and father standing with Liddy and Bill and hurried over to me. She was trembling. "What are we going to do? I've never been so scared."

"Honey, stay calm. Don't panic."

She took a breath and steadied her voice. "Daddy doesn't know what Keith was using to blackmail me, but that's bound to come out as soon as the police search Keith's house and find the tape. Daddy'll never be able to prove he didn't know about it. I don't care for myself anymore, but what Keith did to me could make them charge Daddy with murder—and it's all my fault."

"It is *not* your fault. I have an idea, but I'm going to need you thinking clearly. First, what else in the house might link you to Ingram?"

"What do you mean?"

"Are there pictures of the two of you together?"

"No. We never went out in public, except sometimes to an out-of-the-way restaurant. Keith said we should be discreet, so people wouldn't think he'd praised our fudge business because of . . ." She blushed.

"Forget about that, honey. Think hard now. Did you leave clothing at his place? Jewelry? Anything at all that could be traced back to you?"

"No. Not a thing. There's just that that awful video. Why are you asking?"

"I'm going to keep you out of this, but I need your help."

I saw a glimmer of hope in her eyes. "What can I do?"

On the corner of a display table to my left there was a pile of program sheets, listing the celebrity contestants and the location of each of their stoves. I picked one up, turned it over to the blank side, and handed it and the pen from the top of my clipboard to Eileen.

"Go into the bathroom and lock yourself in a stall. Sketch out a floor plan of Ingram's house. As many details as you can remember. And where the doors and windows are in the back."

"What are you—?"

I shook my head to silence her. "If you don't know you won't have to lie. Does Ingram's house have an alarm system?"

"Yes."

It would have been too good to be true, but I asked the next question anyway. "Do you know the code?"

"No. I was never in the house when he wasn't there."

"Do you know if his alarm system has interior motion detectors?"

"It did have, but he told me he got rid of them because his maid kept setting them off accidentally."

Bless that maid, I thought.

I saw Liddy heading toward me and gave Eileen a nudge. "Go. Put down every detail you can remember."

Liddy came over to where I was standing by the door.

"Eileen's going to stay at John and Shannon's house tonight," Liddy said. "John's going to take them home. Why don't you stay over with Bill and me?"

"No, thank you. I can't leave Tuffy alone all night. Just drop me off at home."

"We'll pick Tuffy up, and get a change of clothes for you."

"I can't." I drew Liddy a few feet away from the person nearest to us and lowered my voice. "Ingram had something that I can't let anyone find. The police are going to be searching his house for clues to his murder, probably as soon as tomorrow morning, so I've got to go there tonight."

Liddy's eyes widened with excitement. "If you're going to break into somebody's house, I'm not letting you go alone."

■ ■ ■

The first thing I did when I got home, after greeting Tuffy and Emma, and assuring Tuffy that we'd go for a walk shortly, was to take off my once-beautiful gown and get a good look at the damage.

It was awful. While I was wearing it, I could tell that it was bad, but studying it on the hanger I knew that it was hopeless. Beyond even the best dry cleaner's art. The stains on the front of the delicate peach chiffon fabric had hardened, and turned from the vivid red of fresh blood to a dull shade of old rust.

Even though he was a disgusting human being, the fact was that a man had died a violent death tonight; that was far more serious than the loss of a designer gown. I wasn't sure Phil Logan would see it that way. I dreaded calling him, but I knew that I had to. After putting on a sweater and slacks, I sat down on the edge of my bed and picked up the receiver.

Instead of dialing Phil's cell phone, which I knew he answered twenty-four hours a day, I did the cowardly thing and punched in his office number, to get his voice mail.

One ring.

"Hello," Phil said.

Ooops. "What are you doing at the office so late, Phil?"

"Working. I heard about Ingram's murder."

"How did you know? It couldn't have been on the news yet."

"There's no such thing as a secret—if you've got friends

who are cops," Phil said. "I'm writing a press release that mentions your name, but doesn't make it sound as though I'm using somebody's death for publicity. It's a delicate balancing act."

"Must you do that? It makes me uncomfortable."

"Sometimes effective PR is like making sausages—you shouldn't see how it's done," Phil said.

"I make my own sausages, and there's nothing to hide."

"Talking about food is making me hungry. Listen, the story I'm writing says that you ruined a six-thousand-dollar Jorge Allesandro gown trying to save Keith Ingram's life."

Six thousand dollars!

"Two security men worked on him. You can't give me credit for—"

"My hotel source said you were the first to try to administer aid. Right or wrong?"

"Well, I tried to stop the bleeding from his wound, but it was just for a second or two until the security men—"

"But you tried. Right? And in thinking about Ingram, your dress was ruined."

It was useless to try to talk Phil out of doing his job as he saw it. I gave up and moved on to the subject I feared. "You said the dress cost six thousand dollars. Will Mr. Allesandro let me make partial payments over time?"

I heard Phil chuckle. "Are you worried about that? Don't be. Jorge won't ask you for money. He'll get many thousands of dollars of free publicity out of the fact that you were wearing his gown at the scene of a murder. Luckily, my photographer got pictures."

"When?"

"Tonight. There was so much going on, you probably didn't notice."

"No, I didn't." A new thought occurred to me; it was about Phil's boss and mine, Mickey Jordan. "Does Mickey know what happened tonight?"

"No. He and Iva are sailing around the Greek Islands,

and Greece is nine hours ahead of us. He makes his daily check in call at six PM his time, which is nine AM ours. I'll tell him about it then."

"The trip is their second honeymoon. I hope this won't make him cut it short."

"No reason for him to do that. You were just on the scene of a crime—you didn't commit one."

Not yet, anyway.

"Get some sleep," Phil said. "You've got a live show to do tomorrow night. Actually, you'll be going on the air about nineteen hours from now."

I agreed—but with my fingers crossed. Phil told me he would have the dress picked up sometime tomorrow, and we said good night.

My second call was to Nicholas D'Martino's cell phone. He answered in two rings, but sounded sleepy. When he heard my voice, he said, "Hi, Slugger. How'd the judging go?"

"The contest was interrupted. Somebody threw a smoke bomb, and when everybody could see again we found that Keith Ingram had been stabbed to death."

"Details." His tone was brisk, professional. All trace of sleepiness was gone from his voice.

I told Nicholas everything I knew, including the fact that John had hit Ingram close to an hour before the murder. There was no way to keep that a secret to protect John because there had been too many witnesses. Because John was a decorated lieutenant in the LAPD, that detail was sure to be in every report of the crime.

"Do you think O'Hara killed Ingram?"

"No! And I'm not saying that because he's my friend. John is not a murderer. In fact, he's never even killed anyone in the line of duty."

"Okay, okay. Don't get mad at me. I'll give him the benefit of the doubt, but socking Ingram looks bad. It had something to do with Eileen, didn't it?"

I didn't want to lie to Nicholas, but I wasn't going to betray Eileen. Taking a middle course, I said, "Maybe John heard bad things about Ingram and women. Look, I can't talk about this anymore right now. I have a live show to do tonight. When are you coming back?"

"Friday morning. I'm going to call the paper now, see who's on the Ingram story and work with him on follow-ups."

"See you Friday?"

"Without fail." His voice took on a caring tone. "Sleep well. I know it won't be easy." He added something sweet and we said good night.

13

It was nearly two o'clock in the morning when Liddy phoned from her car to tell me she was on her way. As we planned, she had waited until Bill was asleep, and then sneaked out.

I grabbed the gym bag in which I'd packed the items I would need: a pencil flashlight, a roll of duct tape, a spray can of WD-40, a hand towel, a fresh pair of the white cotton "beauty gloves" I wore when I went to sleep with my hands covered in cream—and an auto center punch. The final item was something I had taken from the glove compartment of my Jeep shortly after I got home. It was five inches long and half an inch in diameter: about the size of a stubby pencil. With its alloy steel point, it was the most crucial tool of my new trade: burglary.

Even though I had committed to memory every inch of Eileen's diagram of Ingram's house, I didn't want to risk the smallest mistake, so I folded the precious sheet of paper and shoved it into the pocket of my slacks.

After petting Tuffy and Emma, and assuring them that I would be back soon, I slipped outside to wait in the darkness for Liddy. Lucky for me—for what I intended to do—there was only the tiniest sliver of new moon, and clouds obscured the stars.

My neighborhood was quiet. None of the houses I could see from where I stood in the driveway showed the glow of interior lights. The dogs in this canine-friendly area weren't barking. The only sounds I heard were faint traffic noises in the distance. I knew most of the vehicles carried people who were going to their work, or coming home. Or returning from late night revelry. I wondered if any of the motorists were heading toward commission of a felony. Given the most recent Los Angeles crime statistics, I guessed that there were probably a few villains among the innocent commuters.

A pair of headlights turned onto my street from Montana Avenue, three blocks south. At that distance, I couldn't tell who might be in the car, so to avoid arousing suspicion by standing outside at this hour I retreated to concealment behind the large weeping willow tree in my front yard.

When the vehicle was half a block away, I recognized Liddy's ivory Land Rover and hurried down to the sidewalk to wave at her. She stopped next to me, but didn't cut the engine.

As I climbed into the passenger seat and put the gym bag down next to my feet, she put one index finger to her lips. I nodded agreement to being silent, but when I fastened my seat belt the resulting *click* sounded almost as loud as a car backfiring.

Liddy emitted a barely audible nervous titter. I held my breath. We scanned the nearest houses for any sudden turning on of lights.

Nothing.

. . . not a creature was stirring, not even a mouse . . .

Liddy put the car in gear but didn't turn her lights on again until we came to Montana Avenue and she turned left, toward Hollywood.

Even at this hour, there was strong illumination on Montana. For the first time I was able to get a good look at Liddy. I laughed, because we were dressed almost identically in black sweaters and black slacks. The only difference in our attire was that she wore a black knit cap covering her blonde hair. I'm a brunette, so I didn't need a cap to make myself less noticeable, but I'd tied my shoulder-length hair back in a ponytail.

"We look like twin cat burglars," I said. "Maybe we should stop at a gas station and buy some black grease to cover our faces."

Liddy shuddered. "That would be awful for our skin. Open the glove compartment and take out the baggie."

I did as directed and removed a Ziploc bag. "What's in here?"

"Two pairs of Bill's powder-free latex examination gloves. So we won't leave fingerprints. He keeps a box in the bathroom. Aren't they just like what the police use when they're investigating?"

"Yes. These are better than the white cotton gloves I brought. You have an unexpected talent for crime, Liddy."

"Thanks." In the headlights of cars coming toward us, I saw her grin with pride.

■　■　■

With traffic moving swiftly on Sunset Boulevard at that time in the morning, we reached Laurel Canyon in twelve minutes. At my instruction, Liddy turned left and we headed up into the narrow, winding canyon.

When we were about fifty yards from Kirkwood Drive, I said, "Slow down here."

Just below the Canyon Country Store, I directed Liddy to turn into the shallow turnaround at the foot of Rothdell Terrace. "Park here, in front of the dry cleaners, but face out toward Laurel."

Liddy maneuvered as I'd suggested, then stopped and turned off the engine. No cars were behind us on Laurel, nor, for the moment, were any coming from the valley toward Hollywood. We sat in the darkness for a few moments, listening for the sounds of footsteps, and watching for lights turned on in any of the nearby houses.

When we were satisfied that the neighborhood was asleep, Liddy whispered, "What now?"

"We walk up Rothdell and find Ingram's little pseudo Swiss chalet."

"Walk? That road looks as though it goes almost straight up."

"It's narrow, and I don't know where it would be safe to park. Besides, if we have to get away fast it's better to have the car down here, where we can get right onto Laurel Canyon."

To reduce the amount of noise we made, we opened only Liddy's driver's side door. After she got out quietly, I handed her my gym bag, then climbed over the gearbox, and stepped down onto the cement beside her. Liddy closed the Rover's door with only the faintest *clunk* and locked the vehicle.

Liddy whispered, "Did you bring those lock-picky things Mack gave you when you kept losing your keys?"

Even at this tense moment, I had to smile at that old memory. "No. I have another plan for getting into Ingram's house."

Walking as quietly as possible, we started up Rothdell. I was praying that we wouldn't run into any foraging coyotes. The canyons were full of them, especially during a period of drought such as Southern California was currently experiencing. This was a fear I hadn't mentioned to Liddy, who lived south of Sunset Boulevard, in the woodsless and coyote-free section of Beverly Hills.

Another potential danger we faced was running into some predawn dog walker who would be likely to know we didn't live in this area. In case we did, I'd prepared a story to tell: We're middle-aged fans of the Doors, looking for the houses in which our musical heroes had stayed. It wasn't a very credible excuse for being there, but it was better than admitting we were planning to commit burglary.

Several houses up the steep lane I touched Liddy on the

arm, signaling her to stop. I indicated a structure that resembled pictures I'd seen of Swiss chalets. Nothing else we'd passed looked like that residence. It was constructed of dark wood, with rectangular windows framed in white, each of which contained four to six small panes. The roof had three peaks. One faced front, a smaller one faced to the left, and the smallest was set toward the rear. All that was missing was a layer of snow blanketing the roof shingles, and a pair of skis leaning next to the front door.

As Eileen had described it, this was a one-and-a-half-story house, with the upper level set a third of the way back from the ground floor. Keith Ingram's bedroom was up there.

Liddy whispered, "What do we do now?"

"You hide in the shrubbery at the front while I go around to the back of the house. If I don't manage to get inside in three or four minutes, I'll come back. If I set off the burglar alarm, run fast as you can back to your car and get in. Drive across Laurel, go a few yards down Kirkwood Drive, cut your lights, and wait for me."

"What about the alarm system? He must have one."

"I have a plan," I said, with more confidence than I felt. "Do you have your cell phone with you?"

She patted the side pocket of her slacks. "It's on vibrate."

"Mine is, too. Call me if you see anyone coming up to this house."

I put down my gym bag long enough to pull on the pair of Bill's latex gloves Liddy had provided. We gave each other the thumbs-up sign.

Carrying the bag, I made my way through the darkness around to the back of Keith Ingram's silent house.

There was just enough illumination from a streetlight in front of the next home for me to stay on the dirt path that led to the rear of the property. Eileen had alerted me to the fact that there was a wooden gate leading to the backyard, and told me where to feel for the latch.

The house next door was separated from Ingram's lot by a six-foot fence made of wooden slats. A backyard security light burned. Only a little light came over the fence, but it allowed me to see what I was doing. Careful to make no noise, I set the gym bag down, took out the can of WD-40, and squirted the gate's metal hinges. Seconds later, testing the gate by easing it open a scant few inches, I was rewarded by a welcome silence.

Bless you, whoever invented WD-40.

Through the gate, I saw that the lot wasn't a very deep one. There was just enough room for Ingram's swimming pool and a narrow brick patio.

I'd made it around to the back of the house without doing anything to arouse the neighbors. Fear of what I was doing made my heart pound. I stopped, stood still, and took a few deep breaths to calm myself. Extending my free hand, I was relieved to see that it was steady. A line from an old astronaut movie ran through my head: "All systems go."

"I'm going," I said to myself.

Studying the back of the house, I saw that Eileen's rough sketch of the exterior had been accurate. Next to the rear door was one of the chalet's vertical six-pane windows. It was set waist high. Three panes were on one side, and three on the other. Strips of white painted wood divided them.

I ran the fingers of my other hand along the bottom of the window and felt the wires that meant an alarm would go off when the window was raised.

But I had no intention of raising that window.

I removed the duct tape from my bag, tore six pieces about eight inches in length. After I'd attached them to the glass panes and to the side of the house beside the window, I took the hand towel out of the bag, draped it over my right wrist, and gripped the item I had taken from my Jeep's glove compartment: my auto center punch.

Several years ago, I'd seen this little tool on a documentary about river rescues. It was used to break the windows of submerged cars. As soon as the program was over, I Googled "auto center punch" and found that they were sold on Amazon, for four dollars apiece, plus shipping. I immediately ordered six of them as presents for Eileen, Shannon, John, Liddy, Bill, and myself. I hoped everybody was keeping them in their cars, as I had been. Southern California is essentially a desert, but we do have floods sometimes, and whenever we have a storm, a car or two is swept into the Los Angeles River. For most of the time, it was a cement channel and a river in name only. There was so little water in it between storms that we called it the "Los Angeles trickle," but when there was a sudden deluge from the skies it was transformed into a deadly trap.

At this moment, I had a more immediate danger right in front of me. Holding my breath and saying a little prayer, I knelt close to the window and positioned the tip of the auto punch near the bottom of the glass—as I had seen it demonstrated on television—and *punched*.

I sighed with relief when the pane cracked down the center. The glass didn't fall because it was held in place by the tape. Working faster now, I repeated the punching process five more times, then began removing the pieces of glass, and setting them on the patio beside me.

Ouch! A shard sliced through the rubber glove on my right hand. There was just enough light coming from over the fence next door that I could see blood oozing through the slit. I tore the glove enough to expose the cut on my finger. It wasn't too bad. I pressed the finger against the towel for a few seconds. The bleeding stopped. I went back to work removing the panes.

When all the glass was out of the window, I wrapped my right hand in the towel again. Using that hand, I pressed firmly against the center strip of wood that had held the six panes in place. It cracked. Another press and I'd loosened it enough to push it aside.

No alarm shrieked.

Eileen's sketch had filled me with hope that I wouldn't have to open a door or a window, that I could create my own entrance into the house. By going through the panes and not disturbing the outside frame, as far as the alarm circuits were concerned, that window had remained closed.

I stuffed the towel back in the gym bag, removed my pencil flashlight, and dropped the bag into the house. I clicked on the pencil light, clamped it between my teeth so that my hands were free—and eased myself headfirst through the opening I'd made.

And into the darkness below.

14

Stretching downward inch by inch, my gloved hands touched a tile floor. According to Eileen's diagram, I was in the kitchen.

When I'd maneuvered all of my body inside and twisted around so that I could stand, I transferred the pencil light from my mouth to one hand and aimed the slim beam around the room. Ingram had all the basic kitchen equipment, with everything neatly arranged for cooking convenience. The ubiquitous step stool—there was one in every kitchen that I'd ever seen—fit into a space beside the stove, safely out of the way of foot traffic. I wouldn't be falling over it.

So far, so good, but there wasn't time to think about how well things had gone thus far. At any moment my luck might turn.

Using the tiny beam to guide my way, I found the staircase and climbed.

Ingram's bedroom was a man's lair: a king-size bed with a headboard carved from some dark wood. Above the bed was a wooden canopy, with little lights set into it.

Opposite the bed, as Eileen had described, was a large armoire.

Using the pencil light to examine it closely, I discovered a peephole disguised as part of the raised design. When I opened the door, I saw what had caused Eileen so much terror. There was a video camera, aimed through the peephole at the bed.

Lights. Camera. Action. I had the urge to throw up.

A shelf below the camera contained at least a dozen DVDs. Homemade.

I shuffled through them, looking for labels. No labels, but at the bottom of each case were small initials inscribed neatly in silver paint.

Did all of those cases contain video recordings of women with whom he had sex, taped with or without their knowledge? Thinking about that made me feel sickened to be standing in Keith Ingram's bedroom.

I found a DVD marked with the initials EO'H. After making sure there was only one that had Eileen's initials on it, I grabbed it and closed the armoire.

For a brief moment, I was tempted to open the armoire again and take *all* of the DVDs, to spare the other women. But I knew I couldn't do that. They were properly police evidence; one of the women in that collection could be his killer. I felt justified in taking Eileen's because I knew that she hadn't stabbed Ingram. Still, whether they were tricked, as Eileen had been, or if they were willing exhibitionists, I felt sorry for the women who would soon be exposed. If any of those women were married—

The piercing *ring* of Ingram's bedside phone nearly gave me a heart attack!

Instinctively, one hand went to the pocket holding my cell phone. I clutched at it, but it wasn't vibrating. The ringing phone that had startled me really was Keith Ingram's. Either the person on the other end of the line was someone who didn't know he was dead, or it was the police calling to see if there was anyone else in Ingram's house.

I doubted that Detective Hatch—*Hatchet*, I was calling him to myself—could obtain a search warrant before midmorning, but he might send a patrol car to guard the outside to prevent anyone from entering until the police searched Ingram's residence.

I knew I had to get out fast. My luck had been good so far, but good luck could turn bad in an instant. I didn't dare

stay in this house I'd broken into even a few minutes longer. I shoved Eileen's DVD into my bag and hurried down
the stairs and climbed out through the broken window.

On the patio, I took a few deep breaths of the cold night
air to calm my racing heart as I listened for any sounds that
might mean trouble for me.

But the houses on either side of Ingram's place were as
dark and silent as when I'd arrived.

Liddy was still crouched in the shrubbery in front of the
house when I let myself out through the back. As soon as I
whispered her name, she emerged and grabbed my arm.

"I'm so glad you're all right! You were gone so long I
was getting worried."

I pressed my index finger against my lips. She nodded,
and we scurried down Rothdell Terrace as quickly and quietly as we could.

Liddy's ivory Land Rover was exactly where we'd left it,
and I was relieved to see that there were no other vehicles
nearby. We scrambled inside and made our escape from
the scene of my crime.

By the time we reached Sunset Boulevard we began to
relax.

"Whew. We made it," Liddy said. "Did you find what
you were looking for?"

I paused to think before I spoke. I didn't want to lie to
her, but I couldn't tell her the truth.

Liddy was smart enough to realize what my silence
meant. "Forget the question. If I don't know anything, I
can't slip up, right?"

I gave her hand an affectionate squeeze. "Thank you.
You are the best."

In the headlights of cars coming toward us, I saw her
smile. "Yeah, yeah—that's what all the burglars say to
their getaway drivers."

■ ■ ■

Tuffy must have heard Liddy's Land Rover pull up outside because as soon as I unlocked my front door, he was there to greet me, wagging his entire back end with excitement. I gave him some loving strokes, and hurried toward the kitchen at the back of the house. He followed me.

In the kitchen, I opened the plastic case and took out the DVD Ingram had made of himself and Eileen. Then I realized that I had a problem. It would bend, but it wouldn't break.

Oh, for the good old days of videotape that I could have ripped out of its cassette and burned in the sink.

I glanced around the kitchen, searching for something that could destroy the disk beyond repair.

Poultry shears?

Opening my tool drawer, I spotted something even better: the heavy-duty clippers I used on my rose bushes. I went to work on the disk and in a matter of seconds I had cut it into little pieces.

I took the key to the rear gate from its hook on the kitchen wall, and let Tuffy and myself out into my backyard. While Tuffy relieved himself against his favorite tree near the rear fence, I unlocked the gate and slipped out into the alleyway. Thursday was garbage pickup day, and it was already three hours into Thursday morning. Up and down the alleyway I saw that the big plastic garbage cans had been set out for collection. Starting at the far end of the alley, and moving farther and farther from my own block, I deposited bits of the DVD beneath the trash in a dozen garbage receptacles until the last little piece was thrown away.

Four blocks from home, I inched my arms up into the sleeves of my jacket so that my hands were covered, and wiped the DVD case clean of finger prints, then broke it in half at its spine. Without leaving prints, I shoved each of the halves beneath smelly bags of trash in two different receptacles.

Now that I was sure no trace of the DVD tormenting Eileen could ever be found, I went home to stand under a hot shower and scrub away any trace of tonight's activities.

Later, with Tuffy lying at the foot of the bed and Emma curled up on the pillow beside me, I tried to sleep, but wasn't having much luck. A line from *Macbeth*—a play I taught in my old high school English classes—kept running through my head:

Sleep that knits up the raveled sleave of care . . .

But my "sleave" stayed raveled. For me, sleep was fitful, and full of cares.

15

Thursday morning I was returning with Tuffy from his morning walk when I saw John O'Hara's black Lincoln parked in front of my house, and John sitting alone on my doorstep. Tuffy saw him, too, wagged his tail, and tugged at his leash. I released him and he raced toward his old friend.

John stood when he saw us, said "Hi" to me, and greeted Tuffy with the gentle roughhousing Tuffy enjoyed with him.

"Where's Eileen?" I asked. I knew if she had come here with John, she would have let him into the house.

"With her mother. Shannon's still pretty upset over what happened last night."

"How are *you*?" I asked.

"Sidelined. Not suspended, but that's only because the squad's undermanned. The fact that I slugged a civilian goes in my jacket with a reprimand."

"That's not so bad." I tried to sound cheerful, but a reprimand wasn't good.

"Maybe . . . Hey, can you spare a cup of coffee for a guy who doesn't have a case at the moment?"

"Of course. How about some breakfast, too?"

"That would be great."

As soon as I opened the front door, Tuffy dashed into the house. After our vigorous walk I knew he was heading for his water bowl. John and I followed him into the kitchen.

John sat down at the table, as he had hundreds of times over the years, but this was a different John, one who was less confident. He almost looked lost.

"Del, I need your help."

"What can I do?"

"Obviously, that smoke bomb was set off to cover Ingram's murder. Weaver told me he asked you about this last night, but I wondered if you might have had some new memory since then, or even a guess, about who could have set it off."

"No, I'm sorry," I said. "Those things are so simple to make just about anyone in that room could have prepared it before the gala. All that person had to do was bring the cooked sugar and saltpeter mixture in a sheet of foil, set it on fire with a match or cigarette lighter, and toss it into the crowd."

Interest replaced the look of dejection in his eyes. "How do you know how to make a smoke bomb?"

"From the Internet. A few years ago, when Eileen was taking high school chemistry, she wanted to make one for a demonstration. No, John—I'm sure Eileen was across the room when—"

"You haven't told anyone she knows how to make a smoke bomb, have you?"

"Of course not."

"Thank you," John said.

"You're *thanking* me for protecting Eileen? That's insulting! I don't care how worried you are, I deserve better than that."

John looked at me in amazement. He'd seldom seen me flare up in anger, and it had never before been directed at *him*.

"I'm sorry," he said.

I heard the sincerity in his voice, and saw that he was embarrassed. To let the awkward moment pass, I poured him a mug of coffee.

After a few sips, his said, "You've got good powers of observation, Del. I know you probably told it all tõ Weaver, but Hatch confiscated his notes, so let's start fresh. Think back to a few minutes before the smoke bomb went off. Who was standing in your area?"

I closed my eyes, focused my mind on the ballroom, and began to visualize the scene. "This wasn't a show with assigned seats. People were moving all around. The ones closest to me and to Ingram were watching the celebrities in Sector Four cook. But then the comic actor on the other side of the room started a spectacular juggling routine, and it caught everybody's attention."

"Name?"

"Wolf Wheeler. He stars in those raunchy comedies with food fights, explosions, and topless starlets."

John added Wheeler's name to his notes. "Go on. Who were the celebrities in Sector Four?"

"Francine Ames—the actress from Eileen's favorite TV soap opera when she was growing up. Oona Rogers and Coupe Deville—they're husband and wife movie stars, but they were cooking at separate stoves. The one nearest me was Roland Gray, the novelist." I opened my eyes. "I'll make a sketch for you."

As I had been visualizing, John had been writing in the notebook he carried in his jacket pocket. He flipped to a clean page and handed it to me.

"I'll be this little circle, here," I said. "I'll use initials for the others. Roland Gray was facing me, but when people started to watch the juggling he came out from behind the stove and stood near me. Deville was at the stove next to Gray's, on Gray's right. To Deville's right was Oona Rogers, and on the other side of Oona was Francine Ames. Everyone was close together, and all were working at their stoves until the show started on the other side of the ballroom. While I was watching the juggling, I'm afraid I didn't see what anyone else was doing."

"Let's go over who was standing nearest to you and to Ingram."

"Roland Gray was somewhere on my right, but slightly behind me. Ingram was a few feet away—maybe two or three yards—on my left. Yvette Dupree was somewhere on Ingram's right, but she had moved up closer to where Oona Rogers was cooking. I think Yvette had her back to Ingram. There was a couple in their fifties just behind Yvette. I don't know their names, but I'd recognize their faces. I think that's pretty much where people near Ingram were standing when we were watching the juggling act. There were other people behind us, but I couldn't see who they were, or exactly where they were standing when the smoke suddenly started filling our area and people panicked, bumping into each other and screaming."

Remembering the brief sensation of pain on my skin, I said. "Just before the smoke erupted, a drop of something hot hit my hand. I think the lighted foil was tossed from behind me."

I had a momentary flash of excitement, but one glance at John's sober expression quashed it.

"That's no help unless you know who was behind you," he said.

I studied the sketch I'd made: all those little marks around the circle that represented me. "This isn't much help, is it?"

"It might be. Some. It eliminates the crowd on three sides of the room, so that cuts down the list of suspects."

"That must leave at least a couple dozen people in my area who were in the right spot to set off the smoke and kill Ingram."

"They'll be scrutinized for any connection they had to Ingram," John said. "Unless someone is shooting at us, most police work is the process of elimination, putting the shoe leather on the concrete, asking questions and checking answers until somebody slips up, or we find enough evidence for an arrest.

"You weren't watching the four celebrities in your section, or the French woman. Any one of them, or someone else you didn't see, could have tossed the smoke bomb and stabbed Ingram. Based on my slugging the vic earlier, Hatch thinks I could have sneaked in behind the crowd, set off the bomb, and killed him."

"That's ridiculous," I said. "If you were going to kill a man, why would you have hit him earlier and called attention to yourself? Besides, where could you have cooked up a smoke bomb? You said you were walking around the hotel grounds. You wouldn't have had time to go somewhere, concoct that thing, and come back in after your . . . fight."

"It wasn't a fight. I punched him and he went down. That's assault and battery, and you know it. As for the bomb, I could have made it before we got to the hotel and just lighted it when people's attention was on something else."

"You didn't know that Wolf Wheeler would start performing," I protested.

"I didn't," John said, "but someone might have."

"He wasn't scheduled entertainment. Apparently, he saw an opportunity to start showing off and be the center of attention. That's hardly unheard of for an actor."

"Wheeler could be an accessory. He might have a history with Ingram, or ties to someone on your side of the room. Those possibilities have to be checked out."

My wall phone rang. John clenched his jaw, signaling his irritation at the interruption.

"I'll make it quick," I said.

In response to my hello, I heard the voice of one of the Better Living Channel's telephone operators. "A man named Roland Gray is trying to reach you," she said. "Of course I wouldn't give him your number, but if you like I can transfer him to your line now."

"Yes, that's fine," I said.

"Hello? Della Carmichael? This is Roland Gray. I hope I'm not disturbing you."

"No," I said, "but I don't have much time to talk at the moment."

"I'll be brief. According to my private investigator, Sherlock Google, you teach cooking classes in Santa Monica. Correct?"

"Yes, I do."

"I was wondering if you would like me to come there some time, to demonstrate one of my puddings. I don't mean to be self-aggrandizing, but I am something of an expert on the subject of pudding. It's the forgotten pleasure."

I was about to put him off when I had an idea. "How about being the guest on my live show tonight? I can cut the dessert I was going to make and we can substitute pudding. Your thrillers are so popular, I'm sure the viewers would enjoy the surprise of watching you cook. Are you available?"

"I can be . . . Yes, definitely," he said. "I'll bring all the ingredients and my favorite utensils."

"That's wonderful. Would you bring a finished pudding, too, so we can display the end product? And also a copy of your latest book. I'll show it to the audience and to the viewers at home."

"How delightful of you. Where is your studio, and what time shall I be there?"

I gave him the address. "We go on the air at seven PM, but you should arrive by six so the director can walk you through your segment."

"I'll see you this evening," he said.

After replacing the receiver, I turned to John. He was looking at me with curiosity.

"That was the British author from the contest. Roland Gray."

I picked up the receiver again, dialed the studio, and left a message for director Quinn Tanner, telling her that the famous novelist Roland Gray was going to be a guest on the show tonight.

"He'll be making his special pudding for the audience, so I'm cutting the dessert I'd planned to make," I told Quinn's voice mail. After letting her know what time Gray would arrive, I said that I'd see her later, and disconnected.

"It appears you've made another conquest," John said. "Roland Gray's a bad writer, but I have to admire how fast he works."

I ignored John's sarcasm. "He's a good writer, or at least a good storyteller, or he wouldn't sell so many millions of copies. I like his books—but I invited him to be on the show so that I can talk to him about last night. *We* can talk to him, if you want to come this evening."

"You can bet I'll be there. You shouldn't be alone with someone who could be a murderer."

"After the smoke bomb went off, Roland Gray kept me from getting hurt by the stampeding crowd. We were both crouched under his preparation counter. Before that, he was facing me. When the juggling started, he moved around to stand on my side of his stove to get a better view of Wolf Wheeler's act. I'm hoping that he saw something or someone in the crowd behind me and has not realized that it's significant."

John looked skeptical. "It's a long shot."

"Practically everything in life is a long shot. If he knows something that helps the investigation, and you solve the murder, that should get you reinstated."

"Instead of arrested," John said glumly.

"Arrested?" I felt a jolt of fear for him. "You're not serious?"

"Manny Hatch is going to try to hang Ingram's killing around my neck."

Tuffy, who had been relaxing while we talked, lifted his head to stare toward the front of the house. He got to his feet. I heard a growl low in his throat—and a second later the doorbell rang.

16

I started at the sound of the doorbell. John's posture stiffened. I guessed John had the same concern as I did: that the visitor was Detective Manny Hatch, clutching handcuffs and a warrant for John's arrest.

I calmed down when I realized it was too soon for Hatch to make a move against John. He didn't have evidence other than John's confrontation with Ingram. Thanks to my early morning burglary, he wouldn't find a motive for John to have killed Ingram.

"It's probably just Phil, or someone from his office," I said. "He's having the dress I wore last night picked up."

I started toward the front door. John got up and followed me.

Through the living room window I saw that the person pressing my bell wasn't Detective Hatch. I let out a little sigh of relief.

I opened the door to be ignored by Hugh Weaver, John's LAPD partner. Without so much as a blink in my direction, he looked past me at John.

"We gotta talk," Weaver said.

"Has there been progress in the investigation?" I asked.

"One of the SID guys found the smoke bomb foil balled up and shoved down into one of those palm tree containers."

"Prints on the foil?" John asked.

Weaver grunted in frustration. "We got zilch."

"Come into the kitchen and have breakfast," I said.

Weaver's scowl cracked, and he almost smiled.

A few minutes later I was cooking for the three of us. Scrambled eggs and bacon for me, and the same plus large pancakes for John and his partner. I'd learned years ago that John liked pancakes the size of a salad plate. No "dollar size" griddlecakes for this crime-fighter.

"The f***in' captain—excuse me, Della."

"That's okay. I've heard the word before."

"Anyhow, he put me on deskwork, taking calls from our grateful public." Weaver's voice dripped sarcasm. "Grateful, my left nut. Nothin' we do is good enough or fast enough for the knuckle-draggers who scream when we can't send detectives to find their missing dogs, or when they're given the wrong order at McDonald's."

"At least you aren't a murder suspect," John said.

" 'Big whoop,' as my ex-wife used to say. I'd rather been suspended than turned into a desk jockey, 'cause then I could get out of payin' Candy her f***in' final year of alimony. Hell, she's makin' more now at her hairdressing job than I take home."

Weaver calmed down when I put a plate of bacon and eggs and a platter of the large pancakes in front of him. He inhaled the aromas and sighed with pleasure.

"Candy cooked up a storm when we were goin' together," Weaver said. "She stopped after the ring went on her finger. I shoulda sued her for false advertising."

Before the first forkful of eggs reached his lips, Weaver's cell phone rang. Glancing at the faceplate he said, "The house."

I knew that was cop shorthand for their station house.

After listening for a few seconds, Weaver said, "Does anybody know what was taken?"

John and I put down our forks. I looked at John, but he was staring tensely at Weaver.

Weaver grunted, nodded at John, told the person on the other end, "Keep me in the loop," and ended the call.

"That was Duff. A neighbor who was looking for a lost dog went into Ingram's backyard and discovered some windows in the house had been knocked out. He called in to report it. Hatch and forensics are on the way over there to search the place."

"Doesn't he need a warrant to go inside?" I tried to keep my voice steady to make the question seem innocent, but guilt had caused a sudden ringing in my ears.

"Exigent circumstances," John said. "When the home of a murder victim is burglarized that makes it an ancillary crime scene. No warrant necessary."

Weaver and John put down their napkins, pushed their chairs back, and got up, leaving their food untouched.

"I'm going back to work," Weaver said.

"I'm coming with you. I'm sidelined, not barred from the premises."

"You need to eat." I quickly filled two of the large pancakes with scrambled eggs and strips of bacon, rolled them into pancake burritos, and wrapped the concoctions in paper napkins. I handed them to the two detectives "Here. Mobile meals."

"Thanks, Del," John said.

Weaver immediately took a big bite. Nodding, with his mouth full, he mumbled something that sounded like "good."

At the front door I watched them get into their separate cars and speed away. With the discovery that someone had broken into Ingram's house, I was both elated and worried. The elation came from my hope that the police would find evidence to point them toward the murderer.

In another part of my mind, I was praying that I hadn't left any trace of myself behind. I told myself that I was being silly to worry. I knew I'd been careful in Ingram's house.

But I also knew there was no such thing as a *perfect* crime.

17

By five o'clock, when it was time for me to leave for the Better Living Channel's studio in North Hollywood, there hadn't been any news—either from John or on TV—about the break-in at Ingram's house. While walking Tuffy, I kept my cell phone in my pocket, with the ringer on "Loud."

No one called.

It was nerve-wracking, not knowing what the police had discovered, but there was nothing I could do to get information without calling attention to myself, so I said good-bye to Tuffy and Emma, gathered what I needed for the show that night, and climbed into my Jeep.

I wished Nicholas were here. In order to protect Eileen, I couldn't tell him that I'd broken into Ingram's house, and certainly not my reason for it, but he had good sources of information in the LAPD. Because of John's behavior at the gala, he was being kept out of the loop. As John's partner, Weaver, too, had been sidelined. I was sure Nicholas was more likely to be able to get confidential information, but he wouldn't be back in town until tomorrow afternoon. I'd have to be patient. To play it cool.

Traffic through Beverly Glen Canyon and into the valley was heavy at that hour of the day, so I'd left home in plenty of time to allow for delays. Naturally, because I allowed for traffic tie-ups, they didn't happen, so I was early when I turned into the driveway leading to the studio's security gate. I stopped at the call box, pressed the button, and heard the always-cheerful voice of Angie Johnson.

"You got a visitor inside, Della. And I'm impressed," she said. Angie, who was usually blasé, sounded as though she meant it.

"Impressed with what?"

"Your Mr. Roland Gray," she said.

"You've read his novels?"

"No. It's his car—a blue Rolls-Royce. It's just like one I saw Will Smith riding around in."

"Gray was supposed to be here at six. I wanted to get here first, to greet him and show him around," I said.

She snickered. "Don't worry 'bout it. From what I saw when he came in the front door, he's being taken care of real well." In an amused tone, she's turned "real" into a two-syllable word.

Angie opened the security gate and I drove around the building to park near the studio entrance.

The first thing I saw was a sapphire blue Rolls in one of the spaces marked "Visitors." It was an older, classic model with the distinctive boxy shape and the Spirit of Ecstasy hood ornament that distinguished it as the automobile equivalent of royalty.

I parked my Jeep Compass, grabbed my tote bag, and hurried through the open studio doors. Car Guy's TV show repair shop was closest to the big, barn-door entrance so that he could drive his demonstration vehicles in and out easily. His set was dark, except for a couple of safety lights to keep people from tripping over cables or bumping into equipment.

On the far side of Car Guy's set, I saw my lights had been turned on and that a gaffer on a tall ladder was methodically testing the security of each light casing. This was done before every show, ever since one had crashed down onto the preparation counter during my Halloween show. No one was hurt, but it gave me and my in-studio audience a heck of a scare.

Quinn Tanner and Roland Gray were perched on stools

at my preparation counter, drinking from china cups that I'd brought from home and kept in the dish cupboard next to the refrigerator. On the counter in front of them was a Wedgwood teapot I'd never seen, and a little silver tea strainer on a saucer beside it.

Quinn was laughing at something Gray had said.

Laughing? In the nine months that I had known her, I'd barely seen Quinn smile, and I'd never heard the cheerful soprano trill that was coming from her throat until now.

I should have been pleased that Quinn was entertaining my show guest with such uncharacteristic warmth. Instead, I was a bit annoyed. Not that they were getting along so well, but that they were doing it in my kitchen. Granted, it was a set constructed in the studio for use in broadcasting shows, but it was a replica of my cozy, yellow and white kitchen at home. I didn't care what either Quinn Tanner or Roland Gray did socially, only that they were doing it on *my* turf. The feeling surprised me, but then I'd never seen anyone else using my set as a café. It was unreasonable, I knew, but I couldn't help feeling proprietary.

The two of them were so engrossed in their conversation that they didn't look up until my "Hello."

"Oh, Della, you're here at last," Quinn said.

"I'm fifteen minutes early."

Roland Gray stood up, smiled, and greeted me.

I said, "Please sit down." But, gallantly, he remained standing.

"Join us for a cuppa," Quinn said.

"Quinn has been kind enough to give me true English tea," Gray said. "Steeped in a china pot, made properly with leaves."

"From my private stash," Quinn said, smug as the Cheshire Cat.

"I'll take a rain check. Unfortunately, I have too much to do right now." The truth is that I'm a devoted coffee person, just short of being a coffee addict.

"Ah, brewed tea," Quinn said, inhaling steam from the cup. "The hallmark of a civilized people."

Ignoring Quinn's little dig, I moved around past them and into the kitchen, took my small handbag out of what I called my "cooking tote," and bent down to put it away on the bottom shelf of the utensil cabinet. When I straightened up, I almost collided with Roland Gray, who had followed me.

"Ooops. I seem to always be running into you," he said, grinning.

"It's all right." Out of the corner of my eye, I saw Quinn glaring at us. She folded her arms across her chest and crossed her legs: the human body language equivalent of a coiled snake.

Gray indicated the fluted mold encased in foil resting on the rear display counter. "That is my finished steamed pudding. The shopping bag on the floor contains what I need to demonstrate how to make it."

"Good," I said. "Let's unpack both our bags and Quinn can walk us through what we'll be doing on camera."

The first item my guest took out of his bag wasn't an ingredient for making pudding. "This is for you," he said, handing me a hardcover book. "My latest."

"*The Terror Master*. Thank you. I'd planned to buy a copy."

"You must not have read my reviews." His tone was wry.

"I don't pay attention to them," I said. "When I was teaching I wanted my students to learn how to survive the harsh criticism that we face in life, so I brought in a collection of terrible reviews for some books that later became great classics. A reviewer at Russia's *Odessa Courier* said that Vronsky in *Anna Karenina* showed more passion for his horse than he did for Anna. A British critic said about *Moby Dick* that it was full of the biggest collection of dolts to be found in all of 'marine literature.' And a critic in Boston called *Leaves of Grass* obscene. He said Walt Whitman should be publicly flogged for writing it."

Gray laughed. "At least none of my reviewers have suggested that."

"Haven't you noticed that very popular authors are resented by some critics because their books sell so well? It's as though the elitists think that if millions of people like a novel then it can't be any good."

"Thank you for cheering me up," he said with a rueful smile.

Quinn saw me holding the book and came over to us. "Isn't Roland marvelous?" she said. "This afternoon he telephoned the studio to find out how many people would be in the audience. When he arrived, it was with a case of his novels, enough for everyone who'll come to our broadcast, and for all of us here at the channel."

"That was a very generous thing to do."

"I'm unscrupulous in my pursuit of readers," he said with a smile that seemed almost embarrassed. I had the feeling that with all of his success he was shy in the face of compliments.

Quinn held her hands out. "Let me have your jacket. I'll hang it up for you in my director's booth."

"How nice of you," he said, slipping out of the navy blue cashmere blazer that was almost the same shade as his Rolls.

Beneath it, he wore a pale blue silk shirt and steel gray slacks, secured by a black belt with a silver buckle in the shape of a badge with the raised monogram "MI 9." The department Gray called MI 9 was the fictional antiterrorist division of British Intelligence for which his series hero, Roger Wilde, was the top secret agent.

Quinn removed a clean dishtowel from one of my equipment drawers and tucked it carefully into his belt. *Very* carefully.

"This is to protect your trousers from kitchen splatters," Quinn said.

In my opinion, Gray was in more danger from Quinn Tanner than from getting stains on his clothing.

Quinn was supposed to be married, but no one at the channel had met her husband. Camera operator Ernie Ramirez once voiced the theory that Quinn's husband, the never-seen Mr. Tanner, had been killed and stuffed, like Norman Bates's mother in *Psycho*.

After the bit with the dishtowel, Quinn took her teapot and strainer and Gray's blazer and went up to the director's booth. She usually held her body in a posture stiff as a fireplace poker, but today there was a definite sway to Quinn's narrow hips.

18

In my earpiece, I heard Quinn start her countdown to air-time. The show's theme music began, Camera One's red light flashed on, and we were broadcasting.

I smiled into the lens and said, "Hi, everybody. Welcome to *In the Kitchen with Della*. Tonight I have a special treat for you at home, and for you here in the studio audience."

Camera Two swung around to take a shot of the audience in the studio. There were lights above the seats because I'd learned that people liked to see themselves on TV and programmed their sets to tape the shows they attended.

More than half of the members of the audience were women, their ages ranging from early twenties into the seventies. The men appeared to be in their late sixties, and older. I had often wondered if they were widowers, or for other reasons needed to learn how to cook. John O'Hara, at fifty, was the "kid" among the men. I'd seen him arrive just a minute or two before we began broadcasting and pointed to the only empty seat: on the aisle in the last row, nearest the entrance. I'd saved it for him by putting a cardboard "Reserved" sign on it.

I told the audience, "A famous guest cooker is here with us, a man who has kept me awake many a night—long before I met him. Let's give a warm welcome to one of the world's most popular novelists, Roland Gray."

As the audience applauded, Camera One drew back from its close-up on me into a two-shot that included Gray, standing on my left, relaxed and smiling.

Facing the camera, I held up my copy of *The Terror Master*. "This is Roland Gray's latest spy thriller." Turning to Gray, I said, "I think it's been on the *New York Times* best seller list for a month now."

"Six weeks, actually," he said. "But who's counting?"

Twenty-nine out of the thirty people in the audience chuckled appreciatively. The one grim face belonged to John O'Hara.

Speaking to the audience again, I said, "If those of you here in the studio will look underneath your seats, you'll each find a copy of *The Terror Master*. They're a gift from Roland."

Everyone, including John, bent down to retrieve the books. Most people smiled or made sounds of delight at the surprise.

"Don't start reading now," I joked. "We've only got an hour together, soooo let's get cooking." I smiled at Gray again. "What are you going to make for us tonight?"

"Spotted Dick," he said.

I heard a few giggles.

Playfully, I chided the audience. "Now, now. Let's not jump to conclusions." Turning to Gray, I said, "You're talking about a classic steamed pudding."

"Absolutely. It's a timeless staple of British comfort cuisine. I'm going to make my mother's recipe, which was taught to her by *her* mother. In fact, I've learned that the earliest recipe of Spotted Dick dates from 1847. And as an aside, regarding the name of this dish: Some years ago, in Gloucestershire, England, certain hospital authorities, fearing that patients would be too embarrassed to ask for Spotted Dick, changed the name to Spotted Richard. British comedians had a great time with this, until administrators restored the original name."

As Gray talked, I helped him by organizing his ingredients in the order he would use them. We had rehearsed this bit, to have physical action during his explanation to the audience. I knew how to make pudding, but he'd briefed me on the particulars of his family recipe.

"The 'spots' in Spotted Dick come from the fact that it's studded with currants and raisins," he said. "Also, it can be made in the shape of a log and then sliced after it's cooked, but I like to make it in what's called a 'pudding basin.'" Gray held up a round mold, about half the size of a Bundt pan.

"We start by sifting a cup of self-rising flour into a bowl, then we add the salt and half a cup of suet . . ."

Although I knew the answer, I asked Gray, "Where can people get suet?"

"Funnily enough, I buy my little tins on the Internet, but one can find it in British shops. You could even have a friendly butcher shred some up for you."

"Suet is fat," I said to the audience. "It performs the function of butter or solid Crisco. Roland, if people at home can't write down your instructions, may I put the recipe on my Web site, www.DellaCooks.com?"

"I would be honored," he said with an elegant bow.

I ran water into the Dutch oven Gray would use to steam his pudding, put it on the stove, and lighted the fire beneath it. It was another piece of business we'd preplanned.

Gray smiled at me in appreciation. "Thank you for the help," he said. "You're very gracious to this amateur."

In my earpiece, I heard Quinn's voice. "Ten seconds to commercial, Della . . . nine . . ."

"We have to take a little break now," I told the audience. "Roland will keep working on his pudding and when we come back he'll show you how to steam it."

In the audience, a fifty-something woman in a bright pink pantsuit called out, "Yes!" Several other people laughed and clapped.

The camera lights went off.

I told Gray, "It sounds like you're a hit."

"Free books make friends," he said with a wry smile.

As commercials began going out over the air, the audience in the studio could watch them on the large TV monitors, which were placed on either side of my kitchen set. Their purpose was to allow those on the premises to see close-up shots of the cooking in progress, which otherwise only the viewers at home could watch.

Gray strolled to the refrigerator on the back wall of the set and beckoned for me to join him. Puzzled, I moved over to where he was standing.

Gray leaned close to me and whispered, "I know that the plan was for me to be on the first half, and then watch the rest of the show from your director's booth, but do you suppose you could let me stay down here, to help you prepare your stew?"

"Yes, of course." I was happy to have him continue on camera, but he must have seen the question in my eyes.

"To be frank," he said, answering the unspoken query, "I'm not entirely comfortable around your Ms. Tanner."

I wasn't going to say anything negative about Quinn, but I felt a sympathetic smile twitching the corner of my mouth.

"I'm happy to have your company," I said. "This isn't a scripted show, and we're only shooting in one small set, so there's no technical problem if you're here. Stay near me and I'll give you things to do."

"Consider me your *sous* chef. Or your scullery maid."

"Deal. I have a favor to ask of you, too."

"Anything."

"After the show, I want to introduce you to a friend of mine. John O'Hara. He's here tonight."

"Ah, the man with the flying fist. Certainly. I recognized his face in the audience, but it took a few minutes for me to recall where I'd seen him before."

I used the intercom microphone beneath the prep counter to contact Quinn.

"Little change of plans," I said. "The audience likes Roland so much he's going to stay down here for the rest of the show. I'm putting him to work."

I half expected to hear Quinn object, but after a moment of silence, she said in an icy tone, "Take your place. Ten seconds." She hissed the S in *seconds*, sounding like a snake whose nest had been disturbed.

When we were broadcasting again, I told the audience, "As soon as Roland's pudding is steaming, he's going to help me make our main dish, Italian Chicken Stew. It's one of those meals you can prepare one day and keep reheating for the next two or three nights, and it just tastes better and better because the flavors soak in."

■ ■ ■

The show went off without a glitch. I didn't burn the chicken pieces I sautéed for the Italian stew, and Gray didn't cut himself while he was chopping prosciutto ham and slicing red, yellow, and orange bell peppers for me. The show had been timed so that I could have done the chopping myself, but to make Gray look necessary, I wiped the stove top clean of grease spots from the sautéing, and brought the Dutch oven full of my completed Italian Chicken Stew I'd brought from home in my tote bag up to the counter.

"Here's what our Italian Chicken Stew looks like when it's finished," I told the audience. Camera Two moved in for a close-up "beauty shot" of the stew.

In the show's final segment, Roland and I chatted about pudding while we made the custard sauce for his Spotted Dick. Because what he'd demonstrated on the show was still steaming, Roland placed on the prep counter the Spotted Dick he'd made at home.

"That looks delicious," I said sincerely.

"Something sweet is just the prescription to take one's mind off the disappointments of the day. Or as a reward when things go well."

"In other words," I said, "any excuse will do."

He chuckled. "Ah, Della, you have cracked my code, so to speak."

The clock ticked down to the final ninety seconds. Roland placed his pudding on the crystal dessert dish he'd brought with him, and I ladled warm custard sauce over it.

As we'd planned during the previous commercial break, I took a handful of plastic spoons from a box in the drawer beneath the preparation counter, handed them to him, and told the audience, "Now Roland's going to offer some volunteers a taste." I was careful not to say, "a taste of his Spotted Dick."

Most of the spectators applauded enthusiastically.

Jada Powell on Camera Two swung around and followed Gray as he strode to the front row of seats. With a theatrical flourish, he made a show of inhaling the pudding's sweet aroma, then passed out spoons. He walked along the row, holding the plate, as people dug into the pudding. I saw appreciative nods at the taste from those with their mouths full.

As the end credits rolled over the scene, I was aware that Quinn did not instruct Ernie Ramirez, manning Camera One, to conclude the episode on me, as was the usual practice. Ernie must have realized that Quinn was punishing me, because he leaned around his camera and gave me a helpless shrug.

When the show was over, it took half an hour for Gray to finish autographing books and for the last of the audience members to leave.

The moment the final spectator had left the studio, Gray and I sat down on the stools behind the preparation counter. John O'Hara joined us and I introduced them. Gray's response was warm. John's was polite. The book was tucked under his arm, but John didn't ask Gray to sign it for him.

"I'm sure Shannon's going to enjoy *Terror Master*," I said to John. To Gray, I added, "John's wife is one of your fans. Whichever of us buys one of your books first, as soon as we've read it, we pass it to the other."

John speared Gray with what Eileen calls "the look that makes bad guys beg to confess." Without preamble, he said to Gray, "How well did you know Keith Ingram?"

"I didn't. Not really. We'd met, casually. In passing, so to speak."

Uh oh. Gray's tone was level—no nervous wobble in his voice—and he was meeting John's gaze, but instinct told me he wasn't telling us the truth. Starting back when I was a high school teacher, I'd noticed that when people were lying they tended to say too much. One "I didn't" was enough. A string of denials undercut credibility.

John reached into an inside pocket of his sports jacket and removed a sheet of paper.

"This is a photocopy of the judging card Keith Ingram made out about you." He held it up for me to see that it was a replica of one of the cards we were issued. My eyes widened in surprise at what I saw on it.

"There were four criteria for judging the dishes you all were creating," John said. "Organization of the workspace, quality of the ingredients, the appearance of the dish, and the taste. Ingram gave you the lowest score on all four categories."

"But the dishes weren't finished," I said. "Nothing had been displayed yet, and nothing was tasted."

"Exactly." John stayed focused on Gray. "So, what was the problem between you and Ingram?"

I turned to look at Roland Gray and saw that his complexion had lost its color.

19

After a moment of silence, Gray stood. "That is not a subject I care to discuss with you, Mr. O'Hara."

"It's Lieutenant O'Hara. LAPD. And you'll either discuss it with me here, or you'll do it down at the station."

Color returned to Roland Gray's cheeks. "I'm not a *naïf*, Lieutenant. Or, as we are in a television studio kitchen, perhaps it would be more appropriate to say that I did not just fall off a turnip truck. You, sir, laid Keith Ingram out flat. I'll take your word that you are with the LAPD, but I think it highly unlikely that you are being allowed to take part in this investigation. In fact, I'm sure that you, yourself, are under suspicion for Ingram's murder. Clearly, you had some severe grievance against the man, or you wouldn't have attacked him in public, before dozens of witnesses."

Gray began to gather up his cooking equipment. "I had a delightful time with you, Della. Perhaps you will allow me to take you to a restaurant, without cameras present, and where neither of us must cook."

"You're making a mistake, Gray." John said. But he'd dialed his attitude down from confrontational to calm reasonableness. "If you tell me—us—about your problem with Ingram, we might be able to help you so that you're not thought of as a suspect."

Gray stopped collecting his gear and looked from John to me, and back to John. "But I will be of interest to the police when they see that judging card. I'm surprised that there hasn't been a knock on my door yet."

"There would have been, and there probably will be at some point," John said, "but their immediate focus is on me. Cooperate here, informally, and I may be able to help us both, and keep the investigation from getting to you."

Gray opened his mouth to speak, but something he saw over John's shoulder stopped him. I turned my head to follow his line of sight. Quinn Tanner was coming toward us, carrying Gray's blue cashmere blazer. He lowered his voice and said to me, "I'll call you tomorrow."

"Call *both* of us." John handed him a card. "My cell phone number's on the back."

■　■　■

It was nearly midnight and I was about to get ready for bed. I'd given Tuffy his final walk, Nicholas D'Martino and I had completed our nightly call, and I had just taken the cap off the tube of toothpaste when the phone rang again. I thought it must be Nicholas, with something he'd forgotten to tell me, but the caller ID number was unfamiliar.

An automatic jolt of concern tightened my stomach muscles.

Was it Eileen again? She was supposed to be with her parents tonight, but I knew all of her phone numbers, and her father's and her mother's. And those of my friends and coworkers. None of those numbers was on the faceplate.

As I reached for the receiver, I guessed that someone had misdialed, but if it was an obscene call, my reaction would be to laugh. On the two occasions that had happened, laughter took the wind out of the pervert's sails—so to speak.

I said hello and heard Roland Gray's Henry Higgins accent.

"Della, please forgive me for phoning you so late. I hope I didn't wake you."

"No, you didn't."

"I need to talk to you," he said. "In person."

"We could meet for breakfast—"

"I mean *now*. Right now. I'm in my car outside your house."

My pulse quickened with anger at that, and I didn't try to keep it out of my voice. "How did you find out where I live?"

"As a writer, I've developed many contacts. Discovering anyone's location rarely takes more than a single phone call, but I do apologize for invading your privacy."

"You should apologize. I don't like this one little bit. You had no right—"

"Of course, no right at all, but I have an explanation. I know something about Keith Ingram that I am sure is relevant to his murder. I don't want to discuss this over the telephone. Now, I'm not suggesting that you invite me into your home at this hour. Will you allow me to take you out for a drink, a glass of wine, or coffee?"

I thought about that for a moment. One of the things I hate in movies and in mystery novels is what I call the heroine who is Too-Stupid-To-Live: the one who goes to meet a murder suspect in the middle of the night, in a remote place, all alone. Or who goes upstairs in a dark house when anyone with an IQ higher than that of a carrot could guess that the villain is hiding there.

I didn't want this virtual stranger in my house at this hour, and I didn't want to get into a car with him, but I did want to hear what he had to say. Maybe it could save John.

"All right. Where shall I meet you?" I said.

I heard him chuckle. "I'm flattered that you consider me so potentially dangerous that you're proceeding with such caution. I must be sure to make the heroine in my new books as smart as you are. When the case has been resolved and Ingram's murderer is in custody, perhaps then you will trust me enough to allow me to call for you and take you out to dinner?"

"Thank you for the invitation," I said, "but I'm seeing someone."

"Are you engaged?"

"No."

"Then I will feel free to ask you again sometime. Regarding tonight: There is a place nearby where we could meet, if you like. I want you to feel safe."

Feel safe? *He's making me sound positively antediluvian.* Nevertheless, I wasn't going to let a twinge of embarrassment turn me into one of those T-S-T-L women.

I kept my cool and said, "Where?"

"There's a sidewalk café I know on Montana Avenue, near Twelfth Street. It's called Caffeine an' Stuff," he said. "Good coffee. Do you know it?"

"Yes."

"How soon can we meet there?"

"Ten minutes," I said.

"Excellent." With a quick good-bye, Gray disconnected.

I didn't bother to change clothes from the slacks and sweater I was wearing, but I did brush my hair and dab on some lipstick and mascara. Looking *completely* natural wasn't as attractive as it had been twenty years ago.

Before I left the house, I wrote a note for Eileen, telling her about Roland Gray's call, and that I was going to meet him at Caffeine an' Stuff. Even though she wouldn't be home tonight, I put it on the little table just inside the door, where we always left messages for each other. The note was one of my little personal voodoo rituals, like carrying a raincoat and umbrella so that the weather forecast of rain *wouldn't* come true. Tell someone where I was going and I would get home safely. I know it was silly, but it did no harm. And just in case . . .

I gave Tuffy and Emma a few strokes and told them that I'd be back soon.

20

Montana and Twelfth Street was only six blocks from my house. During the day, I would have walked down to the café, but not at night. I wasn't shy about taking chances—my life was pretty much testimony to that—but I didn't believe in taking foolish risks.

Montana Avenue was almost as busy at this time, shortly after midnight, as it was during the day and early evening. With its great variety of businesses, small restaurants, pubs, and coffeehouses, it was the shopping, strolling, and meeting-friends-for-whatever heart of the northern end of the city of Santa Monica. I knew the area well because my little cooking school was located in the back of a kitchen appliance store on Montana, near Fifteenth Street. And the library on the corner of Seventeenth was one of my regular stops.

Caffeine an' Stuff occupied the ground floor of a two-story structure that looked like an old English pub. A dark green, weather-faded wooden sign hung above the entrance. The words "Caffeine an' Stuff" were painted on it in gold script, below a drawing of a mug of coffee, steam curling up in the shape of a question mark. In similar, but larger, gold script, the name of the café arched across the front window.

I spotted Gray's Rolls parked in front of the entrance. The man himself was standing in the middle of the empty parking space directly behind his car. When he saw me, he stepped back onto the curb and waved me into the slot. There were no other empty spaces on that block.

When I parked, Gray appeared at my driver's side door and offered his hand to me. I took it, and hopped down onto the street.

"Did you drive yourself tonight?"

"Yes. Will Parker assists me—he doesn't come along when I'm out with a lady."

I indicated our cars. "Either you are the luckiest driver in the state of California, or you bought these two spaces."

"It was partly luck. Someone was pulling out of my spot as I arrived, and let's just say I *rented* yours," he said with a smile. "It's a bit chilly to sit outside, so I secured a table by the window. I hope that's all right with you?"

"It's fine," I said.

In spite of the fact that the temperature was in the fifties tonight—frigid by Southern California standards—three of the four outside tables were occupied by young couples. I remembered being that young, in college at UCLA, and being that impervious to cold when I was on a date and in the first heat of attraction.

Caffeine an' Stuff was comfortably warm inside. Soft lights, soft voices, and tables arranged just far enough apart to give the customers a sense of privacy. Being overheard wasn't going to be a problem, I saw, because fewer than half of the tables were occupied. At the wide front window, there was no one closer to us than two tables away.

Gray pulled out a chair for me, waited until I was settled, then took his place across the wooden divide. With the name of the café on the window just above our heads, we had an unobstructed view of the people strolling along Montana Avenue.

As a college-age waiter in a letter sweater came toward us, Gray asked me, "What will you have?"

"A cappuccino."

"Decaf or regular?" the waiter asked.

"Regular, the more regular the better," I said.

Gray looked at me and asked, "Perhaps a pastry with it?"

"No, thank you. I can't stay very long, Roland." He appeared so disappointed I added, "It's just that I have a lot to do."

"Two regular cappuccinos," Gray told the waiter. "Nothing else."

"You got it." Joe College flashed us a professional smile and hurried toward the service counter to relay our order to the barista.

Roland Gray was staring down at his hands. It seemed as though he was inspecting his manicure, looking for flaws, but his nails were trimmed and his cuticles neat. Even if he hadn't phoned so late and insisted on talking to me right away, it was obvious from the troubled expression on his face that something was bothering him.

I was about to urge him to tell me whatever he knew about Keith Ingram when the waiter returned with our cappuccinos. I kept silent until he'd delivered them and withdrawn again.

Gray picked up his spoon and stirred his coffee in a slow, contemplative way.

"What I have to tell you is difficult for me," he said. "I wasn't frank with either the police who questioned us in the ballroom, or earlier tonight, with you and your friend O'Hara. The truth is that I knew Ingram quite well at one time. It came to be an introduction I wished that I could have avoided."

"Why did you agree to be in the cook-off? The names of the judges were announced weeks ago."

"Will and I were researching an aspect of my new book in some recently released records in Eastern Europe when my publicist e-mailed me the opportunity to participate in the gala. He told me who some of the celebrities were who had accepted, but he didn't mention the names of the judges, and it didn't occur to me to ask. I only returned to my flat in Los Angeles this past weekend, and didn't know Ingram was involved until I arrived at the ballroom that night. Seeing him there was a dreadful shock."

"Did you speak to him?"

"There were other people around, so we just nodded at each other. Actually, I nodded. He smirked. In spite of my discomfort, I certainly couldn't withdraw at that point without raising questions I didn't want to answer, so I decided to just get through the evening—ideally without a confrontation. To stiff-upper-lip it, so to speak. I resolved to change my original plan of writing in Los Angeles and instead finish my book in London. That was a hard decision for me, because I much prefer to work here. This is where Alan Berger lives—he's my literary agent. I don't trust electronic transmission with something so important as my book, and certainly not the mails. Alan always reads my manuscripts first—and in my living room. I insist. What I need from him are his *immediate* reactions. More than once, he's saved me from veering off course in a plot."

"You'd go to London and change your professional routine, just because Keith Ingram happened to be in the same city? Hadn't you ever run into him in California before?"

"No. When I'm here, primarily I'm writing. I seldom socialize. Changing my established pattern might seem extreme to you, but . . ." He took a breath and clamped his lips together.

I squelched the temptation to fill in this conversational "white space" and interrupt whatever internal struggle he was having. If I didn't say anything, sooner or later the silence should pressure him to continue.

After a few seconds of quiet, his mouth relaxed and he sighed. "This is difficult for me. Because of my past association with Ingram, I have—had—reason to believe that he might try to harm *me*."

That was a shocker, but before I could ask the next question, Gray began to massage his left temple, pressing hard against his skull.

"Are you all right?"

"I'm getting a tension headache," he said. "It happens when I'm under stress, but it's nothing, really—it will pass."

"Have you seen a doctor?"

He shrugged dismissively. "I can handle it."

"You're going to 'stiff-upper-lip' it again?"

"I hate doctors." He said it with a finality that closed the subject.

I thought his attitude was foolish, but Roland Gray's headaches were his business. Mine was to try to pry out of him anything that might be helpful to John. "Roland, do you have any idea who might have killed Ingram? Or did you see anything that—"

CRACK!

Something pierced the café's front window from outside, spiderwebbing the glass.

My immediate reaction was that someone had thrown a small stone at the window, but suddenly Gray jerked backward, and began to topple sideways toward the floor. I tried to grab his wrist to stop his fall, but I wasn't quick enough.

A woman screamed—and a man yelled, "Gunshot!"

The instinct for self-preservation kicked in. I threw myself onto the floor, below the level of the window.

More screams. A babble of voices. A table turned over. Silverware clattered, dishes broke. Footsteps pounded toward the rear of the café.

Roland Gray lay a few feet in front of me. He was still, and his eyes were closed. Icy tentacles of fear knotted into a ball in my chest. I stretched my arm to give him a gentle prod on his shoulder. "Roland?"

He didn't move.

On my hands and knees, I inched closer to Gray's body.

Blood oozed from a red crease that ran across his forehead.

In the distance, I heard the faint shriek of sirens.

•

21

I searched for a pulse in Roland Gray's throat and found a beat. It was faint, but he was alive. The blood from his head wound was matting his hair. Praying that the bullet had only grazed him, instead of penetrating deeper, I grabbed a handful of paper napkins from the table and pressed them against his bleeding forehead.

"Roland, can you hear me? Roland?"

No answer.

The sirens were closer now. Mercifully, there hadn't been any more shots.

"Hang on, Roland. Help is almost here. Hang on."

A paramedic van screeched to a stop in front of the café, double-parking next to the blue Rolls. Two emergency medical technicians jumped out. A man and a woman. The woman carried a medical kit. The man wheeled a gurney.

As soon as they were in the doorway, I waved my free hand at the EMTs and yelled, "In here—he's been shot!"

The paramedics reached us at a trot. Immediately, I stepped back to get out of their way. Quick and focused, they bent over Roland, working on him. I couldn't see what they were doing, and I couldn't hear what they were saying. All I could do was stand with my fingers laced together tightly in front of my chest and hope.

Seconds behind the paramedic van, a City of Santa Monica police car zoomed into view and came to a squealing stop. Two officers in uniform got out: one young and short—probably the minimum height for admittance to the academy—and the other older and a head taller. The older officer began to clear people away from the entrance to Caffeine an' Stuff. The younger one hurried into the café, surveyed the scene, saw the EMTs at work, and used his mobile phone. I guessed he was calling for reinforcements.

Shocked customers watched the paramedics and the arrival of the police. Some started to chatter among themselves. Others moved toward the paramedics, craning their necks to get a better look at the star of this drama. The police officer ordered them to back off.

Two middle-aged men, in nearly matching leather jackets worn over T-shirts advertising a rock group I'd never heard of, demanded to know when they could leave.

"When we've taken statements," the younger officer said. "Stay calm, everybody. Complaining won't make things go any faster."

He conferred with the paramedics. I saw the female EMT nod at me. The officer headed in my direction, taking a notebook out of his shirt pocket. When he reached me, I saw the nameplate on his chest identified him as Officer Currie.

With his pencil poised over his notebook, he said, "You were sitting with the guy who got shot?"

"Yes."

Looking past Officer Currie, I saw the paramedics lifting Roland onto the gurney. They'd put an oxygen mask over his face.

"Officer, you talked to the paramedics—is my friend going to be all right?"

He shrugged. "Don't know."

"What hospital are they taking him to?"

"I can't give you that information. Your name, ma'am."

"Della Carmichael."

"Address?"

I gave it to him.

"Do you have some ID, ma'am?"

"Of course." I fumbled in my purse and found my wallet. I opened it to the driver's license window and showed it to him.

"Remove the license, please, ma'am."

I did as instructed and watched him study my photo as though he was trying to connect it with someone he'd seen on *America's Most Wanted.*

He handed it back to me and nodded toward the direction of the stretcher the paramedics were placing in their van. "And who was he?"

Was?

"Please don't talk about my friend as though he's dead!"

"Sorry, ma'am. What is the name of the victim?"

I told him. He didn't seem to recognize it.

Officer Currie was about to ask another question but I stopped him. "Wait. You should notify Detective Manny Hatch at West Bureau about this. He's handling a murder case that could be connected to what happened here."

He cocked his head and frowned at me with doubt, but he used his mobile to call West Bureau.

■ ■ ■

Twenty minutes later, more police officers had arrived on the scene. They used their vehicles and road flares to shut the street down. The area around the café was marked off with crime scene tape. A team from the Scientific Investigation Division had arrived. The SID technicians were photo-documenting the scene and searching for clues.

Three members of this law enforcement army were taking statements and contact information from the customers and employees of Caffeine an' Stuff. Two more were questioning the people who had been sitting outside when the shot was fired.

Per Officer Currie's order, I'd remained at the table and was watching the activity outside through the sunburst of cracks around the bullet hole in the front window. It wasn't long before I saw a brown Crown Victoria with a red bubble light clapped to its top being let through the police barricade. It slammed to a stop next to Roland's blue Rolls.

Detective Hatch got out of the Crown Vic. I'd expected to see him because I'd suggested he be called, but I was surprised to see Hugh Weaver with him.

The two detectives stepped carefully around the area where the techs were working and came into the café. They flashed their badges at Officer Currie. A few brief words were exchanged. Hatch pivoted toward me. Weaver's eyebrows lifted in an expression of surprise when he saw me. The two detectives marched in my direction.

Detective Hatch demanded of me, "What happened?"

Choosing my words carefully to keep Hatch from learning that I was here to try to find out who killed Ingram—and possibly inviting a charge of interfering with a police investigation—I stuck to the barest of facts. "Roland Gray phoned to invite me out to coffee. I met him here."

"You and that writer hooking up?" Weaver asked bluntly.

"Certainly not." I said that with a touch of heat. I was hiding my reason for being here, but I didn't want anyone to think it was romantic. "It was just for *coffee*. Roland Gray was a guest on my television show earlier tonight. I'm worried about his injury. Where did the medics take him?"

Hatch retrieved that standard law enforcement notebook and pen from his jacket pocket. "My questions first. So you agreed to meet Gray for coffee. Who picked this place? You?"

"No, he did. What possible relevance—"

"I'm asking the questions. When you got here, what did you two talk about?"

This was dangerous ground; I had to step carefully.

"We were only here for a few minutes. The waiter had just brought our coffee. We didn't have time for more than a sip." I let my eyes light up with what I hoped looked like a sudden memory. "Oh, Roland told me he was getting a headache. He started rubbing his forehead. I asked him if he was all right, but that's when the window cracked. At first I thought someone threw a rock, but then I saw Roland had been hit. Things happened so fast. As I said, I thought that—"

"Yeah, a rock." Hatch's mouth twisted into a grimace. "But it was a bullet. Tell me who wants to kill you."

"What?" My heart lurched with a sudden rush of fear. I froze, unable to think.

"Kill *her*?" Weaver said.

The sound of Weaver's voice penetrated the shock that had momentarily paralyzed my brain. "No one has any motive to kill me."

"Think about it," Hatch said. "Wednesday night somebody offed a judge at that celebrity thing. Not much more than twenty-four hours later another judge is sitting near where somebody gets shot. Two nights, two judges in the same contest. Maybe the shooter wasn't aiming at Gray, but at *you*."

"We better find out where that third judge is," Weaver said. "A Frenchwoman. What was her name?"

"Yvette Dupree," I said.

"Do you know where she is?"

"No, but if one of your officers didn't get her contact information at the gala, I'm sure Eugene Long knows."

"Have somebody put a guard on her until I can question her." Hatch turned back to me and gestured toward the table. "Show me exactly where you were and where Gray was."

I sat down in the chair I'd occupied. As my mind worked to recreate the scene, my initial fear began to recede. I was sure I hadn't been the target. While I couldn't explain why in any rational way, it was a powerful conviction.

"Think about it," I told Hatch. "Keith Ingram's throat was slashed, and whoever killed him took a huge risk by doing it in the middle of five hundred people. Even acting under the cover of smoke, it was an enormous gamble. That was an intensely *personal* murder. Nothing random about it. I'm convinced that whoever killed Ingram intended to shoot at Roland Gray. You should be looking for a link between those two men."

Hatch's features twisted into a sneer. "If you're such a great detective maybe you should be leading this investigation instead of me. Where'd you earn your badge, at the Betty Crocker Police Academy?"

I decided that the "better part of valor" at this moment was to be quiet. Hatch and I locked eyes.

He broke the silence. "As I said before, show me exactly where you and Gray were sitting."

Tapping the tabletop, I said, "I was here. Roland sat across from me."

Hatch took Roland's place and fixed me with a skeptical stare. "Do you always sit up straight like that?"

"Yes, I do. My parents brought us up to have good posture. What you're *really* asking is: Was I leaning forward so that my head was close to Roland's. The answer is no, I wasn't. And he wasn't leaning toward me."

I motioned to Hugh Weaver. "Roland was sitting about the way Detective Hatch is. How far apart would you say our heads are?"

Weaver squinted. "Three feet, give or take a couple inches."

Hatch looked disappointed. I didn't know whether he was upset because I hadn't told him anything helpful, or whether his sour expression was one of the interrogation techniques cops used to get the person being questioned to keep talking. I stared back at him and kept my mouth shut.

A Scientific Investigation Division tech who had been

kneeling in front of the bar called, "Hey, Detective." He summoned Hatch with a wave.

"I bet he found the bullet," I said.

Hatch told me to stay where I was. He and Weaver went over to talk to the SID tech. The tech photographed the front of the bar, then, with great care, he began digging an object out of the wood. In less than a minute, he'd extracted it. With a ceiling light directly above him, I could see that the object was a bullet.

I watched the two detectives examine it, after which the tech dropped it into a clear plastic evidence bag, sealed and initialed it. If they were following procedure, the bullet would be taken to Ballistics for microscopic examination.

Hatch and Weaver came back to my table.

"What kind of a bullet is it?" I asked.

Weaver said, "Sniper—"

"Shut up! What's the matter with you?" Hatch said.

Weaver's face turned crimson. While he kept his hands down at his sides, I saw his fingers curl into fists.

I stood up and grabbed my handbag. "I've answered your questions, Detective. Now, I want to know where the paramedics took Roland Gray."

Hatch and I stared at each other.

He blinked first.

22

St. Clare's Hospital was the city's newest facility and covered half a block on Colorado Boulevard between Sixth and Seventh Streets. I'd never been there, but a recent article in the *Los Angeles Chronicle* had listed its emergency room as one of the best in the state.

It was nearly two in the morning and there were plenty of parking spaces available in the hospital's visitor lot. I picked a spot beneath the nearest security light. Before I got out, I stuck to my woman-alone nighttime habit of scanning my surroundings for potential danger. Seeing none, I climbed down to the pavement, and looked around again. Still nothing to cause my mental alarm to go off. I locked the Jeep and hurried toward the entrance to the emergency room.

In contrast to other emergency room reception areas I'd been in, these walls were painted a cheerful yellow, the lighting was bright but not harsh, and there was only the faintest trace of disinfectant in the air. Half a dozen people occupied chairs around the room. Some sat in tense postures, others seemed sunk in weary resignation.

One man was at the reception counter, bent across the expanse of Formica, speaking quietly to a young woman wearing a floral print medical smock. Even though his back was to me, there was something familiar about his stocky frame, the short, curly hair, and the tweed jacket.

Approaching the reception counter on his right side, I saw the young woman smile at him. He scribbled something on a slip of paper, handed it to her, and she took it. It struck me that this exchange was more social than medical.

"Excuse me."

She looked up at the sound of my voice, and the man turned toward me. Now I saw why he'd seemed familiar: This was the man who'd appeared at the entrance to the ballroom Wednesday night, asking to speak to Roland.

"You're Will Parker," I said.

"And you are Della Carmichael, the cooking lady." He pronounced "lady" as "lie-dee." In contrast to Roland Gray's upper-class British accent, Parker's was pure Cockney.

"Mr. Parker, do you know how Roland is? Have you seen him?"

"Just left 'im. They're going to move 'im up to the second floor for more tests. An' call me Will. Mr. Parker's me dad."

Eager to get the informalities over, I said quickly, "Yes, all right. I'm Della." I turned to the woman behind the desk. She was typing something into her computer. "I'd like to see Roland Gray."

She paused, one hand poised over her keyboard, and eyed me skeptically. "Are you a relative?"

"No, a friend. I was with him tonight—"

"Sorry. Family only." She went back to whatever she was typing.

Will Parker cupped my arm under the elbow, steered me away from the desk, and lowered his voice. "They let me in 'cause I told the medical blokes I'm 'is brother."

"Is he going to be all right?"

Parker lifted his shoulders an inch. "Dunno yet. A bullet grazed 'is fore'ead. Wot the bloody 'ell 'appened?"

Briefly, I told him the little I knew. Then a question occurred to me. "How did you know he was here?"

"There's a card in 'is wallet says I'm who to call in case of emergency."

The receptionist held up a form and waved it at Parker. "More bloody paperwork," he said. "Be back in a jif."

Parker returned to the reception desk and I thought about the card in Roland's wallet. I didn't have any such instruction in mine, and resolved to take care of that oversight. But with Mack gone, whom should I name? My mother and sisters live in San Francisco, too far away in an emergency. Nicholas D'Martino and I were having a relationship, but there was no commitment—except that we see only each other for as long as we're together. Maybe the right person was my best friend, Liddy Marshall. I decided to talk to her about it tomorrow.

Parker wrote something on the form and handed it back across the counter. Returning to me, he asked, "Did the cops catch the bloody sodden bugger who shot 'im?"

"No. Do you have any idea who might want to hurt Roland?"

Parker bit his lower lip and closed his eyes for a couple of seconds. "The women 'e stops seeing tend to cry, not pick up weapons. No jealous husbands 'cause 'e doesn't trifle with the marrieds." Parker shrugged. "Look, miss, there's no point our waiting around tonight. 'Ow about letting me buy you a brandy?"

"I appreciate the invitation, but if I can't see Roland I'll go home and get some sleep."

"Need a lift?"

"My car is in the lot. Oh, but Roland's car is in front of the coffeehouse where we were. Caffeine an' Stuff, on Montana Avenue and Twelfth Street."

"Good to know. I'll go over there, leave me own wheels, an' drive the Duchess."

"The Duchess?"

"That's wot we call the ol' girl." Will Parker cupped my elbow again. "I'll take you to your car and follow you to be sure you get 'ome safe."

"That's not necessary."

"Me mum would be ashamed of me if I didn't at least escort you to your vehicle." He guided me toward the exit, but before we took more than two steps, the outside door opened and in strode Detectives Hatch and Weaver.

The two investigators saw me and headed for my spot on the waiting room's industrial carpet. Neither one of them looked happy, but next to Hatch's angry glare, Weaver's frown seemed almost cordial.

"If you talked to Gray before I questioned him, you're looking at an obstruction charge," Hatch snapped.

"I haven't even seen him. I told you that I only wanted to find out his condition."

With a grunt, Hatch stalked off toward the woman at the reception desk.

"Who are you?" Weaver demanded, looking at Will.

"Will Parker. I work for Mr. Gray."

"Yeah? Wha'daya do?"

"General factotum."

Weaver squinted at Parker. "What's that?"

"Whatever me boss needs done." Parker inclined his head closer to Weaver and lowered his voice. "I told the girl at the desk I was 'is brother so I got a quick look at 'im, but 'e wasn't conscious."

I was getting impatient. "I didn't see Roland. I've told you and Detective Hatch everything I know about what happened tonight. I'm exhausted and I'd like to go home."

"Stay here, Parker," Weaver said. "I have some questions for you about your employer." He nodded to me. "I'll walk you out to your car, Della."

"Wait." Parker took a small white card from his pocket, scribbled something, and handed it to me. "Me numbers. Call if there's anything I can do for you."

I thanked him and we said good night.

Outside in the cold night air, I shivered. To my amazement, the ordinarily chivalry-challenged Hugh Weaver offered to give me his jacket.

"No, thanks. My car is right over there."

As I unlocked the Jeep, Weaver said, "Keep this to yourself, but I figure you deserve to know what we learned so far. One of the SID guys is ex–Special Forces. Even before Ballistics gets a look, he says he's sure the sniper's bullet came from a Walther WA 2000. If the shooter had that kind of weapon, it's unlikely he could have missed if he really was shooting at you, so Hatch dropped that theory. Good news for you—you don't have to look behind you on every corner—but it puts John back as Hatch's number one suspect. The other thing we know is that the shot came from the roof of that two-story building directly across the street from the coffeehouse. SID measured the angle the slug hit the window at and traced the trajectory backward."

"Did they find a shell casing?"

Weaver shook his head. "The shooter policed his brass."

I knew what that meant: Whoever fired the weapon was smart enough not to leave a shell casing behind for evidence.

"I'm guessin' we're not dealing with some 'disadvantaged youth' out to pop one off at the folks drinking designer coffee," Weaver said.

"If the shot wasn't random, then Roland Gray really was the target."

"That's how I see it." Weaver glanced back toward the hospital. "But Hatch still has a hard-on for John. Tomorrow he's going to start looking for a connection between John and the writer."

"There isn't one, Hugh." I wanted to scream in frustration, but I forced myself to stay calm. "You've got to make Hatch look at the facts. Keith Ingram was murdered on Wednesday night. Less than twenty-four hours later, someone tried to kill Roland Gray. I know that John lost his temper and slugged Ingram in front of a room full of witnesses, but he had no argument with Gray. He never even met the man until earlier tonight, after my TV show. Whoever killed Ingram had a reason to try to kill Gray. John did not."

"I hope you're right about that, but you can bet that if John ever so much as gave Gray the finger, Hatch is going to find out about it."

23

Because there was very little traffic at this early hour of Friday morning, I drove home from the hospital concentrating on two nagging questions: Who killed Keith Ingram, and who tried to kill Roland Gray? I visualized this puzzle as a triangle, with Gray and Ingram at opposite sides of the base but with a question mark at the triangle's apex.

Who is that third point?

Thinking of the father and daughter I loved, my stomach roiled with concern. Weaver believed in John's innocence, but Detective Hatch didn't. Or perhaps the truth was that he didn't want to. According to Weaver, Hatch was focusing his energy toward linking John to Roland Gray. I knew he wouldn't be able to find anything, but Hatch was wasting precious time looking in that direction when his efforts could be put to much better use trying to find the real killer. But Hatch was stubborn, and because of the old grudge he held, it looked as though he was determined to find evidence against John. By the time he abandoned that course of investigation it might be too late to find the person who murdered Ingram. Statistically, the longer that a case was unsolved, the less chance there was of it being solved. Unless there was an unexpected lucky break, and it was foolish to count on that happening.

The only evidence against John was his fury at Ingram. That was flimsy, but people had been arrested on flimsy evidence before. The longer John was under suspicion, the harder it would be on the O'Hara family. Because of her relationship with Ingram, Eileen already felt responsible for the trouble her father was in. I was worried, too, about what the pressure would do to her emotionally fragile mother, Shannon.

A block from home, my cell phone rang. I pressed the "Answer" button, said hello, and heard a man's voice that always made me think of dark clover honey with biceps.

"Hey, baby. Where are you?"

"Almost home," I told Nicholas D'Martino. "Where are you?"

"Standing on your doorstep. That will be me, waving at you."

As I turned into the driveway my headlights swept the front of the house and illuminated his muscular body. The stray lock of black hair that perpetually fell across his forehead brushed the top of his thick eyebrows.

I jammed on the brakes and cut the ignition. No sooner had I reached for the door handle than it was opened from the outside and Nicholas pulled me into his arms.

We kissed, and held each other tightly. The deeper he kissed me, the louder my heart pounded.

When we came up for air, he asked, "Do you have to walk Tuff?"

"I'll let him out into the backyard for a little while. I have so much to tell you."

Caressing me through my clothing, he whispered, "I want to hear everything, but later. Okay?"

My responding kiss signaled that was definitely okay with me.

■ ■ ■

Later, happily spent, and Tuffy now curled up on the rug next to my side of the bed, I told Nicholas all that had happened earlier that night.

"You have to be right about Ingram's murder being connected to the shooting of Gray," he said. "Nothing else makes sense. The question is *how* are they connected?"

"I don't know, but I have to find out."

"Hold it. I'm not going to let you put yourself in danger," he said.

"You hold it." I sat up in bed, looked down into his dark Mediterranean eyes, and said firmly, "You should know by now that I do not let you tell me what to do."

His full lips curved in a smile that I found hard to resist. I softened my tone. "However, if there's something you want me to do, you may *suggest* it."

Nicholas reached up and started gently caressing my breasts. "Fair enough." Still lying flat, he inched his body closer to mine. "May I *suggest* that this time you be the one on top?"

A hot charge of desire shot through me again. I laughed, shifted my position, and whispered, "I am happy to take that suggestion."

In another moment, there was no more talking.

■　■　■

After breakfast, I was saying good-bye to Nicholas at the front door when I saw Hugh Weaver's personal car, a maroon Chevy Malibu with primer paint on the left front fender, a missing hubcap, and a faded red, white, and blue "Buy American" bumper sticker, screech to a stop in front of the house.

Weaver wrenched himself out from behind the wheel. Crimson-faced and sweating, he hurried up the path and demanded, "Are you crazy?"

With a sly smile, Nicholas asked, "Which one of us are you talking to?"

Weaver ignored him and aimed a worried glance back at the street. "Hatch managed to roust one of the ADAs and get him to talk a judge into signing a search warrant. Soon as he's got the paper, he'll be over here."

A lump of dread formed in my chest. "Why? What are you talking about?"

"SID found your bloody fingerprint on the broken back window of Ingram's house. Hatch knows you broke in. That's probable cause for a warrant to search your place for anything belonging to Ingram."

The lump of dread balled into a big fist and pushed hard against my heart and lungs. The worst had happened.

No, not quite the worst. Hatch doesn't know about Eileen's video.

Nicholas gripped my arm. "You don't have to say anything."

"I wasn't going to." My voice sounded hollow in my ears, as though it was coming from a far-off place.

Weaver's cell phone rang. He glanced at the faceplate and scowled. "It's Hatch." He answered with a brusque, "Yeah?" and listened briefly. "I'm getting coffee, that's where the f*** I am . . . In Westwood . . . No, of course I didn't *call* her—the Carmichael dame means nothin' to me . . . 'Kay. I'll meet'cha at her place in ten." Weaver snapped the phone shut. "He has the search warrant an' he's madder than a tiger who missed a meal. You got ten minutes to think of a story, or do what you gotta do. And don't thank me. I'm not doing this for you, it's for John. In fact, I was never here."

Weaver double-timed it back to his Chevy and tore off.

Nicholas looked at me with concern. "Is there anything you want to get rid of before Hatch arrives?"

"No."

"No?"

"I've got nothing to hide," I said.

"I want to ask if you broke into Ingram's house, and why you're not worried about Hatch finding whatever he's looking for."

"It's better if you don't."

"O . . . kay."

From the way he stretched the word, it was clear he knew my reply had been a silent admission of guilt.

"Do you have a criminal lawyer?" he asked.

"No."

"I know a good one. I'll call her for you."

Her . . . He knows a lot of women. "Thank you, but I hope I'll never have to meet her," I said.

"I think you'd like Olivia. Maybe someday I'll get the three of us together. You two have something in common."

From the smile on his face, I was sure now that I didn't want to meet "Olivia" and find out what the two of us had in common.

"Before Hatch gets here, I want to walk Tuffy," I said.

I took my Tuffy-walking jacket—the one with the pockets full of plastic bags for picking up after him—from the hall closet.

"I don't think I want to know what your lawyer friend and I have in common."

Nicholas chuckled. "You'd be surprised."

I shoved my house keys into a pocket of my slacks and hooked the leash onto my excited poodle's collar. Tuffy fairly bounced beside us as Nicholas and I headed for the street, where Nicholas's prized silver Maserati Quattroporte was parked. He'd bought it several years earlier in a police department confiscation auction and was so careful with it he'd never turn it over to parking attendants.

"You don't have to stay here," I said. "Why don't you go home, or go to the paper?"

"I'm not going to leave you alone with Hatch. He can be one nasty SOB."

"All in the valley of death Rode the six hundred . . ." I quoted that grim passage from "The Charge of the Light Brigade" as we started down the street.

"I know a poem that's a lot more cheerful," he said. " 'There once was a soldier from Lutz, who was a—' "

"Stop." I poked him on the shoulder. "I've heard that one." Remembering the naughty rest of it made me laugh.

We were going south toward Montana Avenue. It was the route I usually took with Tuffy in the morning, and it was the direction from which I was sure Hatch would be coming.

"Speed it up, Tuff. We don't have time to linger this morning."

As though he understood the situation, or at least understood my need for him to hustle, Tuffy picked out a spot on the grass between the sidewalk and the curb and made a firm and generous deposit. Quickly scooping it up with the plastic baggie, I put that into a larger, Ziploc bag.

Nicholas watched me and chuckled. "Don't be half safe. That's like using a condom when you're on the pill."

"That's not a very good analogy. I double bag it so there won't be any odor in the trashcan. Garbage pickup isn't until Thursday."

As we resumed our walk, I said, "If something bad happens this morning—I mean if Hatch arrests me—would you call Liddy Marshall, tell her about it, and take Tuffy over to stay with Liddy and Bill until . . ."

"Until we can spring you." Nicholas gently squeezed my hand. "Don't worry."

"And please call Eileen. She's at John and Shannon's house. You have that number. Tell her where I am and ask her to take care of Emma."

"I like that cat of yours," Nicholas said. "Maybe it's because she's the only cat that has ever seemed to like me."

I was about to remark that he does well charming females, but the words died unspoken in my throat because I saw a four-car convoy turn off Montana and head up in our direction.

In the lead was Detective Manfred Hatch's brown Crown Victoria. Following Hatch was a police black-and-white with two uniformed officers in it. Behind them was Weaver's Chevy.

The fourth car in the line was the one that I hadn't expected.

It was John O'Hara's black Lincoln.

24

When Hatch saw me, he stopped beside us so abruptly that the three sets of brakes behind him screeched. I thought I caught a faint whiff of tire material left on the pavement.

"What do you think you're doing?" Hatch demanded.

I held up the plastic bag containing Tuffy's deposit. "Being a good citizen." Pretending I didn't know, I gestured to the line of vehicles behind him. "What's this parade about?"

"Go back up the street to your house."

■ ■ ■

By the time Nicholas, Tuffy, and I returned a few minutes later, Detective Hatch and the two uniformed officers were standing on my doorstep. Weaver and John were just getting out of their cars. Weaver hiked across my lawn to join Hatch. Knowing that I care about the condition of my lawn, John took the brick path that led up to the front door.

I smiled at John, and said, "Hi."

Nicholas nodded at him. "Morning."

John glared at Nicholas with his usual expression of disapproval, but his responding "Hello" was polite.

Hatch had parked in front of the Maserati. Behind Nicholas's "silver bullet," as I referred to it, was the squad car. Weaver's vehicle and John's were strung out behind the black-and-white in a line that took up a good portion of the block.

With the arrival of four more adults—Nicholas, Weaver,

John, and me—and a standard poodle, there was so little room at my front door that the uniformed officers and Weaver took positions on the lawn. John positioned himself on the walk behind me. Hatch blocked my front door with his body, reached into his jacket, and withdrew a folded sheet of paper.

"Search warrant," he said, waving it in front of me. "These officers and I have permission to search your premises and your vehicle."

I held out my hand. "I don't have X-ray vision, Detective. Let me read it."

He handed the paper to me, and I gave Tuffy's leash to Nicholas.

"All the Is are dotted and the Ts are crossed," Hatch said. "Signed by Judge Newton Carter."

Nicholas peered over my shoulder, reading the warrant as I did. Deliberately, I took my time, while in my peripheral vision I saw Hatch fidgeting.

When I thought I'd let him wait long enough, I said, "The scope of your search is pretty narrow. You only have permission to look for DVDs or videotapes."

Those restrictions told me he'd had trouble getting this warrant. It wasn't an open invitation for a fishing expedition. It also told me that the police had found Ingram's personal pornography collection, had viewed at least some of them, and thought that I might have taken one or more. Given I'd left a fingerprint, it was a pretty easy deduction.

"Why videos?" Nicholas asked.

"Evidence of an extremely *personal* relationship with Keith Ingram." The innuendo in Hatch's voice made the nature of that video unmistakable to anyone, but to embarrass me further he added, "Think about that Paris Hilton tape on the Internet."

I saw Nicholas's face flush with anger, but he kept his temper in check. John's expression was stony. It was clear to me from John's rigid lack of reaction that he'd already

learned about Ingram's sex tapes and was deliberately re-
fusing to show any reaction.

Nicholas handed Tuffy's leash back to me and pulled his
camera phone out of his jacket pocket.

"I'm going to be with you and the officers while you
search, photographing any destruction you commit."

Hatch's grim expression hardened. "If you put one
foot in that house while we're working there, I'll bust
you for obstruction." He planted his feet, as though daring Nicholas to try to get past him. "Nobody except the
officers, Detective Weaver, and myself goes inside until
we're through."

"Before you start," I said, "I want to put Tuffy out into
the backyard with a bowl of water. And I want to put my
cat into her carrier so that nobody steps on her, or opens a
door that lets her out into the street."

"All right," Hatch said. He beckoned to one of the uniformed officers. "Roy—go with her. Make sure she doesn't
do anything else."

■   ■   ■

A few minutes later, I was back on my front doorstep with
Emma in her carrier. It had been a struggle to get my little
gray and gold calico into it because to her it meant she was
going to Dr. Marks, her veterinarian, for a shot or some
other unwanted intrusion into her furry person. I'd put one
of her favorite soft toys in with her, but she ignored it.

I set the carrier down in the shade next to the doorway,
removed the small bowl I'd shoved into my jacket pocket,
and quickly filled it with water from the garden hose.

"Here, sweetie," I whispered to Emma as I maneuvered
the bowl of cool water into the front of the carrier while
blocking her attempt to exit. "We're not going to the doctor
today, so just relax and enjoy watching the birds."

John said, "God knows how long we'll be here. I'm going on a coffee run."

"That would be great."

I wanted coffee, and the timing was good for John to run that errand. From the tightness of his mouth, I knew that Nicholas was upset about something. He wasn't likely to talk about it with John around.

"How do you take yours, Martino? Black?"

"A little half-and-half with one packet of sugar. Thanks—*Hara*."

If I hadn't been aching at the thought of Hatch and company pawing through my possessions, I would have been amused at John O'Hara and Nicholas D'Martino deliberately misstating each other's names in a childish game of tit for tat.

John ignored Nicholas's jibe and marched down the path toward his car.

"I notice he didn't ask how you take *your* coffee." There was a sharp edge in Nicholas's voice.

"For heaven's sake, John and I have known each other for more than twenty years. But that remark isn't about who takes what in their coffee. What's bothering you?"

"In the past few months you've figured out a couple of murders. I think you're smart enough to know what's on my mind."

"Four apes with badges are pawing through my belongings. I have no idea what damage they're doing, and the thought of it hurts like hell. I don't have the patience for sarcasm right now."

"Okay. Here it is. What was going on between you and Ingram?"

"Nothing," I said. It was a relief to tell the truth.

"Hatch couldn't have got a search warrant without showing probable cause. Their fingerprint evidence suggests you broke into Ingram's house. I didn't need the Paris Hilton cheap shot to know he's looking for a sex tape. Did you have sex with Ingram?"

I felt my face grow hot with anger. "I told you there was

nothing going on between us. What part of 'nothing' don't you understand?"

"Hatch obviously thinks there's a tape of you and Ingram." Nicholas was angry, too. I could tell from his stiff shoulders and the muscle tic in his right cheek. "You asked me what kind of a man Ingram was. You said you were concerned for Eileen, but it must have been yourself you were worried about. You met Ingram while we've been seeing each other." He let out a snort of disgust. "I thought we had a deal."

"A *deal*? Is that what you call our relationship? An exchange of services?"

"No. I'd thought it was more. But I've been wrong about women before."

"I'm not going to defend myself to you," I said.

"Ha! The old non-denial denial. Now you sound like a politician. I think you missed your calling, Toots."

"Don't you dare call me 'Toots.' After all these months, if you won't take my faithfulness for granted then I don't want you here."

"You don't have to ask me twice."

"I wasn't *asking*!"

Nicholas stomped off, ignoring the brick path and digging his heels into my lawn with every step of his heavy stride. The path was a more direct route to his car, but he knew how much I prized my lawn.

"Hurting my grass is childish," I yelled.

He ignored that. When he reached his car he hurled himself inside and—uncharacteristically—slammed the door. Nicholas usually treated his silver bullet as gently as I treat my pets.

Nicholas gave his steering wheel a hard yank to the right, barely missed hitting Hatch's rear bumper, and roared off up the street, spewing a cloud of pungent gray exhaust fumes behind him.

"I hope you get a ticket for polluting," I yelled.

I didn't know which of us was the more furious: Nicholas because he thought I'd slept with Keith Ingram, or me because the only man I'd been to bed with since Mack died didn't trust me.

I sat down next to Emma's carrier, unzipped enough of the top of it to fit my hand inside, and stroked my sweet cat. Her responding purr made me feel better.

"As long as you and Tuffy and I, and the people I love, are okay, then nothing else really matters," I whispered to Emma. "My possessions are just *things*."

I hoped I'd still feel that way when I finally got back into the house.

25

When John returned fifteen minutes later it was with only two containers of coffee. He handed one to me.

"Thanks. Didn't you get any for Nicholas?"

The slightest hint of a smile twitched the corner of his lips. "I was pretty sure he wouldn't be here."

I took a welcome swallow. The coffee was hot enough, without burning my throat, and he'd put the right amount of Sweet'N Low and half-and-half into it. It was my favorite flavor: Vanilla Nut. Caffeine an' Stuff was on the container, but when I tasted it I would have known where it came from. In my coffee-craving opinion, that café brewed the best Vanilla Nut.

After a few minutes of comfortable silence, John asked, "Anybody come out while I was gone?"

"No." Fortified with the coffee, I asked, "Why did you think Nicholas would have left?"

John watched two birds twittering at each other on a low branch of my willow tree. He didn't look at me as he said, "Because he doesn't know you as well as I do, that you'll take a bullet for someone you love."

I knew he was making a subtle reference to Eileen and Ingram. I didn't respond to that because Eileen's involvement with the dead man was the last thing we should be discussing right now. Surely John had realized that if I broke into Ingram's house, it had to have been for Eileen's sake. He couldn't ask me and I couldn't tell him what I knew, or admit what I had done. Even though he wasn't part of the Ingram murder investigation, as a member of the LAPD who'd sworn to uphold the law, he was obligated not to withhold pertinent information. What John didn't *know* didn't have to be revealed; he was allowed to keep his theories to himself. By our shared silence, we were protecting his daughter. Come to think of it, we were protecting me, too, from a charge of breaking and entering. With that subject out of bounds, it didn't leave much for us to talk about, so we drank our coffees and watched cars go by. Neighbors left for work, or took their children to school. Several noticed the police car. It was impossible to miss. Several sent curious looks in my direction. I smiled, trying to give the impression that it was the most natural thing in the world to have a police car outside my house, and for me to be on the front steps with a tall man and a cat carrier.

The woman next door, who had lived in her house even longer than I'd lived in mine, called out "Hi" and waved at us as she hurried to her car. We waved back.

"I've seen her somewhere before," John said.

"Julie Coombs. You met her and her husband at Mack's funeral. She works at a talent agency and he's in computers."

"Oh, yeah." I could tell from his inflection that he did remember her. John had a remarkable facility for recalling names and faces.

A few minutes later a familiar ivory-colored Range Rover came up the street and parked behind John's Lincoln.

"That's Liddy," I said, getting up. John stood, too, but remained in place as I hurried down to the street to greet her with a hug.

"I'm so glad to see you," I said. "But why are you here?"

"Nicholas called to tell me police were doing their cop thing in your house. He said you needed me."

"I do."

Liddy waved at John. "Where is your Sicilian stallion? Did Big John chase him off?"

"We had a fight," I said.

"A bad one?"

"Very bad."

"So, he stalked off in a snit, but he didn't want you to be alone. I like him."

John greeted Liddy with a quick squeeze of her hand. "Glad to see you. Do you know what's going on?"

"Nicholas phoned her." Something occurred to me. "John, if he contacted Liddy he might have phoned Eileen, too. You'd better get hold of her and tell her not to come here. Tell her I need her to go to our shop and handle the business until I call her later."

"Good idea." John pulled his cell phone out of his jacket, pressed a number on his speed dial, and walked down to the street for privacy.

"The forensics techs found my fingerprint at the back of Ingram's house, where I broke in."

Liddy's eyes widened. "How? You were wearing gloves."

"Latex. I cut myself on a piece of broken glass that sliced through one of the fingertips. I didn't think I'd left a print, but I must have. It was enough for a match to the prints they had of me from before."

Liddy nodded, remembering that I'd been suspected of murder a few months ago. At that time I'd volunteered to give the police my prints to prove that I'd never touched anything belonging to the victim. Eventually, I'd been cleared, but they had my prints in their system.

I saw John close his phone. He came back to join us at the front door.

"Your friend didn't call Eileen," he said. "So I didn't tell her what's going on here. I just said you were giving Hugh Weaver and me some additional information about people who'd been at the gala, and that you'd asked me to give her the message about going to your shop."

Liddy opened her tote bag. "I brought us a deck of cards

and a pad to keep score. How 'bout some three-handed gin while we're stuck out here on the doorstep?"

For the first time in several days, I saw John smile. I guessed what he was thinking: that it reminded him of the "old days" when Liddy and Bill, and John and Shannon, and Mack and I played gin on Saturday nights.

■ ■ ■

Three hours and twelve hands of gin later—I owed Liddy six dollars and John owed her eight—Detective Hatch and his Merry Pillagers finally emerged from my house.

With a cardboard box full of DVDs and VHS tapes.

"Those are my favorite old movies," I told Hatch. "After you've had your film festival, I want them back."

"If they're really what you say, they'll be returned."

In a low voice, Liddy said, "At least they're not carting off huge garbage bags full of stuff, like I see on the cop shows."

"That's because Della's house wasn't the scene of the crime," John said.

"We're going to search your vehicle," Hatch announced.

"I'll get the keys," I said.

"No need." Hatch held up the keys to my Jeep. "They were on your dresser." He tossed the ring to one of the uniformed officers. "We're taking this to the LAPD garage to look it over there. You'll get it back in a day or two."

That further indignity infuriated me, but I couldn't prevent it. "I know the mileage and how much gas is in the tank," I said, "so no joyriding. And keep my radio on the setting where I have it."

They ignored me and headed toward the driveway, where I'd parked. I hadn't put the Jeep into the garage last night because Nicholas was there, and we'd started kissing.

The thought of Nicholas made me remember that I hadn't made my bed this morning, after he and I . . . And

Nicholas had left a wet towel on the bathroom floor after he showered. *Hatch must think I'm a slob.*

It suddenly struck me as funny that I'd worry about such a ridiculous thing, under the circumstances. I started to laugh.

John picked up Emma's carrier. "You're taking this well."

"I was a cop's wife," I said. "We're tough."

Then I opened my front door, stepped into my house, and began to cry.

26

"Oh, no . . ." Liddy's voice was a wail of despair. She put her arm around my shoulders in sympathy. "This is awful."

Awful didn't begin to describe the condition of my living room.

"Bastards," John said. "I'm sorry, Del."

Every book had been taken from the shelves and left on the floor. Chairs were turned upside down; the drawer was removed from my Grandma Nell's little antique writing desk and the contents scattered on the floor; sofa cushions lay in a heap in a corner. The heavy glass top on my carved wooden coffee table was leaning up against one wall, with the table upended. The two area rugs were rolled up and pushed aside. The pictures on the walls had been taken down and leaned against the baseboards. The family photos on surfaces had been taken out of their frames and left lying facedown where they used to stand upright.

Liddy handed me a packet of tissues. I wiped away the tears, blew my nose, and took a long, deep breath.

"I'm okay now." It was a lie, but I figured if I kept saying that to myself, I could make it true.

I picked up the little wastebasket that had been under the writing desk, placed it back where it belonged, and dropped the tissues into it. "Let's keep going."

John lifted the cat carrier a little higher and asked, "Where do you want Emma?"

The fact that John remembered the name of my cat cheered me. In the middle of chaos, little things mattered.

"For now, in my bathroom," I said.

At the door to my bedroom, I felt tears filling my eyes again. The linens had been torn from the bed and lay in piles on the floor. The mattress had been turned over but not put back on the box springs. All the clothes in my closets had been taken out and dropped onto the bed. The lingerie in my dresser had been dumped out and the drawers turned upside down. Even all of my handbags had been opened, shaken out, and thrown aside. Old tissues, crumpled receipts, loose coins, and partial rolls of breath mints that had been in the bottoms of the purses were left on the linen pile.

Reaching for the only positive thing I could think of, I said, "At least they didn't slice up my cushions and mattress and pull out the stuffing."

Relatively speaking, my bathroom was in the best shape. Towels and washcloths had been swept from the shelves and left on the floor. The top of the toilet tank had been taken off but not put back on, just leaned up against the corner of the shower stall. The contents of my medicine cabinet had been hauled out and left in the bathroom sink. Even Emma's box has been emptied out onto one of the used towels.

Adding insult to injury—I hate a cliché, but in this case it expressed exactly how I felt—the toilet seat had been left up. Nicholas never left it up, so it meant that one of those rampaging "Protect and Servers" had relieved himself here. That made me mad enough to stop the tears.

I closed the lid, resolving to scrub out the toilet later, before I used it myself.

"Let me straighten this up quickly," I told John, "and then we can settle Emma in here for a while."

While John stood holding the carrier, Liddy quickly put dirty laundry into the hamper and replaced the clean towels on shelves. I folded the spilled litter into the dirty towel where it had been dumped and refilled Emma's box with fresh crystals from an unopened box beneath the sink. Finally, I refilled Emma's water dish and spread a fresh towel out on the floor and took the carrier from John.

I unzipped it and coaxed her out. She was tentative. I know how upsetting it is to an animal when their familiar territory is changed in some way. It's hard on human beings, too. I stroked her and said, "Don't worry, sweetheart. You'll be comfortable here until I can let you back into the rest of the house."

Emma crept over to examine her litter box, and I backed out of the bathroom and closed the door.

■   ■   ■

Eileen's bedroom and bathroom were an ugly mirror image of mine. Total disarray.

"We'll have this put back together before she sees it," I told John.

Jaws clamped, John nodded. I guessed that he didn't trust himself to speak at that moment.

As bad as the living room and the bedrooms had been, the worst pain whacked me in the heart as soon as I came to the kitchen.

Liddy groaned, and John muttered a string of expletives I'd never before heard him use.

All of my dishes and cooking utensils had been taken out of their cabinets and left on the counters, the table, and the floor. All of my cleaning products had been removed from the area beneath the sink and my brooms and mops and vacuum cleaner cleared from the utility closet. My large crockery jars of dried pastas, sugar, and flour had been emptied onto paper towels and obviously pawed through. Rendered unusable by hands I was sure were dirty, those supplies would have to be thrown away.

They hadn't opened Tuffy's and Emma's sealed bags of Natural Balance dry food, but they'd emptied the already opened bags onto newspapers. I'd have to discard that, too.

With growing dread, I opened the refrigerator. Hatch and his team had taken everything out, but at least they'd put back the items that needed to stay cold, although not in the logical arrangement in which I kept my supplies.

Last came the freezer. This news was semibad. The frozen items in sealed supermarket packaging had been left alone, but everything that I'd wrapped in foil or freezer bags had been opened and not resealed. I'd have to get rid of that food, too, because I didn't know what contamination had occurred and I wasn't going to risk my health, or anyone else's.

John's expression was grim, but—perhaps trying to sound a positive note—he said, "For anything that they've destroyed, you can be reimbursed. There are forms. Want me to pick one up for you?"

"No, but thanks. Figuring out the cost of the ruined food will take more time than it's worth."

As I stared at the disaster that was my kitchen, heartsick and virtually paralyzed, Liddy stooped down, picked up a stack of dinner plates, and put them onto the cabinet shelf where they belonged.

"It's a start," she said.

My best friend's simple act—and her encouraging smile—were just what I needed to snap myself out of the emotional morass I'd sunk into.

I indicated the lone pile of plates that Liddy had put back on the otherwise empty cabinet shelf. "One thing done. Only a thousand more to go."

Filling a bowl of fresh Natural Balance for Dogs, I said, "I'll take this to Tuffy."

It was a relief to go out into the fresh, cool air. I hadn't realized it until that moment, but the search party had managed to raise dust that I didn't know I had. I resolved to be more thorough when I vacuumed.

Seeing me at the back door, Tuffy trotted over from where he'd been playing with a rope toy I'd hung from the limb of my one orange tree. I put the bowl of Natural Balance on the bottom step.

Ignoring the food, Tuffy nuzzled me, and I hugged him. His warm body and soft fur in my arms was a comfort.

"I'll let you inside soon, Tuff. In the meantime, you've got food and water and shade and toys."

He looked at me with his dark, intelligent eyes and I felt he understood. In any case, having Tuffy and Emma reminded me that it didn't really matter how big a mess Hatch and company had made of our home. Whatever was ruined were only *things*, and things could be replaced.

Back in the kitchen, John was closing his cell phone.

"I gotta go. There's a double homicide in the Hollywood Hills." He looked around at the chaos. "I hate to leave you girls with all this."

"We'll be fine," I said. "Liddy knows where everything goes as well as I do."

Liddy blew him a kiss. "Go solve the crime, Big John. We'll work faster without having to tell you what to do."

As soon as we heard the front door close, Liddy tugged at my sleeve. "We're alone now. So tell me why the Sicilian isn't here."

"He thinks I was sleeping with Keith Ingram."

Liddy huffed. "Men! We can't do without them and it's illegal to kill them. Where's the justice in that?"

■   ■   ■

It took us two hours to put the kitchen and my bedroom back together. While we worked, I filled Liddy in on what had happened at the coffee shop.

"I love his novels," Liddy said, "but he's not exactly a darling of the *New York Review of Books*. Maybe it was one of those snobby critics who shot at him."

I smiled. "When he's well enough, I'll tell him your theory."

I'd opened the bathroom door and was enticing Emma into the bedroom, when I heard the doorbell ring.

"I'll go," Liddy said.

"Thanks."

I lifted Emma up and put her on top of my freshly made bed. After giving her a few gentle strokes, I closed my bedroom door to keep her inside until we put the rest of the house right.

My bedroom was finished. Now it was time to begin restoring Eileen's room and bath. I'd started down the hallway when I heard Liddy's voice from the front door.

"I don't know if I should let you in," she said. "Is your medical insurance paid up?"

27

I met Liddy and Nicholas in the archway that led to the living room. He carried a large bag from Junior's Restaurant and Deli on the corner of Westwood and Pico Boulevards. He knew it was my favorite place for sandwiches. I could smell the wonderful scent of Junior's pastrami from twenty feet away.

Nicholas held the bag out in front of him like a shield. "I come in peace."

"I'm so hungry if you won't forgive him, I will," Liddy said.

Nicholas kept his eyes on me and waved the Junior's bag so as to waft more enticing aromas in my direction.

"Extra lean pastrami on fresh-cut rye," he said.

I took a few steps forward, but kept ten feet between us. "What's on the sandwich?"

"Russian dressing on one side of the rye, mustard and coleslaw on the other. No pickle. I got you your favorite extra lean corned beef, Liddy. And sides of potato salad, and three slices of New York cheesecake for dessert."

"I forgive you," I said.

"Thank God." Liddy took the bag. "I'll set us up in the kitchen. You two need a few minutes alone." She winked at me as she left the room.

"I was a total jerk," he said.

"Agreed. But what made you come to that conclusion?"

"When I cooled off, I thought about the kind of person you are and figured out that you must be taking heat for Eileen.

I'm guessing Ingram made a video of her. That's why O'Hara decked him and why you broke into the bastard's house."

"Off the record?"

Nicholas nodded agreement.

"You're partly right," I said. "John didn't know about the video when he hit Ingram. He just knew that Ingram had done something that hurt Eileen badly. I'm sure John's put it together now because he knows what Hatch got the search warrant for, and that SID found my fingerprint on Ingram's back window."

"O'Hara stuck around while I left. He really does know you better than I do."

I smiled at him. "In one particular way he doesn't know me at all. Now, I'm trusting you, that you're not going to write about this."

"Not unless somebody else in the media gets the story, or parts of it. If that happens I'll have to report it, but I'll keep you and Eileen out of it as much as I possibly can."

"Fair enough," I said.

"I noticed O'Hara's car is gone."

"He was called away on a double homicide in Hollywood. Shouldn't you be covering that?"

"Ted Jaffe is. I wanted to see you." Nicholas looked around at the disaster in the living room. "Is the rest of the house as bad as this?"

"It was even worse, but we started in the back and have been working our way forward. We just have Eileen's room and the living room yet to do."

"I'll help," he said.

"After we eat."

I turned and began to walk toward the kitchen, but Nicholas caught my hand. Gently, he pulled me into his arms. We kissed until I felt all the tension of the day drain out of my body.

■   ■   ■

After eating lunch, the three of us finally managed to restore the house to the way it had looked before Hatch and his invaders tore it apart. Miraculously, they hadn't broken anything, but cleaning up took most of the rest of the afternoon.

Liddy went home to take a bath and to make dinner for Bill.

I gave Tuffy and Emma their dinners, and made a fresh pot of coffee for Nicholas and me. When it was ready, and I'd poured mugs for us, I took out a pen and one of the pads of paper I kept in a kitchen drawer, and joined Nicholas at the table.

"What are you doing?" Nicholas asked.

"I'm going to try to make some sense out of what's happened," I said. "I think better when I write things down. Let's make an investigation plan."

Nicholas smiled.

"Don't laugh at me," I said.

"I wasn't going to. That was a smile of recognition. When I'm working on a complicated story I make lists, too. I start with what I already know."

"Here's what I know." I talked as I began to write. "One: Ingram had a hidden video camera in his bedroom and taped women with whom he was having sex."

"Some of them might have been all right with that," Nicholas said. "Exhibitionists."

"Eileen didn't know about it, and I'm guessing some of the others didn't either. One of those women might have been angry enough, or frightened enough, to have killed him."

"Did the tapes have names on them?" Nicholas asked.

I shook my head. "Only initials. As soon as I found Eileen's—and I made sure there was only the one tape of her—I grabbed it and left the house."

"Can you remember any of the other initials?"

I squeezed my eyes shut, trying to recall what I'd seen in

the collection of DVDs, but no images came into my head. I opened my eyes. "Nothing. I was so nervous about being in his house the only label that registered with me was Eileen's. The police have those other DVDs. They've probably figured out who at least some of the women are." I made a note. "I'll ask John to find out from Hugh Weaver."

"What makes me doubt that one of those women killed Ingram is that the attempted murder of Roland Gray was done by a sniper."

"There have been female snipers." I said it a touch defensively, as though I was trying to stand up for the equality of female killers.

"But a female sniper in Beverly Hills? I think we'll find that all of Ingram's sex conquests were wealthy, either married to or divorced with a big settlement from rich men."

"Eileen isn't wealthy."

"She's young and beautiful. That's its own kind of wealth. I'm sure Ingram went after her out of lust. She must have been a nice change from targeting women whose most attractive qualities were their fat checkbooks. You told me that when he connected with Tina Long, the only child of a billionaire, he dropped Eileen, but was still trying to force her to be available for booty calls."

"If Ingram had married Tina Long, her father would have been smart to hire a food taster." I felt my eyes widen. "Hey, I thought I was making a joke, but I just realized that if Eugene Long figured out exactly what kind of an unscrupulous opportunist had captivated his daughter . . ."

"It could be a powerful motive for murder," Nicholas said. "He wouldn't have had to do it himself. He can afford to hire a thousand hit men."

That was an exciting thought, until I fell back down to earth with a thud.

"But then why would he, or his hit man, try to kill Roland?" I said. "I have to find out what the connection is between Long and Roland."

"*We* have to find out a lot of things," Nicholas said. "I'll use my sources to see what I can dig up."

"Most of us were watching Wolf Wheeler's juggling act when the smoke bomb went off. It might have been coincidence, or—"

"Or part of a plan." Nicholas nodded and made a note of Wolf Wheeler's name.

"Next: I want to get the guest list for the gala. Maybe one of the people attending had something against either Ingram or Roland, or both."

"I can get the list from the *Chronicle*'s entertainment editor. And I'll get copies of the pictures our photographer took."

"Perfect. I'll ask our publicity man, Phil Logan, to get a guest list, too. Double-check of who was there." I made another note. "Yvette Dupree. I want to talk to her. She seems to know Long, very well, and she's close to daughter Tina. About Tina: I'll have to figure out how to do it without Hatch going crazy, but I want to talk to Tina."

"I'll check our files to see what we have on Dupree and the Longs."

"Ah!" I stood up. "I've got an idea. Don't move."

I hurried to the bookcase in my bedroom and found the copy of Roland Gray's new thriller, *Terror Master*.

Back in the kitchen, I showed it to Nicholas. "Roland gave this to me when he came to the studio Thursday night."

"So?"

I opened the book to the Acknowledgments and scooted my chair around so that Nicholas could see it, too.

"There's a lot of information in these author 'thank you' pages."

We studied the names, but I let out a sigh of disappointment when we didn't find any we recognized.

"Most of these people gave him information about nuclear weapons," I said. "It's not likely we'll find any of them on the gala list."

"Let's see who he dedicated the book to." Nicholas turned a page. "Hey. What do you make of this?"

I read the dedication aloud: " 'To the one who got away . . .' "

"Jeez—novelists! They think they're so clever. Do you have any idea who that 'who' is?"

"No, but I'll see him tomorrow. Right now I'll call Phil Logan and ask him for the list of people who attended the charity cook-off."

Nicholas got up from the table. "I'm going to the paper to get our entertainment editor's list, and copies of the file pictures. I'll e-mail them to you. Then I'm going home to sleep."

"You're welcome to stay here."

"That's not called 'sleeping.' "

Inside the front door, we kissed. For quite a while. Finally, Nicholas stepped back. "I want us to make a rule."

"What rule?"

"We don't have sex *every* time we're alone together," he said.

"All right. Do you play gin? Poker? Scrabble? Do crossword puzzles?"

He smiled, but his tone was serious. "What I'm saying is that I want to live to be a very old man, and have you there to wipe the drool from my chin."

That declaration veered too close to a subject I wasn't anywhere near ready to think about: the future. More specifically, our future.

I kept my tone playful. "What woman could resist such an appealing prospect?"

And then I kissed him lightly on the chin. "Good night."

28

By the time Eileen came home that evening, Phil Logan's messenger had delivered the gala's guest list, and Nicholas had e-mailed the *Chronicle*'s list, as well as copies of thirty-six pictures taken by the paper's photographer.

I was at the kitchen table again, with the two lists and the photos spread out in front of me. Tuffy must have been alerted by the sound of Eileen's car, because he stood up and began to wag his hindquarters before I heard her open the front door.

"Hi, I'm home," she called.

Tuffy loped off to greet her.

"I'm in the kitchen, honey."

Eileen came in with Tuffy close at her heels.

"I've got interesting news—actually, delicious news—from the shop," she said. "We're going to have a new line to sell."

Her excited smile gave my heart a lift. It was the first time I'd seen Eileen smile since the night she told me about Keith Ingram's repulsive threat.

"What's happened?"

"That school friend of yours, Carole Adams, e-mailed from where she lives in Delaware. She saw Roland Gray making pudding on the show and started experimenting. After a bunch of tries she came up with a pudding version of our nut butter fudge."

"That's Carole," I said. "She's always loved a challenge, and if someone didn't give her one, she challenged herself.

I never thought of trying to alter the fudge ingredients to create a pudding. How does her recipe sound?"

"I didn't just read it. The cooks were busy filling the orders for brownies and fudge, so Walter and I bought a hotplate and a pot at the hardware store down the street. We tried out the recipe in his office."

Walter was so knowledgeable about the equipment left from our building's days as a bakery that we asked him to stay on with us. An extra plus was that his many stories about Old Hollywood were very entertaining. He'd developed a personal following among many of our regular walk-in customers. It was at his suggestion that we'd added a small coffee bar in the front area where he could regale people who stayed to drink coffee and eat our brownies.

"Walter made the pudding. I just read out loud Carole Adams's recipe and handed him what he needed. It's so easy, and it's really good. Now I've got to figure out the cost of packaging and what we need to do to ship it. If we're able to add the nut butter fudge pudding to our line, I'm convinced we'll have a winner."

"Let's do it," I said. "And we need to decide how to compensate Carole."

Eileen went to the refrigerator and peered inside.

"Are you hungry? I can make something for you," I said.

"No, thanks. I had a hamburger with Walter. I'm thirsty." She took a bottle of orange juice from the top shelf, poured herself half a glass, and drank it. "I didn't see your Jeep in the driveway," she said.

"I'll have it back sometime tomorrow, I expect."

Eileen must have sensed that I was being evasive, because she turned and looked at me. She wasn't smiling anymore.

"What happened? Were you in an accident?" I heard a note of concern.

"No, nothing like that." I gestured to the chair across

from mine. "Come sit down. I'll tell you what happened today."

I didn't let Eileen know how truly awful Hatch's search had been, but even my much milder version brought tears to her eyes.

"Oh, Aunt Del, I'm so sorry! This is all my fault."

"Stop it," I said, squeezing her hand. "It is *not* your fault. It's Keith Ingram's fault because of what he did to you, and it's mine because I stupidly left a fingerprint when I broke into his house."

"I'm afraid to ask, but did Detective Hatch find my DVD?"

"There wasn't anything to find. I destroyed it."

Eileen and I had been so close for so many years that she could tell from the slight shake of my head that I didn't want her to ask any more questions.

"Thank you," she said softly.

Eileen took a deep breath and wiped her eyes with a paper napkin from the blue dragon napkin holder on the center of the table. She'd made it for me when she was in a middle school craft class. All grown up, she'd urged me to get rid of the dragon holder, saying it was ugly. "It looks like something done by a child with no talent at all for crafts," she'd said.

"That's exactly why I like it," I had told her, "because one particular child made it for me." I think she was secretly pleased that I kept it.

Getting back to what was important right now, I said, "Look at these pictures and the guest lists from the gala. Tell me if there's anyone here that you ever saw with Ingram. Or if he'd mentioned any of these names to you."

Eileen studied the photographs. "That's a good one of you." She pointed to a picture in which I was leaning forward slightly as I watched actor Coupe Deville working on his Philly Cheesesteak. "You've got a great profile." She pulled another photo toward her. "Yvette Dupree. Keith really hated her. A couple of months ago we were watching TV late one night and when she came on a talk show, he was so upset he turned off the set. In fact, I thought he was going to throw the remote. I asked him what was the matter and he said he couldn't stand her, that she was a total phony who'd tried to ruin his career. That's all he'd tell me. I'd only heard him speak so negatively about one other person."

"Who?"

"Eugene Long. That's another reason I was so stunned when he told me he was going to marry Tina Long. He'd said her father was an unscrupulous, vindictive drunk who had done so many crooked things, he deserved to spend his life in jail." She shuddered. "When I think back, there were little signs about the kind of person Keith was, but I didn't let myself see . . . Aunt Del, I thought I loved him. I was so stupid!"

"He put up a good front. When I met him the day he interviewed us for his column, he was charming. I'm not surprised you were attracted to him. Neither of us had any idea what he was really like."

"But I learned. Too late," she said bitterly. "And look at the trouble I've caused you and Daddy."

"We'll be all right." I gave her hand a comforting pat.

"I could tell the police the truth and get you off the hook," she said.

"No, you can't. If you did, that would convince Detective Hatch your father had a powerful motive for murder."

"I've put both of you in an awful spot. I'm so sorry."

"Stay strong," I said. "We'll get through this."

Somehow.

I didn't sleep very well that night.

■ ■ ■

The police hadn't returned my Jeep by the time Eileen and I had to leave for the Mommy & Me cooking class I taught every Saturday morning, so we loaded two cardboard boxes full of ingredients into her car.

Before we left, I phoned St. Clare's Hospital, asked to speak to Roland Gray, and was transferred to the second floor.

"Nurses' station," a female voice said briskly.

"Good morning. Would you connect me to Roland Gray's room, please?"

"Mr. Gray isn't taking calls."

"All right. Can you tell me how he's doing?"

"We're not allowed to give out information about patients," she said.

I was getting frustrated, but kept my tone pleasant. "What are your visiting hours?"

"Mr. Gray has is not having visitors."

It was taking an effort, but I remained genial. "My name is Della Carmichael. Would you ask him to phone me? My number is—"

"I'll tell him you called." And then that Angel of Mercy disconnected.

Eileen saw me gritting my teeth. "No luck?"

"I'm not through yet." I dialed the hospital's main number again. When an operator picked up, I asked her when visiting hours were.

"From nine AM until noon, and from three PM until seven PM."

"Thank you."

My cooking class for adults, which followed the Mommy & Me session, ran from noon until three.

I told Eileen, "I going to find a way to see Roland Gray this afternoon if I have to buy a set of scrubs and pose as a hospital employee."

"You won't have to buy anything, Aunt Del."

"What do you mean?"

Eileen reminded me that while Liddy Marshall had given up acting for marriage and motherhood, now that her twin sons were in college she sometimes worked as an extra in movies and on TV shows.

"Liddy's been on *General Hospital* several times as a nurse in the background, and she always supplies her own costumes so they'll fit. You two are the same size," Eileen said. "Why don't you call her while I finish packing up."

I grinned at Eileen and reached for the phone. "I knew there was a reason I put up with you all those years when you were a teenager."

Liddy was delighted at my scheme for getting in to see Roland Gray.

"Of course you can have the outfit, and it comes with an authentic-looking ID badge. Don't worry about the picture. Those things are so bad hardly anybody's recognizable."

"Great."

"I'm coming with you," Liddy said. "In case you need someone to create a diversion. Aren't you lucky you have a best friend who's an actress?"

29

I *was* lucky to have Liddy as my best friend, in more ways than one. She was the person who had set me on the path of cooking for a living.

My father had been a veterinarian and my mother was, and still is, an accountant in San Francisco. Because they both had to work full-time to support us, and I was the oldest of the four children, I'd prepared the meals from the time I was ten years old. My grandmother Nell taught me how to shop carefully for food, and how to make dinners from scratch. The fresh ingredients she showed me how to choose went into meals that were both more nutritious and cheaper than packaged dinners heated in a microwave. Learning what she called her "Nellie Campbell menu magic" was exciting. Cooking never seemed like a chore. As an adult it became my hobby, my relaxation. I enjoyed feeding people I cared about.

When I met Mack, I was a brand-new high school English teacher and he was in his third year as a police officer. I'd loved teaching English, and did it for fifteen years, until the terrible day when a student I'd given an F to for cheating brought a Glock to school and shot at me. I saw the pistol a moment before he pulled the trigger, and ducked. The bullet streaked past my head and smashed into the wall. When I saw where it had lodged in relation to where I was standing, I realized that it hadn't missed me by much.

The school's basketball coach had been out in the hallway when he heard the shot. He'd rushed in and subdued the boy before he could fire again. The young gunman glared at me, cursing. "Next time I'll pop you when you ain't looking."

I stayed home for a week, jumping at every unfamiliar sound. At night, even with Mack's arms around me, I dozed only in snatches. I stopped leaving the house, ordered groceries over the phone, and asked for them to be delivered. Tuffy was just a year old then. Instead of our jaunts through the neighborhood, I walked him around our backyard.

Liddy told Mack she was afraid I was becoming agoraphobic. It was her idea that I make a professional switch and teach that other thing I loved: cooking.

It took most of our modest savings, but with Mack's and Liddy's unwavering encouragement, I found the perfect space—in the back of a kitchen appliance store—and jumped through all the hoops that the State of California requires when someone wants to open a small business. By the time I was ready for students, I felt like my pre-gunshot self, and Tuffy and I were strolling around Santa Monica again.

Liddy rounded up most of the people who enrolled in my first classes, but within a few months word of mouth was sending students to me. Soon they were bringing their friends. The business grew to the point where I was almost breaking even. The first month when the school actually earned a tiny profit, I celebrated by treating myself to a professional manicure. That night I had another celebration, an especially sweet one, with my husband.

The next morning, Mack suffered a fatal heart attack while he was jogging. That same afternoon a vase of yellow roses arrived. They had been ordered the previous day. The card said, "Congratulations, Cookie. I knew you could do it. Love you always, Mack." Cookie had been my nickname since the first time I'd made dinner for him when we were dating.

The little school that I called The Happy Table was barely surviving financially, until I had the good luck to be hired to host a cooking show on the Better Living Channel, replacing the previous host, who had been fired. Depending upon whom one talked to, she'd lost the job either for drinking on the air or for being impossible to get along with. Or both.

Taping three half hours a week, and doing one live hour-long show on Thursday nights, had made me cut back on the number of classes I taught, but I never wanted to give up my little school. The TV exposure had increased enrollment to the point that the weekend courses were filled, with a waiting list. The school still wasn't making much money, but at least it wasn't drowning me in debt any longer. While I enjoyed teaching cooking to a television audience because the shows reached a great many people, the fact was that I got the most pleasure out of watching people who were standing right in front of me learn new kitchen skills. And the excited expressions on the faces of the children, when they learned how to make something they could eat, was priceless.

My cooking school was located in the back of Country Kitchen Appliances on Montana Avenue, between Fourteenth and Fifteenth Streets. The front of the building was white clapboard siding, accented by dark green shutters. Customers entered through red Dutch doors.

At ten minutes to nine o'clock on Saturday morning, Montana Avenue in front of Country Kitchen Appliances was not the busy thoroughfare it would be in another hour, so it was easy to find a parking place near the store's entrance.

I fed a handful of quarters into the meter while Eileen removed the two cardboard boxes, one at a time, from the back of her VW and set them on the sidewalk.

"Look, there's Mrs. Tran," Eileen said.

I glanced up to see a tiny, gray-haired Vietnamese woman smiling and waving at us through the front window. We waved back. Mr. and Mrs. Tran owned the store.

Eileen lowered her voice. "I'm afraid to ask Mrs. Tran, but do you know how her husband is doing? He scared me half to death when he fainted last Saturday."

"When I came to visit him on Monday he looked frail. He was supposed to have some tests on Tuesday. Mrs. Tran told me that he hasn't been very strong since his years doing forced labor in a Communist reeducation camp."

Eileen looked puzzled. "I don't understand? What kind of a camp?"

I put the final quarter into the meter. "When the North Vietnamese Communists defeated South Vietnam, many, many men from the educated, professional classes were taken from their homes and families and sent away to do hard labor. The Communists called it 'reeducation.' Some didn't survive. Many of those who did were never the same again." I picked up one of the two boxes. "Mrs. Tran said it took them almost fifteen years to finally get to America. A lot of that time they had to spend in refugee camps."

"They're such an upbeat couple," Eileen said. "After what they must have gone through, I'm ashamed to make such a fuss over my problems."

"Atrocities go on every day somewhere in the world. We've been very lucky," I said.

I try not to forget that. I appreciate the accident of birth that put me in a relatively safe part of the world.

Mrs. Tran held the Dutch doors open as Eileen and I carried the boxes inside.

"Good morning," she said brightly.

Eileen and I returned her greeting.

"How is Mr. Tran?" I asked. "Did he have the tests you mentioned?"

Her smile dimmed a bit, but she maintained a cheerful demeanor. "We are very hopeful. Good doctors here."

I matched her positive tone. "Tell Mr. Tran that I'm sending him my best wishes."

"That will please him," she said.

The store's telephone rang. Mrs. Tran excused herself to answer it.

"She has such a delicate face," Eileen said. "She must have been lovely when she was young."

"She still is," I said. "It's just a different kind of beauty now. Part her bone structure, and part her spirit."

■　■　■

The Happy Table cooking school was in the back of the store; it had been converted from what had once been a storeroom. To get there, we had to carry our boxes past an array of attractive kitchen equipment. The Trans had arranged the merchandise so that it looked as though the store was divided into four separate kitchens, each in a different style, from the sleekest modern to cozy country. The layout worked to the advantage of the Trans, because many of the students bought items that caught their attention as they were walking through the displays.

"One day, when I have some extra money, I'm going to buy a new KitchenAid stand mixer," I said. "In red. The problem is that the one I've had for twenty-five years refuses to wear out or break down."

Eileen chuckled. "That company must have missed the class on 'planned obsolescence.' So many things start going to pieces right after the warranty runs out."

For the past three years, Eileen had worked as my assistant at the school to earn extra money, so the two of us had set up for these classes many times. It didn't take us long to cover the preparation tables with disposable cloths, organize the ingredients for what I was going to demonstrate this morning, and check the four stoves to make sure the burners and the ovens were working.

We finished just as the eight Mommy & Me teams

began to arrive. Eileen handed out disposable aprons for them to put on.

The seven mothers, eight children, and one nanny placed themselves around the preparation tables. They were a nice ethnic mix. The two youngest mothers were about thirty, and the two oldest were deep into their forties. The rest were somewhere in between. The nanny was a Latina in her early twenties, accompanying a six-year-old girl named Alicia who didn't want to let go of her caregiver's hand.

The other seven children—five more girls and two boys—ranged in age from six to nine and were much bolder than little Alicia. One of Eileen's jobs was keeping the children corralled near the prep tables where she could watch over them.

I told the class, "Today's recipes form a theme: They're dishes with family connections. The first one we're going to make is Linda Dano's Italian Meatballs recipe, which was taught to her by her mother-in-law. You moms probably know Linda Dano as an Emmy-winning actress, but when Linda's husband, Frank Attardi, was diagnosed with lung cancer, she stopped working to be with him full-time. After he lost the battle, she became the national spokesperson for the Caregivers Survival Kit and Support Partners. Linda calls her mother-in-law, Marnie Attardi, her role model. Marnie worked in a glove factory while raising her three children. She and her husband, Anthony, never owned a home, but now, through an organization called HeartShare Human Services, and contributions from Linda and Frank, there's a residential home for developmentally disabled adults named in their honor. It's in Frank's home borough of Brooklyn, New York."

I indicated the line of ingredients we'd be using, and picked up the bottle of marsala. "Now, the unusual thing about this recipe is that while it calls for wine, we don't put the wine into the mix. We'll be moistening our hands with it when we roll the meatballs."

One of the boys started making hiccupping sounds and staggered in an imitation of someone drunk. The other children giggled until the boy's mother tugged on his shirt sleeve and shushed him.

We always ate what we made in these classes. When the meatballs had been cooked and consumed, Eileen and I gathered up the used paper plates and plastic forks, dumped them into our trash bag, and set out fresh ones.

"Because this is a Mommy & Me class, what we're going to do next is make two dishes from a Hollywood mother and daughter. One of my favorite actors was Richard Crenna. His widow, Penni, and their daughter, Seana, are terrific cooks and they're sharing with us Penni's Mexican Chicken Kiev and Seana's Quiche.

"Seana told me that when she and her father ate her quiche together, she'd always leave the end of the crust on her plate. He would lean over, wink at her, and eat the leftover piece. It's one of the little father-daughter moments she treasures.

"Now, the crust for this quiche can be bought ready-made at the market, but I'm going to show you how easy it is, and how much fun it is, to make your own crust using just flour, a little salt, some Crisco, and a few tablespoons of ice water. It's my absolute favorite piecrust, and the recipe is right out of the *Betty Crocker Cookbook*. I recommend that everyone have the original *Betty Crocker Cookbook* in their kitchen libraries. Now, I have to warn you kids: You're about to get a little messy."

The children cheered at that. The women groaned.

"Don't worry, moms. We have a big stash of Handi Wipes all ready for the cleanup later."

Eileen and I passed around small bags of all-purpose flour, measuring cups, and mixing bowls. "Since a quiche uses only a single crust, let's start by measuring out one cup of flour . . ."

■ ■ ■

By the time Seana Crenna's Quiches were in the ovens, eight young faces were smudged and sixteen little hands were caked with flour. Eileen helped the mothers and the nanny wipe everyone clean and I started to organize the ingredients to make the final recipe of the class, Penni Crenna's Mexican Chicken Kiev.

I was explaining that this was one of Richard Crenna's favorite meals and that Penni frequently made it for their party guests, when I heard the door from the appliance shop open.

I looked up to see the petite figure of Yvette Dupree, the Global Gourmet, the woman Keith Ingram had mocked to me the night of the gala, the woman Eileen told me Ingram had despised.

Yvette Dupree was one of the people I was most eager to talk to. Now, before I could find her, she had found me.

30

With Eileen and the other women busy cleaning flour off the children, I hurried over to my unexpected visitor.

"Bonjour, Della. *Excusez-moi.* I do not wish to disturb, but I must speak to you." Her French accent was as melodious as it had been the night of the gala, but now there was urgency in her tone.

"Give me just few minutes, Yvette—"

She stared past me and her lips compressed into a thin line. "That girl? Why is she here?" Her pitch had turned icy.

I saw that she was staring at Eileen, who was wiping the face of one of the children and hadn't seen Yvette.

"That's Eileen O'Hara. She's my assistant. Why?"

"*Cherchez la femme.*" Her voice was full of bitterness. "I think that girl killed Keith, and that she will try to kill my Tina out of jealousy."

"Yvette, that's ridiculous." I steered her back toward the door through which she'd entered scant minutes before. "We'll talk outside."

On the appliance shop side of the door I saw that there were customers examining the merchandise. Mrs. Tran was guiding a young couple through the ultramodern kitchen exhibit. The quietest part of the shop was just where we were standing.

"You're wrong about Eileen," I said. "She would never kill anyone. What in the world made you think so?"

"*Merde!*" The woman scorned. "She was—how do you

say in English—*dumped*? For Tina. Keith was *cochon* . . .
pork, *nes pas*?"

"You mean he was a pig."

"*Oui*. One can kill for love. Even love of *espece d'animal,
t'es degueulasse*!"

I didn't have to speak French to know that whatever
she just said was an insult, because she practically spit the
phrase. But her opinion of the late Keith Ingram wasn't what
was important to me. What did she know about Eileen?

"Yvette, what makes you think Eileen had any interest
in Ingram?"

Her raised eyebrows and pursed lips suggested she
thought that I was too stupid to be walking around upright.
"Tina told me. Ever since her mamma died, I have been like
zee mamma to her. *Ma petite fille* has *terreur*. Terror."

"Has anyone tried to hurt her?"

"*Non*. She has protection. But she cannot attend soirees.
It is like prison."

"I can't believe that she's in any danger. You and her
father should let her go on about her normal life. But something else has happened. Did you know that someone tried
to kill Roland Gray late Thursday night?"

Beneath her rouged cheeks, I saw her go pale. She
swayed slightly.

I reached out to steady her. "Yvette? Are you all right?"
She gripped my hand. "Was he alone . . . ?"

Yvette was staring at me so intently I realized she must
know Roland, and yet when were standing together, watching him work at his stove, I hadn't seen any sign of recognition from either of them.

"I was with Roland," I said. "We were having cof-
fee when a sniper shot at him through the café window.
The bullet grazed his forehead. Eileen never met Roland.
Doesn't this prove to you that she's not the killer?"

"I must go." She turned away from me and was gone,
without so much as an "au revoir."

I watched her hurry through the kitchen displays and disappear out onto Montana Avenue.

Eileen opened the door and poked her head out. "Where did you go? Everybody's ready."

"I just needed a breath of air," I said, deciding not to tell her about Yvette Dupree's surprise visit.

I followed Eileen back into the classroom and resumed my place at the preparation table.

When I'm teaching a class, or doing the TV show, I enjoy the activity so much that I have no trouble concentrating on the task of simultaneously cooking and explaining the steps, but Yvette Dupree's accusation against Eileen, and her odd behavior when I told her about the attempt on Roland's life, had left my mind swirling with questions. Part of me wanted to race through this last demonstration, but I couldn't do that. The women in class had paid to be here and they deserved my full attention.

"Penni Crenna's Mexican Chicken Kiev has to be made in advance and kept in the refrigerator before baking," I told the class. "Last night I prepared four casseroles, one for each of our ovens here." I indicated the line of crockery baking dishes on the prep table. "I wanted you to see what they look like after refrigeration and just before they go into the ovens. Eileen and I have the oven temperatures ready at 350 degrees, so let's put them in now. They only take twenty minutes to bake, so by the time you've watched and helped put the recipe together, the ones I prepared last night will be ready to be enjoyed."

I took a package from the refrigerator.

"We start by putting these skinless, boneless chicken breasts between two pieces of wax paper." I smiled at the children and picked up a wooden mallet. "Now who'd like to help me pound them down until they're about a quarter of an inch thick?"

Eight little hands shot up.

31

My noon to three PM adult class was composed of eight men over sixty—five of them were either widowers or divorced—a newly married couple in their twenties, and two women in their fifties or sixties whom I suspected were trolling for second husbands. They always dressed as though they were going to an upscale luncheon and brought their own heavy-duty aprons that protected their clothing better than the paper ones I handed out.

Whatever their individual reasons for enrolling, they were a compatible group and a pleasure to teach. Still, I was eager for three o'clock to come. I had places to go, and a murder to investigate.

"Today's menu starts with dessert," I said as they assembled around the preparation counter. "It's a delicious ice cream cake that we have to make first so it can spend time in the freezer before we'll be able to eat it near the end of the class."

I removed a package from beneath the counter. "This is a store-bought pound cake," I said. "Of course you can bake your own, but if you're in a hurry—say if you have visitors who show no sign of leaving by dinnertime—keep a plain cake and containers of ice cream in your freezer so you can come up with something yummy without leaving the house. The other two dishes we're making today will be my favorite green peppers stuffed with a ground turkey mixture, and Pasta Caruso. That's a recipe created by Fred Caruso, whose day job is producing movies and TV shows. He produced one of my favorite HBO movies, *The Rat Pack*. We'll start on those dishes just as soon as we get this dessert into the freezer."

I held up a loaf pan lined with two lengths of wax paper placed crosswise. "When cutting the wax paper, leave yourself at least two extra inches of paper on each side, because you'll be using them to lift the ice cream cake out of the pan after it's frozen."

I sliced the pound cake into sections and demonstrated how to place several slices around both sides and at the two ends inside the loaf pan. "Next, we take either a quart of one flavor of softened ice cream, or—my favorite—two pints in different flavors. Begin to pack them into the loaf pan, halfway up. Then place the last pieces of cake on top of the first layer of ice cream. Next, add the second layer of ice cream and put the loaf pan in the freezer. Allow an hour or two for the ice cream cake to set, then lift it out of the loaf pan and turn it out onto a dessert plate. Sprinkle some fresh fruit, like raspberries or blueberries or sliced strawberries around the cake. Top it with fresh fruit, or with a few swirls of whipped cream, or Cool Whip, or even with a light dusting of powdered sugar. Then slice and serve. But don't expect to have any left over for a midnight fridge raid."

■ ■ ■

Liddy arrived a few minutes after three. The last members of the cooking class had left and Eileen and I were cleaning up.

She held up the Neiman Marcus shopping bag she carried. "Here's your costume, Nurse Ratched."

Liddy took a folded set of scrubs out of the bag, handed them to me, and reached into the bag again. "And here's your prop."

It was an authentic-looking medical chart, encased in a metal holder.

"When you carry it in front of you, it covers most of the face on your ID badge."

"You've thought of everything," I said.

"Go get changed, Aunt Del. I'll finish up here."

"Thanks, honey."

The tiny bathroom in the corner of the school area was clean, but it was the size of the broom closet it had been before the toilet and the tiny sink were installed. I wouldn't be able to tell how I looked because there was no mirror over the washbasin.

It took quite a bit of twisting and stretching in that cramped space, but I managed to take off my own slacks and sweater and wiggle into Liddy's hospital employee costume without straining one of my muscles, or splitting the seams on her blue scrubs.

I folded up my own clothing and put those items into Liddy's shopping bag.

When I emerged, Liddy nodded in approval and said, "You look very official."

"Does the staff at St. Clare's wear this color?"

"I suddenly thought about that in the middle of the night, so I went over this morning and wandered around to check. Apparently, there's no regulation, because I saw the employees in both blue and green. A couple were in a sort of salmon shade, or maybe those started out orange and faded. Anyway, some of the women wear print tops over scrub pants, but I'd never do that because the contrast cuts the body in half and would make my rear look wide."

Eileen was gazing at me with worry in her eyes. "Are you sure you should do this? Is it illegal to pose as some-body who works in a hospital?"

"I'm just wearing the outfit. I'm not going to work on a patient," I said.

That was mostly true, but I knew that if I got caught in this impersonation by a hospital official and the police were called, I'd be in a fix trying to explain what I was doing there, dressed as I was. And if Detective Hatch caught me questioning Roland Gray, I might get slapped with a charge of interfering with a police investigation. That, on top of having my fingerprint at the scene of the break-in at Ingram's house, could land me in big trouble indeed.

■ ■ ■

During the ride to St. Clare's Hospital, I'd pulled down the passenger seat's visor and flipped open the mirror. With a tissue from the packet Liddy kept in her glove compartment, I wiped off my mascara and lipstick. As a final touch, I'd twisted my hair into a coil and pinned it against the back of my head. The style—if one could call that a style—wasn't meant to look good, and it didn't.

As we approached the hospital, Liddy asked, "Which parking lot? For the emergency entrance, or the main one?"

I pointed to the right. "Main entrance. The last information I had was that he'd been moved to the second floor."

Liddy steered her Range Rover toward the visitor's ticket booth, took one from the machine, and proceeded into the lot.

She'd just nosed into a parking space when I saw someone I recognized exiting through the hospital's large glass front doors.

"Quick—duck down!" I thrust my head below the windshield until my face was level with her gearshift.

Automatically, Liddy bent down, too.

She whispered into my shoulder. "Why are we doing this?"

"Yvette Dupree just came out of the hospital. I don't want her to see us."

"Do you think she went to visit Roland Gray?"

"She must have. It's too big a coincidence for her to be here for any other reason," I said.

A few more seconds passed.

"I'm getting a neck ache," Liddy said. "How long do we have to stay down here like this?"

"Until I finish counting to one hundred . . . seventy-nine, eighty, eighty-one. Okay, that's close enough."

I slowly lifted myself on one elbow until my eyes were above the dashboard. I took a cautious peek outside, and was just in time to see Yvette Dupree getting into a taxicab. "She's leaving," I said.

The cab pulled away from the entrance and moved into the circular driveway that funneled vehicles back to the street. I sat up. "She's gone. In a taxi, but I got a look at the cab's number."

Liddy sat upright behind the steering wheel and handed me the pad and pen she kept in the driver's side door pocket. "Write that number down before you forget. We should try to find out where she went after she left here."

"I love that 'we.' "

"Every investigator needs a partner," she said. "Sam Spade and Miles Archer. Andy Sipowicz and the Jimmy Smits character on *NYPD Blue*, Dirty Harry and the female cop that Tyne Daly played. And, of course, our Big John and your Mack."

I didn't want to point out that each of those relationships had ended in the death of one partner.

"Let's go," I said.

As we'd planned, we separated in the parking lot and approached the entrance to the hospital from different directions. We reached the big glass doors at the same time, but I was behind Liddy. She took her cell phone out of her purse and pretended to be on a call.

Liddy was giving a performance. Dressed in a figure-flattering navy blue designer suit with a short skirt, Liddy strode inside with a slight swagger that was intended to draw attention to her hips and her shapely legs.

In a posh British accent, she said loudly into the mouth-piece, "I've decided what I want: the double strand of pearls . . . The twelve millimeters . . . That's right, with the platinum clasp. And I want the following inscription on my husband's Patek Philippe: 'Less than tomorrow but more than yesterday.' No—I don't want a comma after the 'tomorrow . . .'"

It worked. Necks swiveled toward her from the left and from the right.

When I entered in her wake, no one seemed to notice.

I went directly to the elevators and pressed the Up button while Liddy disconnected her pretend call and studied the board listing various departments in the hospital.

The elevator arrived, discharged passengers, and I got on. Liddy was right behind me.

An attractive man in his forties, his brown hair peppered with glints of silver, was already in the elevator. He smiled at Liddy. She smiled back. To judge from his white coat and badge, he was a doctor. I retreated as far back into the elevator as I could go, and was grateful to the people who crowded in around me.

Liddy, the attractive doctor, and I all got off on the second floor. The two of them started toward the nurses' station, while I lagged a few feet behind, pretending to study my bogus patient's chart.

At the nurses' station, Liddy upped the wattage on her smile. Still sounding like a younger version of Queen Elizabeth, she addressed the woman behind the desk. "I beg your pardon, but I've just come from London to see my brother. I'm a tad jet-lagged and can't remember the number of his room. His name is Roland Gray."

Before the nurse could reply, the attractive doctor spoke. He extended his hand to Liddy, who took it.

"I'm Henry Lyons," he said. "I attended Mr. Gray. Your brother certainly is a popular man."

"Yes, Roland is quite gregarious, Dr. Lyons. May I see him?"

"I'm sorry. He's not here any longer."

Liddy put her hand on his arm and gave him a pleading look. "Is something wrong? Please tell me."

"I would like to have kept him another day or two, for observation, but he insisted on being discharged."

Suddenly looking distressed, she said, "Oh, dear—I hope he didn't go by himself. He might fall—"

"No, he left in the company of two men, one large and the other shorter. The shorter man has been with him most of the time. He had a British accent, too. The big one was dressed like a chauffeur—a black jacket and cap."

Liddy feigned a sigh of relief. "Well, then, I won't worry. Would you know if my brother was going home?"

"He didn't say, but I told him he needed at least another couple of days of rest." Dr. Lyons took a card from the pocket of his white jacket and gave it to Liddy. "If your brother has any questions, please have him call me. Anytime."

■　■　■

When we were back in her Rover, Liddy turned the key in the ignition. "Who do you suppose those men were who left with Gray?" she asked.

"The shorter one must have been his assistant, Will Parker. The big one dressed as a chauffeur might have been a bodyguard, because Roland told me that Parker usually drives for him." I unpinned the ID badge and put it and the prop chart into the shopping bag.

When we got to the hospital's tollbooth, the attendant took Liddy's ticket and said, "Five dollars."

I took out my wallet. "I'll get it."

I handed over a five-dollar bill. The wooden arm went up and we were released.

"What now?"

"Take me home so I can get into my own clothes. I'll wash your scrubs and give them back to you tomorrow. Okay?"

"No rush. I don't expect another call from *General Hos-*

pital right away. They've got a storyline going that's taken them away from the hospital for a while."

My cell phone rang. I pulled it out of my bag, looked at the faceplate, and told Liddy, "It's Nicholas."

She grinned. "No phone sex while I'm driving."

I laughed and pressed the button. "Hello, Nicholas."

"Where are you?"

"In Liddy's car. She's taking me home."

"How soon will you get there?"

"A few minutes. Why?"

"I'm in your neighborhood and I'd like to come over. I'm bringing you a surprise."

"Animal, vegetable, or mineral?"

"Animal."

"Dog or cat?"

There was a slight hesitation before he said, "If those are my only two choices, I'll say cat. See ya." He hung up.

"That's weird," I said, closing the phone.

"What's weird?"

"I don't know. He got off the phone too fast for me to get a clue."

When we got to my house, I saw my Jeep in the driveway. "Thank heaven," I said.

"And the police returned it in one piece," Liddy said dryly. "After what that wretched Detective *Hatchet* did to your house, I wouldn't have been surprised to see parts of it scattered all over the lawn."

I gathered up my purse and the shopping bag containing my clothes. "Thanks for today."

"I like detecting," Liddy said with enthusiasm. "Figure out where we're going next. I'll call you later."

Liddy drove away and I went to take a look at my Jeep. It was locked, but I found the key on top of my left front tire—where any car thief would look for it.

"You could have had the decency to drop the key through the mail slot in my front door," I said to myself.

From inside the house I heard Tuffy barking. I called to him, "I'm coming, Tuff."

He kept barking, and at that moment I heard the sound of a familiar engine. I turned to see Nicholas's Maserati slowing to a stop at the curb.

He wasn't alone.

In the passenger seat beside him was a stunning blonde woman. Her golden hair was styled in a sleek, asymmetrical bob that curled slightly forward to emphasize her high cheekbones and full mouth.

As soon as Nicholas cut the motor, she opened the passenger door. I saw long legs in a short skirt. My first reaction was that her legs were better than mine.

Then I realized that I was standing there without mascara or lipstick, with my hair a mess, and wearing hospital scrubs. On a woman's body, they were the world's least flattering two-piece garment.

Nicholas, who seemed blissfully unaware that I wanted to kill him for putting me in this embarrassing situation, came around from his side of the car. He took the woman's arm and guided her toward me.

"Della, I want you to meet Olivia Wayne—my favorite criminal defense attorney."

32

"Ms. Wayne," I asked, "has someone ever murdered a man right in front of you?"

I could see by his puzzled expression that Nicholas had no idea what I was talking about.

She got it, and she laughed.

"If you mean a certain Italian, I'd probably help you bury the body," she said.

She thinks Nicholas is Italian, but he's Sicilian. That made me feel better.

"I told Olivia that you're under suspicion for breaking and entering and possible destruction of evidence in a murder investigation."

"But you haven't been charged with anything," Olivia Wayne said.

"No." *Not yet.*

"Good. Most people wait to contact a criminal defense attorney until the prosecution is already on track. I like to get ahead of that train."

"Come inside," I said. "I'll make coffee. Or would you like some lunch?"

"No, thanks," Olivia Wayne said. "Nick already fed me."

"That was nice of him," I said.

She chuckled. "Our friend knows the persuasive quality of grilled salmon."

I'll just bet he does.

Inside the house, I greeted Tuffy and Emma. Tuffy

nuzzled me and wagged his hindquarters at Nicholas, but Emma, seeing the stranger with us, scurried away.

Eileen had left a note for me on our personal mail drop, the hall table. I scanned it quickly and told Nicholas, "Eileen walked Tuffy when she got home from the school at three thirty. We must have just missed her."

I turned around to see Olivia Wayne kneeling in front of Tuffy, giving him a two-handed scratch that he was clearly enjoying.

"He's magnificent," she said. "We had a black standard when I was growing up. If I'm ever in a situation where I have the time to give to a dog, this is what I want."

Her affectionate reaction to Tuffy made me warm to her. Just a little. Perhaps this was what Nicholas meant when he said that Olivia Wayne and I had something in common. Then I wondered what kind of relationship they had so that he would know what kind of dog she had when she was growing up.

"Where did you get him?" she asked. "What breeder?"

"He was a rescued puppy," I said. "My late husband found him abandoned on the Rancho Park Golf Course. The groundskeeper said he'd seen him dumped out of a car the night before. Mack took him to a veterinarian to find out if he'd been micro-chipped. No chip, and no one put ads in the paper looking for him. We got lucky."

Olivia Wayne stood up. "It seems to me that he got lucky, too."

If you work a jury the way you just worked me, I'd want you on my side.

I led Nicholas and Olivia into the kitchen, started a fresh pot of coffee, and invited them to sit down at the table.

Eager to put on some mascara and lipstick and get into my own clothes, I said, "Just give me a minute to go and change."

"You're fine," Nicholas said. To my amazement, he

looked as though he meant it. "We've just got a short time before I have to take Olivia back to her office."

"Nick, you go into another room for a few minutes until we call you back in," his favorite criminal defense attorney said.

Apparently, Nicholas expected that. With a pleasant smile on his face, he got up and headed toward the living room. Tuffy stayed with me.

When he was gone, she said, "Della, give me a dollar. I need that so whatever you tell me will be privileged."

I was still carrying my purse and Liddy's shopping bag. I took a dollar bill out of my wallet and handed it to her. "You work cheap."

She laughed. "We'll see if you think so should it turn out that I have to defend you. There was a famous criminal defense attorney way back in the old days. Jake Ehrlich was his name. I read his autobiography, *A Life in My Hands*, when I was in college. To defend someone for murder he charged everything they had. When a client balked, he'd ask, 'What's your life worth to you?' "

I thought, *I'd give up anything except Tuffy and Emma*. But what I said was, "Let's hope it doesn't get to that point."

"What do the police think they have on you?"

She already knew that Keith Ingram had been murdered at the charity cook-off gala. I told her about breaking into Ingram's house, that I'd left a fingerprint behind on a broken window, and that Detective Hatch had used that evidence to get a warrant to search my house and vehicle.

"Did they find what they were looking for?"

"No."

"I'm not going to ask you why they didn't. I can guess." I didn't reply.

Olivia Wayne smiled at me. "You know when to keep quiet. Good. Did you admit to breaking into Ingram's house?"

"No, but I didn't have to, because they have my bloody fingerprint."

"Blood." She frowned and made a *tsk* sound. "That's not good. I can discredit fingerprint evidence against you, and probably get it excluded, but a DNA test will nail you. However, in spite of what those pseudo-science TV shows tell you—I call them *Detecting for Dummies*—you don't get DNA results in an hour, or forty-six minutes plus commercials and promos. A properly run test to a ninety-nine-plus certainty result takes weeks. But because you left blood at the scene, the trick will be to turn police attention away from you and onto somebody else in that window of time.

"Now, before I tell Nick he can come back in, is there anything else you need to say to me in confidence? I'm deliberately not asking what you *might* have taken from Ingram's house, and what *might* have happened to it. If that imaginary thing can't be found, then it can't walk through the door to bite us in the ass. And I'm not asking why you're dressed like a hospital employee. That's peculiar, but it's not relevant to our association, unless you wore it to commit a crime and did, in fact, commit some infraction."

"No crime. No intent to commit one."

"Then I don't need to know about it." She raised her voice, called Nicholas's name, and in a few seconds he resumed his seat at the kitchen table.

"I've told Della that I can challenge the fingerprint evidence against her if I have to, and can probably get it quashed," she said.

"But I don't understand how you could do that," I said. "I thought fingerprint evidence was the gold standard for convictions."

"Yes and no," she said. "When prints are properly harvested and correctly matched, they are proof that a certain person was in a certain place. But they can't tell an investigator *when* that person was in that place. And the Achilles' heel, so to speak, of fingerprint evidence is that there's been so much sloppy lab work that last year the National Academy of Sciences released a scathing report on inept or inexact forensics."

"The FBI is supposed to have the nation's best crime lab," Nicholas said, "but back in 2004 they wrongly identified an Oregon attorney as a terrorist because of a wrong fingerprint match. That's just one example."

"I read that the government had to pay the lawyer two million dollars for that little *ooops*," Olivia said. "But I'm sure he would have preferred not to have endured the hell he went through before the error was admitted. Here's the thing, Della: I can twirl the LAPD lab guys into a bowl of spaghetti on the fingerprint issue, but you better hope that they find Ingram's killer before they get a DNA match on your blood and start leaning on you. They can lean real hard."

Olivia looked at her watch. "I gotta go." She took a card out of her purse and handed it to me. "This has all my numbers." She reached down to give Tuffy a final scratch beneath his ear.

"I'll call you later," Nicholas said to me as he followed his "favorite criminal defense attorney" toward my front door.

33

While I was showering, I thought about my next step in trying to find out who killed Keith Ingram and shot at Roland. Olivia was right when she said that the police had to be turned in a direction away from me. And I wanted them away from John, too. He was in a worse position than I was. Hatch knew that I'd broken into Ingram's house, but he didn't know why. He had guessed that I was one of the women on Ingram's sex tapes, but couldn't prove it because there was no evidence. Even if I had been one of those women, I was single and had nothing to fear from the exposure except, at most, some embarrassment. That wasn't a credible motive for murder.

But Hatch knew John had something against Ingram that was powerful enough to make him lose control and deck Ingram in the middle of a ballroom full of people. Of course Hatch would like to know the reason John did it, but John's action was bad enough to get him sidelined from the investigation, and possibly a suspension in his future. Or worse.

My only comfort was that there was no connection between John O'Hara and Roland Gray, and therefore no way to link John to the attempt on Roland's life. Hatch would not be able to prove that John committed both acts, and he'd look ridiculous if he tried to claim that the two events were unrelated. Also, and I smiled remembering this, neither John nor Mack were very good shots. It was a joke in the department that the two best investigators on the force had to tackle fleeing felons because they'd never be able to bring them down any other way. For his birthday one year, Shannon had John's worst target practice sheet framed. She'd hung it in their bathroom. "To remind him to be careful when he's out there fighting the bad guys," she'd said.

Although the water that poured over me was still hot, I thought of something that sent an instant chill through my body.

What if Hatch came up with the theory that John shot at Roland in order to throw the police off, because he knew that there was nothing at all connecting him to Roland.

But that didn't make sense to me. Unless he had been following Roland around, John couldn't know he would be at Caffeine an' Stuff, or that he'd be sitting at a table in front of the window. And how could he have found the right sniper perch across the street in only a few minutes? No, Hatch couldn't believe he'd be able to sell so wild an idea.

The comfort the realization gave me didn't last long when I remembered that Hatch didn't have to answer all the questions in an investigation—just enough for the DA to get an indictment and bring a case to trial. During the trial a good defense attorney could blast holes in the state's case, but by then John's career would be ruined. The ordeal of an arrest and a trial could send Shannon into a relapse, and Eileen might never get over the guilt she would feel for the damage her affair with Ingram had done to her family.

There was only one path out of this mess, and that was to find out who really killed Ingram and tried to kill Roland.

I turned off the water and got out of the shower. It was six PM by the ceramic poodle clock on my bathroom sink.

Saturday evening. I had no plans to go out, nor did I expect company. I wasn't hungry because of all the food I'd tasted at the cooking school. After I dried off, I put on one of my oversized Bruce Lee T-shirts and a pair of pajama bottoms.

Next, I gathered up the two gala guest lists, the copies

of the photos of those in attendance, a notepad, and pen; piled a stack of pillows against the headboard of my bed; and climbed in.

With Tuffy and Emma snuggled beside me, I made notes about the questions to which I needed answers. In a little while, a plan began to form in my mind.

It required a Summit Meeting.

I reached for the phone . . .

■ ■ ■

Sunday morning. It wasn't going to be a day of rest.

Eileen had spent Saturday night at her parents' house because she planned to take her mother to mass this morning, and then out to brunch with our Della's Sweet Dreams manager, Walter Hovey. Shannon O'Hara loved Walter's movie trivia stories. Eileen thought it would be good for her mother to have a few hours without worrying about what might happen to John.

At seven o'clock, just as I was taking a pan of fresh raspberry muffins out of the oven, the Summiteers began to arrive. First on the scene was Hugh Weaver. He'd barely crossed the threshold when we saw John drive up.

I settled the two partners at the kitchen table with mugs of fresh coffee and a basket of muffins when the doorbell rang. It had to be the last of the Sumitteers.

As soon as I opened the front door, the delightful aroma of fresh bagels hit me. Nicholas shifted the big Junior's bag he carried to one side and leaned down to give me a quick kiss on the tip of my nose.

"I made it a point to come last," he said. "No need to raise O'Hara's Irish by having him think I'd spent the night here."

"Will you stop this nonsense about John? You and I have nothing to hide. I've told you at least a dozen times that John is my friend, and *only* my friend."

"I believe you," Nicholas said. "But I'm sure that if he were free he'd marry you in one minute flat."

"Not without my permission," I said. "I love John, in the same way I love Eileen and Shannon and the Marshalls."

"You didn't mention me," Nicholas said.

"No, I didn't."

I took the Junior's bag from him and started toward the kitchen.

The detectives and the reporter exchanged polite greetings. I unpacked the bagels, arranged the goodies on a platter, and set it in the middle of the table.

Surveying the spread, John nodded at Nicholas. "Thanks."

"We've got four kinds of bagels: onion, garlic, cheese, and pumpernickel," I told John and Weaver. "And at least a pound of lox and a tub of cream cheese."

Weaver smacked his lips. "What are the rest of you going to eat?" He took two halves of a garlic bagel, slathered cream cheese on the surfaces, topped them off with slices of lox, and said to Nicholas, "I'm almost getting to like you."

"Great love stories have started on a less promising note than that," Nicholas said wryly.

The bagel stopped an inch away from Weaver's mouth. "Hey! What are you implying?"

"It was a joke," John said. "Chew."

When breakfast was consumed, I refilled the men's coffee mugs. No more for myself; I'd had enough caffeine. I'd been up since five to do my pet care chores and make the muffins.

John stood and started to clear the table. Nicholas was just behind him and began picking up dishes. Working in tandem, but silently, it took them less than two minutes to rinse the plates and stack them in the dishwasher.

Weaver watched them with an expression that was about

as close to a good-humored smile as he got. "Who says you can't get good help nowadays?"

When John and Nicholas came back to the table, I said, "Time to call this meeting to order." I indicated the guest lists. "I've gone over all these names and the photos with Eileen. She told me she never met any of these people, and that the only ones she ever heard Ingram mention were Yvette Dupree and Eugene Long. According to Eileen, Ingram disliked the two of them intensely. She said Ingram called Long a vindictive drunk and said he was a crook who deserved to be in jail, but he wasn't specific."

I told them about Yvette coming to see me at the cooking school on Saturday.

"She said she thought a jealous woman killed Ingram, and she's worried that Eugene Long's daughter, Tina, might be in danger because Ingram had asked Tina to marry him and she'd accepted." I left out the part about Yvette thinking that the jealous woman was Eileen.

"Yvette acted as though she's very close to Tina," I said, "but she dropped that subject the moment I told her about the attempt on Roland Gray's life."

"You shouldn'ta done that," Weaver said, shaking his head.

"The chief's managed to keep a lid on it," John said.

"I'm sorry," I said. "But her immediate reaction was interesting. All she asked me was if Roland was alone. I told her that I'd been with him, and then she rushed off. I didn't tell her what hospital he was in, but later that afternoon I saw her leaving St. Clare's. She must have found out where Roland was and went to see him. She left in a taxi."

I pushed the piece of paper from Liddy's notepad toward Weaver. "This is the number of the cab that picked her up at three thirty yesterday afternoon. I'm sure you can find out where the driver took her."

John said, "If Hatch finds out you talked to Gray before he—"

"I didn't talk to him. I admit that's what I'd intended to do, but I found out Roland left the hospital, accompanied by two men. From their descriptions, one of them sounded like Roland's assistant, Will Parker. The other was a big man who was dressed like a chauffeur."

I handed the guest lists to John and to Weaver.

Indicating the pages, Nicholas said, "That's not everyone who attended. Three people bought tickets at the door that night. They paid by check."

Nicholas removed a slip of paper from his jacket pocket and placed it between the two detectives. "The first two people on that list are legitimate. That third name, George Green, is a phony. The check was bogus. I don't mean it was rubber. What I'm saying is that the account doesn't exist. Somebody designed and printed the check. The ticket people were so busy that none of them remembers what the guy looked like."

"At least we know the mystery person was a man," I said.

"But we don't know whether he just wanted to get in free, or if he went there to kill Ingram," Weaver said.

"He didn't just forge someone's name on a check," I said. "He went to all the trouble of creating a fake personal check and account number, which suggests to me that he was there for something more important than watching celebrities cook."

John nodded. "I agree with Della. If we find that man, we'll have our killer."

"No description, and by now there hasta be dozens of prints on that check," Weaver said. "Finding him, we got about a snowball's chance in a haystack."

I refused to be discouraged. "We know more than we did the night Ingram was murdered." I looked at John and Weaver. "What have the police found out?"

"Not much," John said. "Apparently, there's no connection between that actor who did the juggling—Wolf Wheeler—

and Ingram. Wheeler's pretty well-known as a compulsive performer whenever he can corral an audience."

"He's got a rep for jumping up on the stage in Vegas during other people's acts," Weaver said. "Not all of them like it. I got the feeling that some of 'em wouldn't be surprised if it had been Wheeler who got offed instead of Ingram."

"I've been doing background checks on the people who were in closest physical proximity to Ingram when he was stabbed," Nicholas said. "One of the things I did was go back through the past eight years of Ingram's *Chronicle* columns. He wrote two negative reviews of Yvette Dupree's *Global Gourmet* books, and, up until a few months ago, he slammed the restaurants in Gene Long's hotel. Then he suddenly did a one-eighty. Lately he started sucking up in print, giving glowing mentions to those same restaurants that he used to call 'insults to the educated palate.' In one piece he accused Long's executive chef of 'a criminal misuse of the gift of fire.' "

"Roland Gray and Ingram had a history," I said. "I think that if I'd had a little more time I could have gotten him to tell me about it. Just before the bullet came through the window, Roland told me he was afraid of Ingram. He said he thought that Ingram was going to try to harm *him*."

"That might be a reason for Gray to strike first," John said, "except that somebody shot at Gray after Ingram was already dead and no more threat to anyone."

"We're going around in a circle," Weaver said. He reached for the last muffin in the basket and took a large bite.

I pulled my notepad closer and turned to a fresh page. "Then let's break out of that circle. Let's list what we know about Ingram and his associations, both those on the premises the night he was killed, and others who might have hired someone to kill him."

John indicated my sheet of paper. "Start with Eugene Long and Long's daughter, Tina."

I wrote.

"Yvette Dupree," Nicholas said. I added her name.

Weaver grunted and pointed to the paper. "John and you." He looked at his partner. "Sorry, buddy, but you did slug the bastard. And we know you broke into his house, Della."

My pen remained poised over the page. "You can't really think of John and me as suspects."

"Hatch is thinking like that," Weaver said. "But okay, scratch your names and put down Roland Gray."

I did. "And I'm going to add the phony name, George Green, as a 'placeholder' until we find out who he really is."

"This is one of those 'locked room' mysteries," Nicholas said. "A smoke bomb goes off in a ballroom with only one entrance and a guard posted there."

"Wait a minute," I said. "There were two ways to get into that room. You're forgetting the door to the kitchen."

Weaver stood up. "We questioned the waitstaff, but only the ones who were in the ballroom when the smoke bomb went off. I'm gonna go track down the all kitchen workers, find out if they saw somebody in the kitchen who shouldn'ta been there."

"I'm going to call a friend at Interpol to see if they have a file on Gray," John said.

Within a few minutes, I was showing the two detectives to the front door.

When I started back toward the kitchen, Nicholas met me in the hallway. Gently, he drew me into his arms and kissed me. Not so gently. Our arms tightened around each other, our lips parted. We kissed deeply. I felt my heart begin to beat faster.

Nicholas grabbed my hand and led me into the bedroom.

"I thought you would rather play gin or Scrabble," I said.

His answer was to pull me around toward him. He tugged my sweater up over my head, dropped it on the floor, and unhooked my bra. "Shut up," he whispered.

34

An hour later, Nicholas and I were luxuriating in each other's arms after making love, when his cell phone rang. He reached across me to the night table, grabbed it, and squinted at the faceplate.

"The paper." He pressed the answer button. "Yeah? . . . How many? . . . Address? . . . I'm on my way."

Nicholas snapped the phone shut. "Three people shot in Long Beach. I hate to kiss and run, but . . ." He gave me a quick peck on the lips, fairly bounded out of bed, and snatched up his clothes from where he'd scattered them.

By the time I'd showered, dressed, and taken Tuffy for a walk, it was still half an hour before noon. I found the card that Will Parker gave me the night I'd met him at St. Clare's Hospital and, for the first time, gave it more than a cursory glance.

Beneath his name were the letters "NID? WCD." I had no idea what those letters stood for, but I like puzzles and would try to work it out. Below that acronym he'd listed his cell phone and fax numbers, both of which were in the Los Angeles area code 310. A third phone number started with what I recognized as the international code for England. In the bottom right-hand corner was his e-mail: WillDo@ swiftmail.com. No address was listed on terra firma.

The "Will" and "Do" in his e-mail address made me think that the W and the D on his card might be "Will" and "Do." But the "C" in between . . . ?

"Can! I'll bet that word is Can: 'Will Can Do.' " Assuming that I was right, then I must give the credit to Eileen for making me watch *Wheel of Fortune* on TV throughout her childhood.

Now what did the first three letters and the question mark mean?

I dialed Parker's cell number. He answered on the second ring.

"Hello, Will. This is Della Carmichael. I hope I'm not interrupting anything."

"Could'na called at a better time. I'm losing at bloody backgammon. Gimme a sec."

I heard what sounded like the creak of a chair and then footsteps.

"Back again," he said. "Out on the balcony where I can talk."

"How is Roland? I found out he left the hospital."

"Blasted 'ospital! Old Rol was goin' bonkers with people comin' an' goin' at all times. Thought any moment 'e was gonna get shot at again."

Parker lowered his voice. I pictured him looking around to be sure he was alone. "The bloke is scared out of 'is wits—'ad me get a bodyguard and bring 'im 'ome. We went to ground, so to speak."

"Where are you now?"

"At Rollie's flat. Gates across the driveway. Gorgons at the doors. Security up the arse—excuse the expression."

"Has Detective Hatch questioned Roland yet?"

"Not bloomin' likely. Rol played possum when the copper came round. I said 'e was still unconscious."

"I'd like to visit him. Would that be all right? I promise not to stay very long."

Silence. It lasted a few seconds, and I let it. Finally, Parker said, "Not today, poppet. Rol's writing on 'is book. Give 'im a couple days to get 'is sea legs again." Parker chuckled. "Some of us Limeys take gettin' shot at better than others."

I gasped. "You were shot at? When?"

"Ah, was a turtle's age ago. In the military, where blokes expect to get shot at. Look, poppet, why don't you come over tomorrow, for tea. Ol' Rol writes until sixteen 'undred, then 'e likes a tucker."

"A tucker?"

"Food. Tea, scones, the lot. Join us."

"I'll do that. Tomorrow at four o'clock. What's the address?"

"Bloody tall white building, corner of Wilshire Boulevard and Garland Street. Rollie's flat's on the third floor."

"The third? His secret agent Roger Wilde has a penthouse suite, and in hotels he always requests the top floor. I had thought that's what Roland likes."

He emitted a short bark of a laugh. "Rollie's not like ol' Rog. Rollie won't stay on any floor higher than the third, once 'e found out that fire truck ladders only go up a 'undred feet."

"But wouldn't that reach to about the ninth floor?"

"True, but Rollie's thought is that if the truck doesn't 'ave a ladder that tall, a bloke could survive a jump into one a them firemen's nets if 'e's just three floors up."

It sounded as through Roland Gray wasn't anywhere near as daring as his literary invention, Roger Wilde. But it wouldn't be kind to make that remark, so I said, "I think it's wise to be cautious."

Another short bark of a laugh. "You might say that's the motto in this 'ouse."

"I'll see you tomorrow," I said. "At sixteen hundred. Four o'clock."

"Before you go . . ." Parker lowered his voice. "'Ave the coppers caught the sod who shot at Rollie?"

"Not yet," I said. "But they're investigating. Detective Hatch wants to ask Roland some questions."

"Wot sort?"

"Does Roland have any enemies?"

"There's a redheaded bird in Plymouth . . . but I don't suppose that's wot 'e means."

"No. Will, just before the bullet came through the window, Roland told me that he was afraid of Keith Ingram. He was about to tell me why. Do you know?"

"No. Sorry. 'E keeps some things to 'imself."

I decided to take that proverbial shot in the dark. "Yvette Dupree was upset to hear about what happened. Has he known her for a long time?"

A second of silence. "Who?"

"Yvette Dupree. Writes the *Global Gourmet* books. She's a very attractive French woman."

"Rollie doesn't like the French." He chuckled. "Well, maybe french letters." Slight pause. "Do you know wot those are?"

"No."

"Just as well. Look, Miss Della, the backgammon shark is calling me back for more abuse."

"Good luck," I said. "I'll see you and Roland for tea tomorrow at four o'clock."

"Jolly good."

French letters?

I went to the computer I kept in the kitchen for listing the recipes I made on the show and researching ingredients and opened it up to Google. Scrolling down past sites offering me the ability to write letters in French, I came across "french letters." Lower case f. Clicking on that, I got Will Parker's joke; the term "french letters" was World War Two military slang for condoms.

That was cute, Will. But I think you're lying to me about Yvette—unless you really don't know about a relationship between the two writers, Yvette and your boss.

Whether or not Parker was aware of Yvette Dupree's interest in Roland, I needed to find out about it because she was the first person I could connect to both Ingram and to Gray. I pictured the diagram of a family tree: Roland was afraid of Ingram; Ingram disliked Yvette; Yvette was upset when she learned about the attempt on Roland's life. Yvette Dupree was the link between murder victim Keith Ingram and near-miss victim Roland Gray.

A glance at the wall clock told me it was only twelve thirty. It would be another twenty-six and a half hours before I'd be able to talk to Roland. That was precious time I wasn't going to waste.

I sat at the kitchen table, idly stroking Tuffy and thinking about who might have pieces of the puzzle . . .

Then it came to me.

Other than Will Parker and Yvette Dupree, there was one person I'd heard of who might have the answers I needed. Who would be closer to novelist Roland Gray than his literary agent, Alan Berger?

Liddy mentioned once that agents worked seven days a week.

I took the telephone book from the shelf below the wall phone and flipped the pages to B . . .

35

I didn't expect to find Alan Berger in his office, and I didn't. But he had an answering service instead of voice mail, so I was able to tell an actual human being that I needed to reach Alan Berger, and that it involved his client, Roland Gray. I gave my name and left my number.

Four minutes later, my phone rang.

"This is Alan Berger. Ms. Carmichael?"

"Thank you for calling me back so quickly."

"You said you wanted to talk about Roland Gray. What is your interest in him?"

"I was with Roland the evening he was shot at, and—"

"Ms. Carmichael, I'm on my cell phone and my hearing is not good. Unless I'm in my home or office where there's amplification, listening is difficult. I was about to go to lunch. Will you join me?"

"I'd like that. Where shall we meet?"

"At the moment, I'm in a bookstore in Santa Monica, but my favorite little bistro is two blocks south. The Secret Garden. It's on Wilshire and Fifth, in a house behind a tall hedge."

"I know where it is," I said.

"In thirty minutes, then?"

"That's fine. How will I know you?"

"I'll know you because I saw you on television when Roland was your guest star, but I have dark hair, thinning and gray around the edges. Dark beard, clipped short. Because there may be more than one man in the area who fits that description, I'll be carrying a copy of Roland's new book, *The Terror Master*."

■ ■ ■

The Secret Garden's wooden front door had four hand-painted panels illustrating scenes from the classic children's novel. At the top was little golden-haired Mary, the lonely child heroine, finding the key; next to that is a robin showing her the door to the garden concealed behind overgrown ivy. The two lower panels depict Mary lovingly tending the dying roses in the garden; then Mary with a little boy who is rising up out of a wheelchair. *The Secret Garden* was a book that Eileen had insisted I read to her many times, until she was able to read it herself.

The restaurant named after the book occupied the ground floor of a house built to resemble an old English cottage, with a peaked, thatched roof, and a window with six small panes, slightly curved, on the upper floor. The window was set whimsically at an angle. The effect created was of a cocked head with six eyes peeking out at the street.

I spotted Alan Berger as soon as I came through the front door, both because his word sketch of himself made for an easy identification, and because he had a copy of Roland's newest book propped up on the table in front of him. When he saw me, he stood and waved.

Berger was cute, in an irregular-weave, Santa's elf sort of way. He wasn't tall, and he was a little round in the middle, but his bright hazel eyes and easy smile made him pleasant to look at. He wore a red cashmere sweater under a navy blazer. The blazer was so well cut that it had to have been custom-made.

As I came close to his table, I saw that he had a very small hearing aid in his right ear.

"Alan Berger?"

"Della Carmichael." His extended hand was soft. If he

had ever done manual labor it had to have been long in the past. His grip was polite instead of hearty, and just firm enough to signal self-confidence.

A good-looking young blond waiter, who was probably also an actor, appeared and seated me. Berger reclaimed his chair opposite.

"I know that as a professional cook you have high standards, but I think you'll find the food here quite good. It's English. English cuisine gets a bad rap—usually from people who've never tasted it and think it consists only of boiled vegetables. Roland introduced me to this place and it's become a favorite of mine."

The waiter asked, "What can I get you to drink?" His voice was pitched low, his diction perfect, and his manner suave. He had to be an actor.

"I'd like some iced tea with extra lemon," I said.

Berger said, "A glass of chardonnay."

The waiter nodded. "I'll bring them right away. Our special today is Crisp-Fried Herbed Halibut." He smiled. "And that is not easy to say. Or perhaps you would like a few minutes to look at the menu?"

I didn't bother to open it. Instead, I asked Berger, "What do you recommend?"

He didn't look at the menu, either. "Do you like fish?"

"Very much."

Berger addressed the waiter-actor. "Bring us two of your—whatever it was you said about the halibut."

"Excellent choice."

The waiter left to give our orders to the kitchen.

"I've had that dish before. It's very good, and it comes with shoestring potatoes that deserve a prize," Berger said.

The waiter returned with my iced tea and Berger's white wine. As soon as he left again, Berger said, "You said you're concerned about Roland. So am I. Being shot at was pretty traumatic, but happily, he wasn't seriously injured."

"His assistant, Will Parker, tells me he's back at work on his new book."

"I'm not surprised. I've learned that no matter what happens in his personal life, nothing deters Roland from writing. He's the most reliable author I've ever represented. Plus, I like him a lot."

"To judge from his warm words about you in the *Terror Master* acknowledgments, he's very fond of you, too. He told me that he needs your reaction to his manuscripts before he sends them to the publisher."

"Roland is too generous in his praise. I'm very little help, except when it comes to his contracts." He flashed a proud-little-boy smile. "Those contracts are my contributions to the world of art. Now, let's get to the point of your call. Someone shot at Roland. Since you were with him, I can appreciate your concern. My understanding is that the police don't know yet whether this was a random example of urban blight, or if it was personal. Frankly, I vote for urban blight, some subhuman out for kicks who can't distinguish between killing people in a video game and shooting at a live person. Roland doesn't go around having feuds or making enemies. He's very easy to get along with. But, having said that, I must admit I'm glad he's safe in his bunker of an apartment while the police are investigating. Those are my thoughts. Your turn. What's on your mind?"

"Just before the bullet came through the window, Roland told me that he was afraid of Keith Ingram. He didn't have a chance to say why. Of the people who were known to be at the gala the night Ingram was murdered, the only one I've been able to connect to both Ingram and Roland is Yvette Dupree. She's famous as the Global Gourmet. Do you know her?"

Berger looked thoughtful. "Not really . . ."

"Mr. Berger—"

"Alan, please."

"Alan." I gave him a teasing smile. "I've lived long enough to know that when a man says 'Not really' it actually means 'Yes.'"

"Well, I did meet her once, a few months ago, when Roland gave a small dinner party. She seemed charming, but I wouldn't say that I *know* her."

"Yvette was Roland's date?"

"I don't remember if she was paired with anyone. The evening was to celebrate the fact that *Terror Master* had reached the high sales threshold that meant the publisher had to pay him a bigger royalty. She cooked the meal— Moroccan dishes, in tribute to the parts of the book that were set in Morocco. It was delicious."

He squinted for a moment, as though trying to recall details of the evening. Then something made him smile.

"She told us that we had to eat the proper way for a Moroccan meal—meaning without cutlery, and scooping food from the communal serving bowls by using pieces of flat bread. Will Parker, who's a bit of an imp, concealed a fork behind the pocket handkerchief in his jacket. When she was in the kitchen, he used his fork to eat. I wished I'd thought of that."

I chuckled. "That is funny. Did she catch him?"

"Oh, yes. She called him incorrigible. That word is almost the same in French as it is in English, so we all laughed. Parker wasn't embarrassed about it. He said something to the effect that if God had meant humans to eat with their hands he wouldn't have let them invent silverware. As a wit, Parker isn't exactly Oscar Wilde, but he is enjoyable to be around."

"Who else was at the dinner?"

"Only my wife, Frances, and Mary Lively. Mary's one of my agents—my backup. Roland calls her if he needs something and I'm out of town."

"Is Mary Lively close to Roland?"

"Not—" He stopped and grinned. "I was about to say

'not really.' Mary is a spry eighty-seven and tells people she's ten years younger. An old-school career woman—still wears hats in the office. I hope she never retires, because she's amazing at spotting new young writers. I run a small, boutique literary agency. Mary's discovered a third of our client list."

The waiter brought our Crisp-Fried Herbed Halibut with shoestring potatoes. It was as good as Alan Berger had promised. While we were eating, Berger turned the conversation around to me, and asked if I had any interest in writing a cookbook.

"Because you're on television, I'm sure I could sell it," he said.

"I've never thought of it, but I don't think I'm qualified. I've never had formal training as a cook."

"That might be an advantage; you'd be representing the majority of people. The audience must like you because your ratings have doubled since *In the Kitchen with Della* went on the air."

"How did you know that?"

His nice hazel eyes twinkled. "I researched you when Roland told me he was guesting on your show. After I saw you, I made a mental note to call at some point to discuss the possibility of a cookbook."

I shook my head. "I'm afraid that what I make is too simple for a book. Anyone who watches the show could make my dishes, and I already post the recipes on my Web site."

"Don't dismiss the idea without thinking about it," he said. "You might enjoy seeing your face on a book cover. And it could only help your show."

To be polite, I agreed to think about it, but at the moment the only thing I was interested in was finding out who killed Keith Ingram and tried to kill Roland Gray.

My lunch with Alan Berger was pleasant, but it didn't yield the "Aha!" moment that pointed me in the right direction to solving the mystery that threatened me, and those dear to me.

I did learn one thing, though. Yvette Dupree was close enough to Roland that she had personally cooked his celebration dinner. That wasn't the act of a mere acquaintance.

As we were having coffee and dessert—marmalade steamed pudding—I planned my next move.

36

It was close to three o'clock when Alan Berger and I were saying good-bye outside the restaurant.

"I've enjoyed meeting you," Berger said. "Perhaps you'll have dinner sometime soon with me and my wife. I'd like to talk to you more about the possibility of doing a cookbook."

The valet brought my Jeep. Berger insisted on paying him.

"Thank you," I said. "And, thank you for lunch."

"I'll call you," he said.

■ ■ ■

The idea that had occurred to me during lunch involved going to the Santa Monica Library. When I had time to read for pleasure, it was one of my regular stops, so I knew that it was open until four o'clock on Sundays. That was perfect. What I wanted to do wouldn't take more than an hour.

The Santa Monica Library, on the corner of Montana Avenue and Seventeenth Street, is a one-story building with a simple exterior, but to anyone who loves libraries as I do, the inside is a magical kingdom for grown-ups, filled with the delights of entertainment and knowledge.

Just as I pulled into a parking space, my cell phone rang. It was Hugh Weaver.

"Our Gang Unit picked up a piece of scum named Victor Raynoso—street name Shoes, 'cause he's got two hundred pairs of shoes." Weaver was speaking hurriedly, his voice low. I heard the hum of voices in the background and guessed that he was at his West Bureau squad room. "They caught Raynoso shooting at cars on the 405 freeway near Santa Monica last night. Hatch decided he's the one shot at your writer."

"He was using the same sniper rifle?"

"No. Like that ex-Special Forces SID tech guessed, Ballistics established that weapon was a Walther WA 2000. The creep last night was using a H & K G3 assault."

"Then what tied him to the Caffeine an' Stuff shooting? Did the police find that other weapon, the Walther?"

"Not so far," Weaver said. I heard anger in his voice. "Hatch doesn't care. His position is that Raynoso shot at the coffeehouse and was caught shooting at cars in the same general area. Raynoso doesn't have an alibi for the Gray attempt. He claims he was dead drunk asleep Thursday night."

I felt my stomach muscles clench with worry. If Hatch believed that Raynoso was person who shot Roland, then in his mind he'd severed that case from the Ingram murder. Which put John O'Hara back in Hatch's crosshairs.

"Does John know about this?"

Weaver gave a snort. "Oh, yeah. After Raynoso's collar, Hatch convinced the captain that John's a viable suspect in the Ingram murder. John's been suspended. Look, Della, he doesn't want his wife and kid to know about this."

I understood. John would be afraid this bad news might send Shannon into a relapse. "But how is he going to keep it from them?"

"By making things look normal," Weaver said. "He's going to keep leaving the house to go on duty, but he'll tell them he's been assigned to work on a big white-collar fraud case for the state, so if they need to reach him, they're to call on his cell."

I sensed Weaver was about to ring off, but I had one more question for him. "Has Hatch identified any of the women in Ingram's sex tapes?"

"Yeah, we know who all of them are. Every guy in the station volunteered to look at the tapes to see if they recognized anybody. The putzes. It was SID using their computer system that matched faces on the tapes to newspaper an' magazine society photos." Weaver chuckled, but it was a dry sound, without a trace of mirth. "We had a bit of drama around here this morning. One of those thousand-buck-an-hour lawyers shows up with legal papers. There was a closed-door conference with Hatch, the captain, and the chief of detectives. A lot of yelling. The chief of Ds was so mad when he left he almost broke the captain's door slamming it. The only one smiling was the shyster, because he had something in his briefcase that wasn't there when he arrived."

"What?"

"Being an experienced detective, later I put two and two together with a thousand-an-hour and checked the evidence log. We used to have eleven Ingram hot-to-trot DVDs. Now we got ten."

"Eugene Long's lawyer," I said. "Tina must have been on one of those tapes."

"If that was a question on *Jeopardy!*, you'da just won a pot of money. I did an info search on the shyster and found out one of his firm's clients is the Long Corp. No big surprise."

"The rest of the women in Ingram's collection—did you cross-check their names against the list of people at the gala?"

"Investigation 101. Except for Long's daughter, there's only one name on both lists."

"I think I can guess."

"*Ooo la la* and *wee wee, Mamzelle*," Weaver said, in a terrible imitation of a French accent.

He was telling me that the woman was Yvette Dupree.

Before I could respond, I heard a man's voice in the background call Weaver's name, and he ended our conversation.

That Yvette was one of Ingram's sex partners was a surprise, and it might or might not be a factor in the stabbing death of Keith Ingram, but at this moment the most important thing to me was the trouble John O'Hara was in. Hatch was now proceeding on the belief that a gang criminal named Raynoso had shot at Roland Gray, which gave Hatch the opportunity to concentrate all of his energy on finding evidence to arrest John for the murder of Keith Ingram. It was bad enough that he had managed to get John suspended, but Hatch had much worse in mind. An arrest would destroy John's career, and maybe John himself, and it would damage his family, possibly beyond repair.

Solving the murder of that detestable, blackmailing food critic had suddenly become a matter of great urgency. The only way to prevent John from losing everything was to find the real killer, and to do it fast.

I dialed John's cell phone number. My name must have come up on the faceplate because he answered by saying, "Della?"

"Weaver just told me what happened to you. Are you all right?"

"I've had better days, but I've had even worse ones, too. I survived."

His voice was strong, but I knew that losing his job, even if it would only be for a while, had been a cruel blow. He was putting up a front. In deference to that, I stopped expressing my sympathy.

"I don't want Shan and Eileen to worry, so don't tell them," he said.

"If you don't want me to, of course I won't. What are you going to do while you're pretending to be working?"

"Working. Investigating on my own. After I found out that Yvette Dupree was one of the women on Ingram's tapes, I asked a friend at Interpol to check her out. He got back to me a few minutes ago. I was about to phone you when you called me."

"What did he tell you?"

"Her real name is Fabienne Talib. I know you said you like the woman, but I want you to stay away from her."

"John, you're making me crazy. Lots of writers and other celebrities change their names, so what's this about?"

"Ten years ago, in London, the woman now known as Yvette Dupree killed a man."

37

"Killed a man?" Stunned, I repeated John's words, trying to process the information. "But if that's true, then why isn't she in prison?"

"She claimed she was defending herself. The man was her husband, Fouad Talib, a Turk. Yvette—Fabienne—brought in three women who signed statements that Talib was violent, had beaten Fabienne in the past, and threatened to kill her if she tried to leave him. Self-defense isn't recognized as a plea in England, so she was put on trial for manslaughter. The jury heard her story and acquitted her. According to my friend, the police thought it was premeditated murder, but they couldn't prove it. There was talk at the time that she'd fallen in love with another man, a Brit. She had just begun proceedings to divorce Talib."

"Her story must have been credible for the jury to acquit her."

"Juries are made up of human beings. They liked her, and sympathized because her barrister painted the victim as a vicious bully. Talib was an importer of antiquities. His business partner and his brother both testified that Talib had never laid a hand on her in anger, but that he was opposed to the divorce and wanted to take Fabienne back to Turkey with him."

"How did she do it? Did she stab him?"

"No. It was blunt force trauma. She smashed him in the head with a bronze bust of Julius Caesar. It was almost an

Olympic feat, because Yvette was a foot shorter than the late Mr. Talib, and almost a hundred pounds lighter."

"Are you saying that she might have had help?"

"According to her, she acted alone, claiming she hit him out of fear for her life. She called the police herself. Without delay, according to the medical examiner in London. Her fingerprints were the only ones on the bust. Still, my friend said it was as though a cat had killed a Rottweiler."

" 'And though she be but little, she is fierce,' " I quoted, almost to myself. But John heard me.

"*Richard the Third*," he said.

"So you managed to stay awake the night we all went to see it."

"Yeah. I was mentally counting up the charges I would have lodged against Richard."

"John, I'm outside the Santa Monica Library. I've got something to look up before it closes at four today."

"Is this for your show, or about the case?"

"The case. It's some research I want to do. I may not find out anything useful, but it's worth a try."

"If I can't keep you out of this, at least I'm glad you'll be safe in the library," he said.

"What are you going to do?"

"Go home. I'm taking Shan and Eileen to an early movie and then out to dinner. But if you need me, during the movie I'll have my phone on vibrate."

When the call was over, I sat in my Jeep for a few more moments and tried to sort out the new pieces of the puzzle I'd acquired. All of them focused on Yvette Dupree.

Alan Berger told me that Yvette had cooked a special dinner for a little party to celebrate Roland Gray's book sales. That was evidence of a connection between Yvette and Gray.

Weaver told me that at different times both Tina Long and Yvette Dupree had been filmed in Keith Ingram's bed.

Earlier, Eileen had told me that Ingram despised Yvette, and yet at some point I knew that he'd had sex with her.

Yvette's protective behavior toward Tina Long the night of Ingram's murder, and Yvette's own words to me yesterday, indicated that she was a mother figure to motherless Tina. I wondered if the young girl knew that both she and Yvette had been to bed with the same man, and what, if anything, that shocker might have had to do with Ingram's killing.

Last, according to John's friend at Interpol, ten years ago, when Yvette Dupree was known at Fabienne Talib, she killed her husband. Her claim of self-defense was believed and she was acquitted of the crime. Not long after that she must have changed her name and became the Global Gourmet.

These were certainly colorful parts of the puzzle, but there were still too many pieces missing for me to be able to see the picture they formed.

The most glaring of those missing pieces was the question of who shot into the window of Caffeine an' Stuff. Hatch was acting as though he had his man. If he believed that, then it meant he could concentrate on proving John killed Ingram.

I hoped that Hatch was wrong about the shooter—but hoping was not good enough with John's life on the line.

Opening my cell phone again, I dialed 411 and asked for the number for Olivia Wayne, attorney at law.

The operator's mechanical voice found the listing and offered to connect me to it. I pressed the button that meant "yes" and heard ringing on the other end of the line. Another mechanical voice answered with the name of the firm. Among the offers it made was the option to hear the list of attorneys and their extension numbers. Another press of the appropriate button. The firm's lawyers were listed in alphabetical order, so it took a while to get to W. When I heard Olivia Wayne's extension number I punched it in.

I'd expected to leave a message on her voice mail, but to my surprise Nicholas's favorite criminal lawyer answered in person.

"Hi, Olivia, this is Della Carmichael, your one-dollar client."

All business, she asked, "Have you been arrested?"

"No. I'm calling to buy an hour or two of your time."

"What's the problem?"

"A friend on the LAPD told me that a man named Victor Raynoso was arrested for shooting at cars on the freeway, but that Detective Manny Hatch also believes that he was the sniper who fired into the front window of Caffeine an' Stuff in Santa Monica in the early hours of Friday morning."

"I hope you're not asking me to represent him."

"No. All I'd like you to do—what I want to hire you to do—is to talk to him in jail and see if you can find out whether or not he was the one who shot into the café. He claims he didn't do that."

"Nick told me you and the writer, Roland Gray, were sitting in the café's window and that Gray was wounded. Is that why you're interested?"

"Partly." I told her that I believed the shooting at the café was connected to the murder of Keith Ingram at the celebrity cook-off Wednesday night, but that if Raynoso was the shooter then they had to be separate acts.

"Why do you want the two events to be connected?"

"Because if the wounding of Gray was just a coincidence, then the detective in charge of the Ingram murder—Manfred Hatch, of West Bureau—will keep trying to prove that John O'Hara killed Ingram. John was my late husband's partner in the LAPD. I know that John didn't commit murder as surely as I know I'm sitting here talking to you."

"So you want me to talk to this Victor Raynoso. What do you expect that to accomplish? You think he'll have a

TV moment and suddenly confess all his sins because I've cornered him with just the right question?"

Her sarcasm was irritating, but I wanted her to do this for me, so I ignored it and applied a speck of butter.

"You're a skilled attorney, Olivia. What I want is your professional opinion, after you've talked to Raynoso, as to whether or not he was the Caffeine an' Stuff sniper."

"I've crossed swords with Manny Hatch—he's an ambitious SOB. And stubborn," she said. "I don't think he'd deliberately frame anyone for murder, but I wouldn't put it past him to try to sweep aside something that doesn't fit his theory of a case."

"Will you go see Raynoso and let me know what you think?"

"All right. I'll polish up my crystal ball to take with me."

"Thank you, Olivia."

"It's not a favor. I'm going to bill you—and it'll include this phone call and my travel time." She hung up.

It was getting late; the library would close in just a little more than half an hour, but that should give me the time I needed.

Before I got out of the Jeep, I took a cautious glance around. All I saw was the usual cast of characters that strolled along Montana Avenue in good weather: young couples holding hands, older people by themselves or in small groups, dog walkers, window-shoppers studying displays in Santa Monica's tempting boutiques. There was no one who seemed to be taking an interest in me, or even looking in my direction.

I stepped down to the pavement, locked the Jeep, and went into the library.

38

Because I used my card regularly at the Santa Monica Library, I didn't need to ask the librarian where the fiction section was. I just gave her a friendly wave, headed toward my destination, and went directly to the G shelf. Eight of Roland Gray's nine spy novels were there; the only one not present—probably checked out—was his current best seller, *The Terror Master*. I didn't need that one because at home I had the copy Roland gave me.

I carried the stack of eight novels to the nearest reading table and started my research. By referring to the copyright dates, I was able to lay them out in their order of publication. Beginning with the first of Secret Agent Roger Wilde's adventures, I opened the book to the Acknowledgments page.

Roland Gray had created MI 9, a fictional department of the British Security Service from which Roger Wilde took his assignments, but it appeared that he had done research, because he thanked "the real-life agents in MI 5 and MI 6, who understandably wish to remain anonymous, for their generosity in sharing their expertise and guidance through the dark and dangerous world of security and espionage."

Because I was a fan of this kind of thriller, I knew that MI 5 stood for Military Intelligence, Section 5, and is the United Kingdom's counterintelligence and security agency. The Secret Intelligence Service, or SIS—also known as MI 6—was the country's external intelligence agency. Roland's fictional MI 9 went back and forth across those lines.

It was in the first book's final authorial "thank you" that I found a name I recognized. The acknowledgement read: "I am grateful to British commando Willis H. Parker for helping me extract Roger Wilde from an impossible situation."

According to the copyright date, that meant Gray and Parker had known each other for at least nine years.

No familiar names, not even Parker's, were in Gray's expressions of gratitude in the second book, but there was an intriguing reference to "the lovely lady who inspired the character of 'French Toast.'"

I remembered that character in the book. "French Toast" was the playful nickname Roger Wilde gave to a woman who was in love with Wilde, but who went to bed with a vicious arms dealer in order to discover information that saved Wilde's life. She paid for that act with her own life.

Thinking back over the novels in the series, all of which I'd read up until his most recent one, Secret Agent Roger Wilde had proved to be very bad luck for women. Every time he fell in love, the object of his affections died some kind of violent death near the end of the book, just when it seemed as though Wilde would be able to retire from fighting international master criminals and settle down in his beautiful seaside cottage on the Costa del Sol in Malaga, Spain.

Was French Toast a tribute to Yvette Dupree?

Books three and four yielded no familiar names, but in Wilde's fifth adventure I found this acknowledgement: "My heartfelt appreciation to Eugene Long for his kind hospitality to Roger Wilde and company."

Flipping again to the copyright date, I saw that book number five had been published four years ago, which indicated that Roland Gray and Eugene Long had known each other for at least that amount of time.

But neither of them had given any indication of it the night of the gala. Are—or *were*—they friends?

They both knew Yvette Dupree—and quite well, judging from what I'd learned so far. She had cooked for Roland and was an affectionate mother figure to Long's daughter, Tina.

Thinking about Long and Tina, I remembered something that Phil Logan had told me the afternoon he announced that I was going to be a cook-off judge. While he was warning me that Eileen was going to be hurt by Keith Ingram because Ingram intended to marry superrich Tina Long, he gave me an example of what a doting father she had. Phil said that when Tina was struggling to graduate from a private high school, Long actually bought the school. Then Long had hired "a novelist" to write Tina's co-valedictorian speech, but that the novelist hadn't told Tina how to pronounce some of the words. The result was public embarrassment for Tina. I shuddered in sympathy, imagining how painful that must have been for the young girl.

And then I imagined how furious Long must have been at that novelist.

Was the novelist Roland Gray? If so, what had happened between that time and what must have been the previous year, when Gray thanked Long for his hospitality? Did Yvette have something to do with it?

Looking into people's private lives made me feel uncomfortably like one of those sleuths who uncovered stories for the tabloids, but at least I wasn't going to make anything I found out public—unless it had to do with Keith Ingram's murder. I made a note to call Phil Logan as soon as I left the library. If anyone could find out the name of the novelist who had humiliated Tina Long, it was Phil.

There were no other familiar names in the Acknowledgments of books six, seven, and eight. So my next act was to see to whom Gray had dedicated these eight books. The first was to his mother, and the second "to the memory of my beloved mother."

The next four books were dedicated to his agent, Alan Berger.

Book number seven broke Berger's streak of dedications, although the agent was thanked warmly on the Acknowledgments page.

The dedication in the seventh Roger Wilde novel was: "To Frank R. Stockton, who understood both Ladies and Tigers."

That one was easy to decode; it was a reference to the classic short story, written by Frank Stockton, called "The Lady, or the Tiger?" It was one of the most chilling tales I'd ever read. I taught it every year in my old high school English classes because the ending always provoked lively debate among the students. Their answers to my questions "What would you do if you were the hero?" and "What would you do if you were the princess?" revealed important clues about their personalities. From time to time what I learned from that exercise enabled me to motivate them to think about their own futures, and inspire them to get the most they could from their years in school. Sometimes; unfortunately, not often enough.

Enough of my memories; I needed to concentrate on my current challenge.

While I hadn't learned the identity of the person to whom Roland had dedicated *The Terror Master*—"The one who got away"—what I did learn was that Roland met Eugene Long several years before the lethal cook-off. It was another piece of the puzzle, but whether it was material to the central picture or just a piece along the edge, I had yet to discover.

I decided I needed to see Eugene Long. Because I wasn't an official part of the investigation into the murder of Ingram, I would have to come up with an innocent-seeming excuse in order to meet with him . . .

Then I realized that the road to Long was through his great big billion-dollar ego.

I closed the covers on Roland Gray's novels, picked up the stack, and replaced them on the appropriate shelf in the library's Fiction section.

As I was passing the checkout desk to leave, I saw a young woman, college age, beckoning to me. I didn't know her name, but I recognized her face; she worked part-time at the library. She glanced around—furtively, it seemed—and gestured for me to come over to where she was organizing books into the cart she would push as she replaced them on their proper shelves.

I whispered, "Did you want me?"

She nodded. "I thought you should know that while you were reading, there was a man watching you. He's gone now, but while he was here that's all he was doing—just watching you."

39

A man in the library had been watching me?

I felt a chill run through my body. "Do you know who it was?" I asked.

"No."

She motioned for me to follow her over to an area in the corner of the library where we could speak privately, but she still kept her voice so low I had to lean close to hear her.

"It might even have been a woman," she said. "The person was wearing a dark green hoodie sweatshirt and baggy sweatpants. I couldn't see the face."

I did a quick search of my memory to recall the people I'd noticed when I came into the library. I hadn't been looking for anyone in particular, but being aware of my surroundings had become a habit ever since someone tried to kill me a few months ago.

"I didn't see anyone in a hooded shirt," I said.

"The person came in about a minute after you did. I noticed you because I recognized you from TV—I watch your show. Then when he—or she—came in after you they caught my attention because they did something peculiar."

"What was that?"

"They took a magazine from the rack, but they didn't actually touch the magazine."

"I don't understand."

"They picked it up using a tissue. I thought the person must be some kind of germophobe. It was strange, and we're told to keep an eye out for anything unusual, so I kept glancing over that way. The person wasn't reading. I could tell because he didn't turn any pages. Instead, he was just pretending while he was watching you. I was positive about that because as soon as you closed the books you had on the table, they put the magazine down and hurried outside. I still couldn't see the face because I was over on the side of the room, behind him—or her. I don't think the person was a fan of yours because wouldn't they have gone over to you and asked for an autograph?"

"Not necessarily." My pulse rate had quickened, but I tried to seem casual about what she'd told me. "In the months I've been on the air," I said, "only a couple of people have asked me to sign something. I think my dog, Tuffy, gets most of the fan mail."

"Oh, don't feel bad. I'm sure that's just because you're a cooking personality."

I wasn't sure what that meant, but I smiled. "I never thought of it like that."

She nodded. "We're in Hollywood—not geographically, but pretty much mentally—so there are different categories of celebrity. Some get bothered; some don't."

I replied with an all-purpose "Ahhh," letting my voice rise slightly at the end of that nonword to denote comprehension, but I needed to get the conversation back to the subject that was important to me. "About the person in the green hood," I said. "I think you should tell the librarian about what you saw, so she can be alert in case that person comes in again."

"You can be sure I will. Look, I hope I didn't scare you."

I faked a smile. "No, not at all. People just do odd things sometimes. I'm sure there's nothing to worry about."

That's what I said, but I didn't mean it. Four nights ago I'd been at the scene of a murder, and then two nights later I'd been present at an attempted murder. Hearing that someone who'd kept his or her face covered, and used tissues to handle a magazine, had been watching me was more than a little frightening.

"Thank you for your concern," I said. "If you ever want to come out to the Better Living Channel to see the show live on a Thursday night, leave your name with the channel's operator and I'll have a seat in the audience saved for you."

"That'd be great," she said with enthusiasm. "My name is Elizabeth Taylor—honest, that's my real name. My parents' name is Taylor and my mother named me after her favorite actress."

"Elizabeth Taylor. I'll remember. And I'll tell the operator at the channel to expect to hear from you."

When Elizabeth returned to her work putting books back onto the proper shelves, I went to the restroom to wash my hands. While my fingers could use a soaping and a rinse after examining the old novels, I was stalling for a few minutes until the library was about to close.

At four o'clock, I left the building in a group with other library patrons. A quick scan of the area didn't reveal anyone in a dark green hooded sweatshirt, but I was not about to linger. As soon as I got into my Jeep, I locked the doors.

Turning onto Montana Avenue, I headed west, but instead of going home to Ninth Street by the most direct route, I drove up Fifteenth Street for several blocks, turned around, came back down to Montana, and then went up Eleventh for a few more blocks. By the time I'd turned around and was headed back again toward Montana Avenue, it was clear I wasn't being followed. When I reached Ninth Street, I made a right turn off Montana and went home.

Back in my house, I let Tuffy out into the rear yard while I refilled his and Emma's water bowls and gave them dinner.

As soon as they were happily munching and crunching, I called Phil Logan on his cell. We exchanged greetings, and I got right to the point.

"Phil, remember the story you told me about Eugene Long buying the private high school his daughter was attending, and then hiring a novelist to write her graduation speech? Can you find out the name of that novelist?"

"I don't even have to look it up. Tell me you're impressed."

"Always," I said. "You can't see me on the phone, but I'm smiling in admiration."

"Okay, I don't want to make you think I'm some kind of 'superhero,' unless you want to, of course. The fact is I know the name because I was surprised when I heard he was going to be one of the contestants in Long's charity cook-off."

"Roland Gray," I said.

"What are you, Robin to my Batman?"

"I'd rather be Wonder Woman to your Superman."

"That's not too crazy," he said. "You've got the dark hair for it—and parts of the body."

Parts?

I refrained from asking which parts. Instead, I said, "How did Roland Gray know Tina wouldn't be able to pronounce some of the words he put in her speech? She could have rehearsed it and asked somebody."

"Tina doesn't like to read, or to study—she brags about it. It was a pretty good guess she wouldn't know words of more than two syllables."

I had one more question to ask Phil. "What do you mean when you called it Long's charity cook-off? I thought it was organized by the Healthy Life Fund, and just held at Long's hotel."

"No. It was Long's idea to promote the Olympia Grand. The charity was delighted to sell the tickets and get all the money without having to do the hard work of corralling celebrities and catering to stars' demands. Why are you interested?"

"Curiosity," I said.

"Yeah, well, just don't forget what curiosity *killed*. I'd hate to have to work with a new show host now that I've gotten used to you."

I laughed. "Thanks."

"Look, if it was Roland Gray who got killed, my number one suspect would have been Gene Long, because that guy has the proverbial memory like an elephant. It's said he's willing to hold a grudge until hell freezes over—or until income taxes are abolished, whichever comes first."

■ ■ ■

After my conversation with Phil, I sat at the kitchen table, watching Tuffy and Emma eat, and thinking about the two new pieces of the puzzle that I'd learned.

Eugene Long had a grudge against Roland Gray. It was an understandable grudge, in my opinion. I couldn't image any parent not being furious at the person who hurt their child, especially in so public a way as what Gray did to Tina Long in not coaching her in the words she didn't know.

Eugene Long, not the Healthy Life Fund, had organized the charity gala and was responsible for choosing the celebrities who would cook, and the judges. (Except for me, who was a last-minute replacement.)

What was Long's motive for including Roland Gray? Long had allowed Keith Ingram to be a judge, but how did he really feel about this man who intended to marry his daughter?

Eugene Long had at least some of the answers that I needed. I didn't have any authority to question him, but I thought that I might be able to get what I wanted by making use of his huge ego.

Knowing that Long had a suite at the Olympia Grand, I

called the hotel, asked to speak to him, and gave my name. The operator put me on hold, but came back in less than a minute and said she was connecting me to Mr. Long. She must have asked if he was willing to take my call. Apparently he was.

I'd cleared the first hurdle. Now all I had to do was persuade him to see me.

When I gave Long my excuse for phoning, I heard a smile in his voice.

"Well, that's worth talking about," he said. "How about tomorrow morning, ten o'clock, here in my suite?"

"That works for me."

"Good. Take the private elevator up," he said.

"See you tomorrow."

I was over the second hurdle.

Now what I had to do was get through the rest of the obstacle course without falling and breaking my neck.

40

Eugene Long had told me to come up to his suite, but he didn't add that he occupied the Olympia Grand's entire penthouse floor nor that there were separate elevators to his private rooms and to his offices. I learned that fact when I presented myself to the man at the reception desk, whose nametag identified him as "Roberto."

"I have a ten o'clock appointment with Mr. Long. He asked me to take the private elevator up, but I'm not sure which one that is."

"Excuse me for just a moment," Roberto said before disappearing through the door behind the desk. I guessed he wasn't going to take my word for it that I'd been invited, and was checking with his boss.

When Roberto returned, having vetted me, he was smiling. "Sorry about that." He didn't specify what "that" was. "The private elevators are at the far end of the bank of public elevators." He pointed. "Between the potted palms and the ladies' lounge. You'll want Elevator A. You don't want B; that would take you to the corporate offices."

I thanked him, and headed toward the palm trees.

The two elevators, "A" and "B," were differentiated from the public lifts by a waist-high brass stand holding a large white card that said "Private." Surveillance cameras above the doors covered all of the elevators, both public and private.

As I approached, I didn't see a button one could press to summon the elevator and realized that access from the lobby required a key, inserted into a brass plate by the doors. But when I stepped in front of Elevator A, the doors opened with a soft *whoosh*.

The doors closed behind me the moment I was inside. This private elevator was half the size of what was usual in a hotel, and it had a small bench covered in burgundy velvet along the back wall. I supposed it was there in case one needed to sit during the arduous journey of twenty floors, up or down. Being of hardy Scottish stock, I roughed it and stood all the way. Above my head was another camera. It was tempting to wave at whoever might be watching, but I repressed the urge to be juvenile. After all, I was a mature woman, secretly investigating a murder. That called for dignity.

Elevator A's doors opened at the penthouse floor with a barely audible whisper. I stepped out into a burgundy-carpeted corridor, which ran to my left, down past several closed doors. A breakfast cart with dirty dishes and a crumpled napkin stood outside one of them. Long's offices, reached by Elevator B, must be located behind the wall on my right. Because I couldn't imagine Long going down to the lobby in Elevator A to take Elevator B back up to the top floor, I was sure access to the office half of the penthouse layout must be through interior doors.

Directly in front of me, golden oak double doors with brass accents opened to reveal Eugene Long. His thick silver mane looked freshly tended; a few silver chest hairs peeked out from the V made by the open top button on his black silk shirt.

The only other time I'd seen the man was at the gala, when he was wearing a dinner jacket. Now, dressed informally in the black shirt and black slacks with no jacket, he exposed a paunchy middle. My brother Sean, a Navy doctor, had said that particular kind of protrusion was usually "a drinker's belly."

Long extended his hand in greeting. "Ms. Carmichael. *Della*. Please come in."

He stepped aside and gestured for me to precede him into a living room that looked to be the size of a tennis court. A wall of windows looked out onto a magnificent view, mostly of the sky. A line from an old song ran through my head: "On a clear day, you can see forever . . ."

Soft lighting came from crystal wall sconces and a crystal and brass chandelier above us that was turned to dim. They weren't needed; the natural light was strong enough even for reading.

Glancing around, I saw four deep club chairs and two sofas, all upholstered in warm earth tones and separated by sparkling glass and brass coffee tables and antique-looking mahogany end tables.

The walls were covered in a pale green fabric and formed the background for several large modern paintings. I'm only minimally familiar with twentieth-century artists, but I did recognize two David Hockney canvases because I'd seen them reproduced in a decorating magazine of Liddy's.

If those were original Hockneys, and the other canvases were genuine and by celebrated artists, then the six paintings in Long's living room were probably worth more than my house in Santa Monica. His chandelier had surely cost more than my Jeep.

"Please sit down," Long said, indicting one of the club chairs. Next to it was a lovely arrangement of fresh tulips in a green crystal bowl.

I sat and he perched on the edge of the sofa positioned at an angle to me. On either side of the living room were golden oak doors. The one on the left side of the room, facing me but behind Long, was slightly ajar. Across the room, the door on the right was closed. Although that one must have led to the billionaire's corporate offices, I couldn't hear any activity. I realized this room must be soundproof.

"May I order you breakfast?" Long asked. "They can make anything you want down in the kitchen."

"Actually," I said, giving a nervous laugh and feigning shyness, "it's Happy Hour in Australia, so do you suppose I could have a little drink?"

In anticipation of this meeting, just before I left the house I'd had a huge breakfast: three eggs scrambled in butter, three pieces of bacon, and four big slices of ciabatta bread that I dipped into a dish of olive oil. This wasn't at all my usual morning meal, but I needed to line my stomach. And it wasn't my idea—it was Benjamin Franklin's. Somewhere I'd read that when he was asked why he thought he'd been such a great success as a diplomat, he'd replied that he owed it to his ability to drink every other diplomat under the table, and his secret was consuming olive oil before getting together with them. After what I'd forced down, I hoped Mr. Franklin had been serious and not joking.

Long aimed a huge smile at me. "Della, you are a woman after my own heart." He stood and headed for a mahogany cabinet below one of the paintings. "Australia just became my favorite continent." He opened the cabinet to display a bar with an impressive array of bottles. "What will you have?"

"I hate to drink alone," I said. "I'll have whatever you're going to have."

"Scotch. The nectar of the gods."

"That's perfect," I said. "My ancestors came from Scotland. But I thought the nectar of the gods was nectar."

"Depends on where you worship." He took two glasses from a shelf and started to pour.

He returned with our drinks and handed one of them to me. This time he didn't perch on the edge of the sofa; he settled back against the big, puffy cushions.

Long raised his glass and toasted: "To that rare woman who knows how to live. Cheers—and may we good people outlast all the bastards."

I tipped my glass in his direction. He took a swallow

and I took a sip. While he added a second sofa cushion to the one behind his back, I moved the bowl of flowers closer to me.

"When you called, you said you wanted to talk about my being a guest on your cooking show."

"Yes. You're such an enormous success in so many fields I thought it would be interesting for the public to see a more *relatable* side to you," I said. "My thought was that you and I would prepare a dish together—any dish you chose—and as we did that, you could talk about what you like to do when you're not out conquering the world."

He chuckled at that; I suspected he liked the image of himself conquering the world.

"The viewers already know Eugene Long, the titan," I said. "I'd like to show them Gene Long, the man."

"What gave you that idea?"

I made a show of looking uncomfortable. "I hate to say this, because it might sound as though I'm taking advantage of a tragedy, but it occurred to me last week at your gala. After the—after the terrible thing that happened to Keith, the way you took charge of the people there and kept everyone calm. I was tremendously impressed with how you handled things in a crisis."

He took another swallow while I touched the rim of my glass to my lips.

"And, too," I said, "it moved me how sensitive you were to your daughter's feelings."

"My baby doll . . . the love of my life." He finished his drink and got up. "Can I get you another?"

"Not quite yet," I said, taking another tiny sip.

He refilled his glass and came back to the sofa. "My Tina's the one you should have on your show. She can cook. I don't know a toaster from a toilet."

"I think you'd learn pretty quickly if you ever tried to make toast."

He either ignored my attempt at humor or he didn't hear

me, because he went on as though I hadn't spoken. "Yvette taught her to cook. Now she's a wonder in the kitchen."

"Having Tina as my guest. That's a fascinating idea." I smiled at him over the rim of my glass. "How is she doing? What happened must be especially hard on her. I heard she and Keith were engaged."

"She's okay. Cried for three days, but it's winding down."

"Tina and Keith would have made a handsome couple. Did you like him?"

Long nodded as he swallowed. "I could talk to him— not like some of those male model types she used to bring around. He'd have made a good first husband."

Looking thoughtful, and a little sad, he swallowed more scotch.

I pretended to take another sip before I said, "Tina's such a beautiful girl. Do you think she'd be willing to cook with me on camera?"

"My baby doll never met a camera she didn't like. She—"

He was interrupted by the ringing of the cordless phone on the end table between us, on the other side of the bowl of flowers.

Scowling, he snatched it up. "Georgie, I told you to hold my calls." He took another swallow as he listened briefly. "That's not my idea of a crisis. Tell him to go—" Long glanced at me. "Tell him to go do something anatomically impossible to himself. And don't ring this line again until I say so." He disconnected and tried to put the phone back in its charger, fumbled, but managed to get it set correctly on the second try.

Eugene Long was getting drunk. A couple more glasses of scotch, and I'd have him in the right state to answer my *real* questions.

41

An hour later, Long had refilled his glass a few more times and was clearly inebriated. He returned to the sofa with his whichever drink and my third. I'd continued to take only sips, and to pour most of my scotch into the bowl of flowers when he turned his head away from me, but I was getting a bit of a buzz.

Drinking had never been a part of my social life. Enjoying a glass of red wine at dinner in a restaurant or if I had guests at home was the extent of my alcohol intake. In spite of my attempt to cushion the hard liquor with a Benjamin Franklin breakfast, my stomach was reacting with mild displeasure. I realized that I had to get the information I needed before it surged into violent rebellion.

As we drank, I kept him talking about what interested him, mostly himself and his daughter. The one possibly relevant tidbit he'd revealed so far was that he and Yvette Dupree had never had a romantic relationship.

"Not that I didn't want to at first, years ago, but she was seeing somebody an' wouldn't play naked with ole Gene." He sighed and drank. "Better this way. If we'da done the nasty an' then broke up, that would have hurt my baby doll. Angel loves Yvette like a mamma. My wife died, ya know."

I didn't know that, but I murmured words of sympathy.

He stared down into his drink for a moment.

"Life's a bitch," he said.

This was my chance. "It sure is. A few months ago I had to deal with a woman who tried to destroy me."

Long grunted. "You shoulda come to me—I know how to handle problems like that." Long swallowed the rest of the scotch in his glass and got up for a refill. He wasn't entirely steady on his feet, but he wasn't stumbling. I was astonished at how much that man could drink and still walk and talk.

He came back with his fresh glass and one for me. As I still held one in my right hand, I reached for the other with my left.

Laughing, he called me a two-fisted drinker.

Long flopped down on the couch and rested his head against the back of it. I put the new drink down on the coffee table and leaned closer to him.

"What did you mean, about knowing how to handle an enemy?"

He chuckled, winked at me, and then stared into space.

"Won't you tell me, Gene? I went through a really terrible time with her."

"Couldn'ta been worse than what that rotten snake-bastard-writer did to my baby doll. But I was gonna get him back—an' get him back good, good, good." He scowled again. "Then somebody killed Keith an' we couldn't go through with it. Damn!"

At last I was getting somewhere—or at the edge of somewhere. I knew I had to dig before the distress in my stomach got worse, so I took a chance and pushed a bit.

Faking awe in my voice, I leaned close to him again and asked, "So Keith was going to help you get back at Roland Gray? That's wonderful."

"Woulda been . . . Jeez, we had a perfect plan . . ."

I widened my eyes to signal fascination. "What was it?"

"Our plan was why I put together the big charity deal. All that work blew up in my face 'cause some scumbag hadda kill Keith *that* night. He couldn'ta waited." Long muttered a curse.

"To organize that spectacular evening as a cover for your plan—Oh! It must have been brilliant," I said breathlessly.

Long nodded agreement. And swallowed more scotch.

"What was it? The plan. I'm dying to know."

He stared off into the distance and smiled. "We were gonna frame that Limey f***er for attempted murder."

"Wow!"

"Yeah, a big wow. A wow an' a half. We were gonna make it seem like Gray tried to murder Keith. Gray was gonna be arrested. I'd make sure he was smeared in the papers an' on TV. All over the world. I was gonna leak all kinds of bad things to friends in the media—like how he plag'd—plazer-size . . ." He couldn't get the word out and shook his head in frustration.

Helpfully, I said, "Plagiarized?"

"Yep. I was gonna plant the rumor that he plaguered— *stole* his first book, from a poor dead guy. Maybe a minority."

"Roland Gray must be a terrible man," I said. "What were you and Keith going to do?"

Long chortled. "I had the idea an' Keith came up with the way. Ya know the three dishes the contestants were gonna serve the judges? For judging?"

"Yes?"

"Keith crushed up nutmegs to slip into the pudding Gray was gonna give him. Keith was gonna taste it—then he'd recognize what was in the stuff, an' accuse that slimy Limey of tryin' to kill him. An' I was gonna call the cops."

"Keith was going to use nutmegs?"

"He said it was a poison."

I knew that three whole nutmegs shaved or ground up made a lethal dose for a human being, but I never imagined that information would be useful to me. As a nationally syndicated food critic I wasn't surprised that Keith Ingram knew that morsel of trivia. I grated fresh nutmeg into a lot of dishes, but only a few grains at a time. One whole nutmeg would last me for at least half a year. Was Long telling the truth? Had Keith Ingram really ground up whole nutmegs with the intention of stirring them into Roland Gray's pudding? If he had . . .

Movement behind the door across from me, the one that was slightly ajar, caught my attention. I saw a flash of red hair and pale skin. I was sure it was Yvette Dupree. Had she been eavesdropping on us?

Long expelled air with an unhappy groan. "Beautiful plan . . . But we never got to do it 'cause somebody killed Keith before it was time to taste the dishes."

No more movement in the crack of the open door. She was gone.

I forced myself to concentrate on Long. "That's a wild story," I said.

"You don' believe me?"

"Well . . ."

Rising to my implied challenge, he said, "I can prove it."

"How? Keith is dead."

"Ask the police, or whoever has his clothes. Just ask 'em wha' they found in Keith's pocket." He let out another long, heavy breath. "A beautiful plan—Keith was gonna accuse, an' the police would have the pudding tested an' found the nutmeg—the proof Gray was tryin' to kill Keith."

"It was brilliant, but there was an obvious hole in the plan. What if Gray had been making a baked chicken, or a meat dish like Tornados Rossini—Keith couldn't have stirred nutmeg into those."

Long grinned at me with boyish pride. "We thought of that. All the celebrities had to turn in copies of their recipes a week before the contest. We said it was so the hotel chefs could prepare enough for the audience to taste. If Gray'd wanted to make something that wouldn't work for us, he would have been asked to switch to a soup, or a stew—a dish with lots of liquid."

My stomach had begun to roil, and talking about food

wasn't helping. I shifted in my seat, trying to ease the discomfort. Didn't work. Trying to will the nausea away, I focused on Long. Although I thought his scheme was ridiculous, I said, "That was clever. Unfortunately, a good defense attorney would have cleared Gray."

"In time, sure. But it woulda cost Gray big-time. Big, big-time. Tha's what I wanted, to make the bastard suffer."

The battle between the scotch and my breakfast was reaching a climax. There was a bitter taste on my tongue and what was in my stomach felt as if it was trying to come up. My scalp was suddenly damp with perspiration. If I didn't get out of that room quickly I was afraid that I was going to throw up all over Eugene Long's living room.

I stood. "It's late. I've got to go." My voice sounded breathy in my ears. My stomach seemed about to explode. I started toward the elevator, although I had no idea how I would open it.

Long got up, took a few long strides, and was beside me in the hall. He pressed a button and the elevator doors parted.

"I'll talk to Tina," he said. "'Bout your show."

I nodded. The only word I could manage to get out was, "Good."

Suddenly the elevator began to descend—fast. I leaned against one wall and clapped my hands over my mouth as gorge rose into my chest.

Silently, I pleaded, *Please, God, don't let me throw up in this elevator*!

As soon as my stomach and I landed on the lobby floor I practically flew into the ladies' lounge.

I just made it to the nearest stall, where I knelt over the toilet bowl and heaved. And heaved . . .

When I was finally able to flush, I got up off my knees and staggered to the nearest of the sinks. I'd just scooped a handful of cold water into my mouth to rinse it out when I heard a soft voice behind me.

"Are you all right?"

Nodding, I spit into the sink, splashed more water into my mouth, and spit again.

"I was just coming in and saw you rush in here. You were all bent over and looked sick. There's a doctor in the hotel—can I get her for you?"

I shook my head. "No, but thanks." I glanced up into the mirror above the sink and realized that the woman who was concerned about me was Tina Long.

"Sit down," she said, indicating an upholstered chair between the stalls and the sinks.

Still a little shaky, I did as she suggested and watched in surprise as she pulled paper towels from the dispenser, wet them in cold water, and came over to me.

"Your mascara ran down your cheeks, from all that barfing." She dabbed gently at my face with the damp towels.

Because of her kindness to a stranger, I was revising my opinion of Tina Long. I had to admit that I was ashamed of myself for making the tabloid stories about her the basis for my judgment of this young woman I had seen at the gala, but never met. The extravagant, party-girl tales might be true, but they were only part of the truth.

With Tina leaning over me, and my eyes at the level of her neck, I had a close-up view of the necklace she was wearing. Six letters hung on a thin platinum chain. Outlined in tiny diamonds, they spelled out the word "Poppet."

Tina Long straightened up again. "All clean. You look okay, but just one more thing." She reached into the small clutch purse that she'd put down on the sink counter and withdrew a tiny bottle. She aimed it at me and gave a little squirt. Cologne. A delicate floral scent.

"Now nobody can smell what happened, but you should change your clothes as soon as you can."

I stood, no longer wobbly. "Thank you for everything."

"You're welcome."

"I couldn't help noticing your necklace," I said. "Is that word 'Poppet'?"

"Cool, isn't it? I love it. That's what my mother-person calls me."

■　■　■

Outside the entrance to the Olympia Grand, I stopped beneath the canopy and took a few deep breaths of fresh air. A uniformed valet approached and asked if I wanted him to bring my car around.

"No, thank you. I'm parked nearby."

With no tip to be had from me, he headed for a couple just exiting the hotel. The man handed him a claim check and the valet scurried off toward the garage.

I'd expected to park at the hotel, but I'd spotted—and took—an empty space on Oakwood Drive, the side street just before I would have turned into the entrance.

It was almost noon. I hoped I'd put enough quarters into the meter because parking fines had become so expensive I couldn't imagine why the city couldn't balance its budget.

Luck was with me. As I came close to the Jeep I saw that the meter had indeed expired, but there wasn't any ticket on my windshield.

I unlocked the door and started to climb into the driver's seat when instinct told me something was wrong. Stepping back from the vehicle, I realized that my Jeep was sitting lower than it should have been.

Then I saw the reason for it: My tires had been slashed flat.

Fear shot through me like the jolt from a cattle prod.

42

My immediate reaction was to run back to the safety of the hotel and call the police.

But when I got to the corner, I realized that I couldn't do that. If I made a police report of the vandalism, my name on it might come to the attention of Detective Manny Hatch. He'd pounce on me like a cat on a mouse, demanding to know why was I near the Olympia Grand. Who was I talking to? What was I up to? And could I spell "interfering with a police investigation"?

No, I couldn't report this to the police.

I felt relatively safe on the busy corner of Oakwood Drive and Wilshire Boulevard. Cars whizzed by in both directions as shoppers and tourists strolled past the elegant stores on Wilshire Boulevard. Peering down both sides of Oakwood Drive, I didn't spot anyone sitting in a car, or walking along the street. It was likely that whoever slashed my tires got away. And now I had to deal with what the vandal had done.

I pulled my wallet and my cell phone out of my bag, found my Auto Club card, and dialed the number for Emergency Roadside Service.

After reciting the make, model, color, and license number of my Jeep, and the location, I told the dispatcher that my tires had been slashed and I needed a tow to the All Tires store on Pico Boulevard near Beverly Glen Canyon Boulevard.

I heard the usual assurance that a driver would arrive

in thirty minutes or less, and thanked the dispatcher. Next, I phoned Liddy, who had a key to my house. Happily, she was home. I told her what happened to my tires and that a Triple A truck would take me to All Tires.

"I don't know how long I'll be at the tire store. Could you go to my place and take Tuffy for a walk?"

"Glad to," she said. "I need the exercise. Where are you right now?"

"On Oakwood Drive just south of Wilshire."

"Oakwood? That's the street that runs next to the Olympia Grand. Were you at the hotel? Were you investigating without me?"

"Yes, but for what I had to do, you couldn't have come with me. I'll call you later, after they put new tires on the Jeep and I get home."

"Okay, but don't leave anything out. After all, I was your wheel woman and lookout while you were—well, I'm not going to say what on the phone."

"Good idea. Thanks for taking care of Tuff."

■ ■ ■

As has usually been my experience with Triple A Emergency Roadside Service, the truck arrived sooner than the dispatcher's outside estimate. Such was the case today.

I showed the driver my two slashed tires and he mumbled something in what sounded like Russian. That would have fit because the name on his shirt said "Ivan."

Ivan examined my membership card, made a note, and handed it back. I told him where to take the Jeep. He nodded, and got into his truck to position it for attaching his chain to my vehicle.

I was on the sidewalk, still scanning the street for anyone who looked suspicious. There was no one. While the driver prepared to tow my car, I walked down the street a few yards, studying the other parked cars. Mine was the only one with slashed tires.

The driver called to me. "Hey—come look." He gestured to the passenger side of the Jeep. "You got a bigger problem than you thought."

When I joined him in the street, I saw what he meant: The two tires on that side had been slashed, too.

All four of my tires had been ruined.

As far as I could see up and down Oakwood Drive, my car was the only one that had been targeted.

■   ■   ■

While the men at All Tires were replacing my four, I sat on a folding chair one of them had brought outdoors from the office for me. I was replaying in my head the story Eugene Long had told me about what he and Keith Ingram had plotted to do to Roland Gray, in retaliation for Gray embarrassing Tina Long four years earlier. It was an outrageous tale that I found very hard to believe.

Sitting in the hot sun was making it hard for me to think. I moved the chair into the shade and felt better. Even though there was a stale taste in my mouth and my stomach was empty and felt hollow, my head was clear.

I decided to do what I would have done more than an hour ago, if I hadn't gotten sick and then discovered the vandalism to my Jeep. I dialed John O'Hara's cell phone.

He answered on the first ring.

"Hi, it's Della. I have a question. When Keith Ingram's clothing and belongings were inventoried and bagged, was anything unusual found in one of his pockets?"

"Unusual—like what?"

"A dry, ground substance, brown in color. Probably in a little packet of plastic wrap."

"How did you know that?" I heard surprise in his voice.

"So they found it. Tell me if it was tested to find out what it was."

"Yes, sure. But it wasn't a drug of any kind. Forensics said it was a spice."

"Nutmeg?"

His voice hardened into his detective-on-the-job tone. "What's going on, Del?"

"Was it nutmeg?" I asked.

"Yes, but it isn't relevant to Ingram's murder."

"Not directly. Or maybe not at all. I don't know yet."

"What have you been up to?"

"This morning I went out drinking," I said.

John laughed. "I wouldn't believe that if you said it with your hand on a Bible. Tell me the truth."

"Okay, but I want you to listen without yelling. Deal?"

Momentary pause. "Deal."

I told John what Long had told me about the plot he and Keith Ingram had devised.

"That's the most idiotic scheme I ever heard of," John said.

"I found it hard to believe, too, until you told me that Ingram had a packet of nutmeg in his pocket."

"Even if I was back on the force, I can't arrest someone for what they *intended* to do." He was silent for a moment. "If Gray had found out what they planned, then he'd be my number one suspect in Ingram's murder, but then somebody tried to kill Gray."

"None of the pieces of the puzzle we have make a picture yet," I said.

Behind me, I heard a car horn honking. Turning my head I saw a familiar ivory Range Rover pulling into the driveway of the tire store.

"Liddy's here," I said. "Talk to you later. Bye."

I disconnected before it occurred to John to ask me how I managed to get that story out of Eugene Long.

Hurrying over to meet Liddy, I saw that she wasn't alone; sitting in the front passenger seat beside her was Tuffy.

"This is a nice surprise," I said.

"Get in and sit with me. I couldn't wait to hear what happened this morning."

As soon as I opened the passenger door and greeted Tuffy, he moved into the back.

"You certainly have Tuff well trained," Liddy said admiringly.

I had to laugh at that. "Not me. He pretty much trained himself. Sometimes I think he reads my mind."

Liddy looked at me and frowned. "You're pale. No lipstick or mascara, and there's a yellowish stain on your blouse. What happened to you? Are you all right?"

I assured her that I was fine. As we waited for the last of my tires to be replaced and balanced, I repeated to Liddy what I'd told John about Long and Ingram's bizarre plot to frame Roland Gray for attempted murder by sabotaging Gray's lemon pudding with a lethal dose of nutmeg. I also told her the things I'd left out of my report to John: getting Long drunk, my increasing stomach distress, Tina Long's unexpected kindness in the women's bathroom, and then returning to my Jeep to find the tires slashed.

"Your idea of getting Long drunk so he'd tell you what he knew about Ingram's murder—that was as weird as the nutmeg story he gave you. Do you believe him?"

"It was hard to. I wasn't sure, so I called John just before you got here. John confirmed that one of the things they found in Ingram's clothes was a packet of ground nutmeg."

Liddy gave a low whistle. Tuffy, who had been lounging in the back, sat up and stuck his nose between our seats.

Stroking his head, I said, "It's okay, Tuff. That wasn't for you. Liddy was expressing amazement at how crazy people are getting."

"If we needed any more proof, all we have to do is watch the news a couple of nights a week," Liddy said.

Tuffy lay down again, and Liddy asked me, "Did they test the pudding Gray made at the cook-off?"

I shook my head. "It burned up. In the confusion when the smoke bomb went off, Gray accidentally left his stove turned on. Anyway, Ingram couldn't have stirred the nutmeg into the pudding until it was finished and dishes were given to the judges for tasting."

"But that never happened," Liddy said.

"No, it didn't."

"What's next on the detecting agenda?"

"I'm having tea with Roland Gray this afternoon at four. Sometime between now and then, I've got to figure out a subtle way to learn if Roland knew what Ingram and Long were planning, and if he has any idea at all about who shot at him."

"Let's examine what we *do* know," Liddy said. "Long hated Roland Gray and plotted with Ingram to frame him for attempted murder. But why would Ingram get involved? I mean, if their scheme was uncovered, it would mean a big embarrassment for Ingram, maybe even criminal charges, since he was actually committing the act of trying to frame Gray."

"My guess is that Ingram agreed to do it to stay on the good side of his potential father-in-law."

"That makes sense. He could have been afraid that if he didn't help Long, Long might have managed to stop the marriage, and it would be bye-bye to the Daddy's billions."

"Let's look at who had a motive to kill Ingram," I said. "Any of the women he taped in bed with him who were afraid of exposure. But only two of the women were at the gala: Yvette and Tina. Tina's acted pretty wild. She might have been taped willingly, or perhaps she didn't know. She seemed genuinely distraught when Ingram was killed. Yvette was near Ingram when he was stabbed, but there wasn't a drop of blood on her. Roland and I ducked under a table together just seconds after the smoke bomb went off. He couldn't have lighted and tossed the smoke bomb mixture and stabbed Ingram in those few seconds."

"So he didn't do it."

"No," I said. "But there was one man unaccounted for at the gala—he paid for his ticket at the last minute with a phony check. My theory, or piece of a theory, is that he's the one who brought the bomb mixture and murdered Ingram. Okay, that makes sense. But where I bump into a cement wall is on the question of why would he, or anyone else in this case, have wanted to kill Roland? No one has suggested yet that Roland and Ingram ever met. That's one of the things I want to find out from Roland."

"Two mysteries," Liddy said. "There doesn't seem to be any connection between them, but there *has* to be. What's the link?"

"There are two, or at least two that we know about so far. Yvette Dupree is one link, and Tina Long is the other. Yvette, because Long told me he made a play for her years ago, but she was seeing someone. Judging from the way she acted when I told her that Roland had been shot, he's probably the man in her life, but I don't think Long knows that."

Liddy nodded. "And Tina's a link because the cruel embarrassment Roland put her through was Long's motive for wanting to frame Roland. But I can't picture either Yvette or Tina lying on her stomach and firing a sniper rifle into a café."

"Yvette is tougher than she looks," I said. "According to John's contact at Interpol, in London a decade ago she killed her abusive husband."

Liddy's eyes lighted up with interest. "Did she shoot him?"

"No—she hit him on the head. The jury believed it was self-defense, but John's contact said there were lingering suspicious because the man was so much bigger than Yvette. If Yvette is involved with Roland, she wouldn't have a motive to shoot him. As for Tina . . . Tina is so thin I can't picture her being able to lift the kind of weapon that almost killed Roland, let alone knowing how to fire it."

"She could have hired a pro," Liddy said. "Or her father could have, when his plan for framing Gray went awry. Did you ask him if he had any idea about who killed Ingram?"

"Not directly, but from what he said, it didn't seem as though he had any idea. He didn't even appear to be interested in who did it, or to care, except for the fact that it ruined his plan. He must have liked Ingram, to some degree; he remarked that Ingram would have made a good 'first husband' for Tina. I've thought a lot about this, and I can't picture Eugene Long putting himself in the power of a professional hit man who would then have had a conspiracy to murder charge to hang over Long's head, and be able to blackmail him forever."

One of the tire mechanics came out of the store and waved at me. I said to Liddy, "The Jeep's ready. I'll take Tuffy home with me. Thanks for looking after him."

"Call me tonight, after your tea party with Gray."

I promised that I would.

Driving home on my four new tires, a plan began to form in my mind.

43

As soon as I let Tuffy and myself into the house, my cell phone rang. The number on the faceplate was unfamiliar.

I answered and heard Olivia Wayne's voice. She started talking without the preamble of a greeting.

"Victor Raynoso has a public defender, but I persuaded the PD to let me go with him into the interview with his client and ask questions about one of the charges against him. To give you a quick snapshot, Raynoso's got tattoos up to his chin, over the top of his shaved head and across the knuckles of both hands. His rap sheet goes back to his first incarceration as a juvenile. He's a total creep with a bad attitude, not worth the price of the air he's breathing."

"But do you like him for the café shooting?"

"No," she said. "He denied it, adamantly, but everybody I've ever met in custody denies everything, so I paid no attention to that. The evidence—I should say, the *lack* of evidence—supports Raynoso's denial. He was caught taking shots at cars on the freeway, and he was carrying drugs. No surprise there. What makes me think he's telling the truth about being so drunk he wasn't even awake at the time you and the writer were having coffee is that he's stupid. And his whole criminal history is one of acting on impulse. I got a—shall we say an *informal*—look at the police report of the café shooting. Whoever did that had to plan it, had to know how to get to the roof across the street and set up for the shoot. I'd bet my year-end bonus that Raynoso has never even planned where to eat lunch."

"Then Hatch is wrong about Raynoso being our sniper."

"I'm sure he is. Look, Della, I told you I'd be billing you for my time visiting Raynoso, but because we have a mutual friend—a very nice guy, even if he's as slippery as a greased eel—I gave you a fifteen-minute freebee."

"What do you mean?"

"After chatting with Raynoso, I went to see Detective Hatch. I volunteered my opinion that he has no case against Raynoso for the Gray shooting, and that he'll look like a fool if he tries to include that charge."

"How did he take it?"

She chuckled. "Not very well, but he listened. You've never seen me in action, but I'm inclined to express myself in somewhat forceful language. Hatch wanted to know why I was interested in Raynoso. I told him it was because I get hot for lowlife scum with tattoos."

I was beginning to like Olivia Wayne. "What do you think Hatch will do now?"

"My guess is he'll realize he's playing a bad hand in trying to tie Raynoso to the Gray shooting and he'll fold," she said. "But he's embarrassed now, and that will make him mucho vindictive. If he really wants to get John O'Hara for the Ingram murder, he'll have to find motive and opportunity for O'Hara to have tried to take down Gray."

"He can't possibly succeed, because John doesn't have any motive to hurt Gray."

"Meaning that he *did* have reason to want Ingram dead. Wait—don't answer that."

"I wasn't going to," I said, "except to repeat that John did not kill Keith Ingram."

"Don't let that belief, or loyalty, make you complacent," Olivia Wayne said. "If Ingram's real killer isn't found quickly, who knows what piece of human excrement with a grudge against O'Hara, and who needs a favor from the cops, might suddenly materialize and tell Hatch some story he would be happy to believe. Good luck."

Olivia Wayne disconnected, once again without saying good-bye. Apparently, she didn't pad her billable hours with unnecessary chitchat.

■   ■   ■

After showering, shampooing, brushing my teeth twice, and putting on fresh clothes, I finally managed to erase all traces of the morning's stomach ordeal.

Tuffy followed me into the kitchen. He already had fresh food and water, so he just glanced at his full bowls and settled down to watch me cook.

The ingredients I needed for what I was going to make were among the staples in my cabinets. No need for a trip to the market. I organized them in front of me on the counter and set about preparing a batch of my friend Carole Adams's Quick & Easy Chocolate Nut Butter Fudge Pudding. I'd planned it as a gift for Roland when I joined him for tea at his apartment this afternoon.

While I melted the honey, sweet butter, chocolate chips, peanut butter, and other components of the recipe together in the top part of my double boiler, I thought about murder.

I visualized the pieces of the puzzle as though they were real pieces, spread out across the kitchen table. That was where Eileen and I used to put such puzzles together when she was a child. But those were easy, because we had the picture on the box to guide us in fitting the parts together.

As I stirred, I began to think again about what I knew. I hoped that if I concentrated hard enough, I would begin to understand what the handful of fragments were trying to show me.

I decided to organize them as if they were points in a mystery story I was reading:

Eugene Long hated Roland Gray.

For revenge, Long and Ingram plotted to frame Gray for attempted murder.

But before they could implement their scheme, Ingram was murdered.

Ingram disliked Yvette Dupree, and it was probably mutual, even though at some point she'd gone to bed with him and he'd taped the event.

Ingram intended to marry Tina Long, in all likelihood for her father's money.

Yvette adored Tina as though Tina were her own daughter. I understood how great a force that kind of love could be, because I felt it for my own honorary daughter, Eileen. I doubted that Yvette was happy about Ingram planning to marry Tina. Could she possibly have been unhappy enough about it to want Ingram dead?

There was one unidentified guest at the gala: the mystery man who paid with a phony check. Because no one at the ticket desk remembered him, he must have been innocuous looking. (It certainly could not have been Victor Raynoso. From Olivia's description he sounded like one big walking tattoo. Anyone would remember seeing him.)

Yvette couldn't have killed Ingram—but could she have hired the mystery man to do it?

Roland Gray must have had a powerful grudge against Eugene Long to have made him humiliate Long's daughter. It didn't seem likely that Roland would have had anything against Tina herself. She was only eighteen at the time he engineered her embarrassment. And, if he did take out anger at Long on his daughter, that was a very cowardly act.

Yvette Dupree killed her husband ten years earlier, in London, claiming self-defense because he was abusing her. Did she have help, as John's friend at Interpol suspected?

And what about the person in the dark green hooded sweatshirt who was watching me in the library? And the fact that someone slashed the tires on my Jeep? Were those little pieces part of the big murder puzzle? And was the person in the hooded sweatshirt the same one who slashed my tires?

If those acts were connected to the puzzle of Ingram's murder, then it had to be because someone knew I was trying to find Ingram's killer.

Thanks to Olivia Wayne's visit to Victor Raynoso and, later, to Detective Hatch, Hatch was probably going to return to the belief that the murder of Ingram and the attempted murder of Gray were connected. But I was as sure as Olivia was that Hatch wasn't going to stop looking for evidence that would allow him to arrest John O'Hara. I didn't doubt that Hatch would be happy if the real killer walked up to him and confessed, but unless that unlikely event occurred, his investigation was focused on John.

I was very glad that I'd broken into Ingram's house and stolen the tape of Eileen. If Hatch had found that tape before I did, it was likely John would be in custody now. A father protecting his daughter was a powerful motive for murder.

Part One of my theory was that the mystery man murdered Ingram. That was easy to say, but how to prove it? If he was a professional killer, he was long gone by now. From what I'd heard and read, they were phantoms, appearing out of the dark to do a job, and then vanishing. How did one find a phantom?

Part Two was that the murder of Ingram and the attempted murder of Gray were connected. Several people had motives to kill Ingram, but who had a motive to kill Gray?

The only person I could think of was Eugene Long, but I didn't believe that he would either kill or hire a killer—unless something was done to Tina that was a lot worse than embarrassment, and there had been no suggestion that such was the case.

That question of who shot at Roland was the wall I kept crashing up against. I had to find a way to climb over, burrow under, or smash through that wall.

This morning I'd managed to pry information out of Long by getting him drunk. *In vino veritas.*

This afternoon I was going to try to use pudding to loosen Roland Gray's tongue.

The nut butter fudge pudding in my pot was thickening nicely. I dipped a teaspoon into the glossy mixture and tasted it. Delicious. This was also the first thing I'd put into my stomach since . . . Since this morning.

And all at once an image flashed into my head: Tina Long's necklace. The word spelled out in little diamonds was "Poppet." When she said her "mother-person" called her that she must have been referring to Yvette. On the phone, when we were arranging my tea this afternoon with Roland, Will Parker had called me "Poppet."

My pulse started racing. Will was an attractive man. Lively. Energetic. Much more energetic and engaging than Roland. What if Will Parker was the man Yvette was involved with, and not Roland?

Where does this line of reasoning take me?

Not very far, unless . . . Unless . . .

I knew that neither Yvette nor Roland could have stabbed Ingram—but Will was on the hotel grounds that night. While the police were keeping all of us inside, he'd come to the entrance and spoken to the guard at the door, asking to talk to Roland. Roland told me Will had driven him to the hotel.

Could Will Parker have been the mystery man who paid for a ticket at the last minute, when the crowd was biggest and the ticket people busy? According to an acknowledgment in Roland Gray's first spy novel, Will Parker had been a British commando. Like members of our Special Forces, he surely would be able to fire a sniper rifle, and to get in and out of places . . . like a phantom.

I remembered the pudding and took it off the stove before it burned. My hands were trembling. In a little more

than an hour, I was supposed to have tea with Roland Gray
and Will Parker. With what I was thinking, I didn't want
to be anywhere near Parker. I decided to make an excuse
and cancel.

I found Parker's card and dialed his number.

The call went to voice mail, and I heard a recording of
Parker say in his Cockney accent, "It's Monday morning.
I've 'ad to go to London for a few days. Returning Sunday
night. Whether you're a bird or a bloke, leave a message."

A wave of relief surged over me.

I didn't leave a message, but I did take a deep breath of
relief.

Then a new thought chilled me: *What if Parker's plans
changed since this morning?*

I called Roland Gray.

"Hello, Roland. It's Della Carmichael."

"I recognized your lovely voice. I hope you're still coming to tea this afternoon."

"Yes, I'm looking forward to it. I'm calling because I'm
bringing you a little something I made and I wondered how
many people would be there."

"Just the two of us, my dear. It would have been three,
but Will's mum had a bit of a scare and he's rushed off to
make certain she's all right."

"I hope it's nothing serious," I said.

"No, I'm sure it's not. But she's quite far up in years and
Will is her last living child."

"I'll hold a good thought for her," I said. "See you at
four."

"Jolly good."

So Parker really is in London.

Okay, this is my new theory: Will Parker was the mystery man at the gala, and murdered Ingram. (Motive as yet
unknown, but my bet was that it had something to do with
Yvette Dupree.)

Now here was my biggest leap, worthy of the Cirque du Soleil: Parker, a former British commando, shot at the window of Caffeine an' Stuff to confuse the police. He probably didn't mean to wound Roland Gray.

I believed Parker did this because it succeeded in complicating the investigation of Ingram's murder. The police were forced to try to find a link between Ingram and Gray. When they weren't able to find that link, Detective Hatch had tried to split the one case into two.

There was one problem with my new theory: How could I prove it?

Stirring the pudding to keep a skin from forming on the top, two ideas occurred to me. The first one involved a call to John O'Hara.

Again, he picked up on the first ring. I wondered if he was sitting in his car, or in a coffeehouse, miserable because he had nothing to do. Well, I was about to give him something to do.

"John, can you get in touch with your friend at Interpol again?"

"You mean now?"

"Yes."

"I have his home number and his cell. Is it important?"

"It could be. I hope so. Would you ask him to check out a man named Willis T. Parker, a former British commando? He's listed in the acknowledgments of Roland Gray's first spy novel—something about helping Gray's hero out of a tight spot. Now he works for Gray. Ask if he can find out if Parker knew Yvette Dupree, when she was Fabienne Talib."

"What's this about?"

"I finally have a theory of the case." I told John what it was.

"Interesting, but you don't have any evidence." I heard the skepticism in John's voice.

"Not yet, but don't you think this is a path worth following? Are you or Hugh Weaver or Hatch on a more promising trail?"

"No. While I'm having your idea checked out, what are you doing?"

"I'm having tea at four o'clock this afternoon with Roland Gray."

"No! I don't want you near Will Parker."

"John, I've told you not to talk to me like that. I'm not a three-year-old. I appreciate your concern, but I wouldn't be going to see Roland except for the fact that Parker is thousands of miles away right now, back in London, visiting his mother who's ill."

John was silent for a moment. I pictured him with his lips clamped together.

"John, are you still there?"

He cleared his throat. "You're having tea with Gray at four. That shouldn't take more than an hour, hour and a half at most. I want—I'd *appreciate* it if you'd call me when you leave."

"I'll do that."

"In case I need to reach you first, keep your cell phone on."

"I always do." We said good-bye, with John promising to call his Interpol contact right away.

After ending the call, I poured the pudding into my white Wedgwood serving bowl and stretched plastic wrap across the top.

When I was ready to leave for Gray's apartment, I put the gift bowl of chocolate fudge pudding into a cardboard box and set the box on the floor in front of the Jeep's passenger seat.

Then I reached into the glove compartment and removed the small, handheld tape recorder I used for making notes about recipes or ideas for the TV show when something occurred to me while I was driving.

After checking that the batteries were working, I rewound it to the beginning of the tape and slipped the little machine into my purse. It was a bag made of loosely woven net, deliberately chosen in order to capture sound in the room.

44

Will Parker had described Roland Gray's apartment building as "a bloody tall white building on the corner of Wilshire Boulevard and Garland Street," with "Gates across the driveway. Gorgons at the doors. Security up the arse."

The big white building with ornamental iron gates across the driveway was easy to spot. An elderly man in a guard's uniform occupied the kiosk just outside the gates.

"My name is Della Carmichael. Mr. Gray is expecting me."

The guard checked his clipboard, found my name, and nodded. "Do you know where it is?"

"No."

"Apartment three twelve, third floor, in the back," he said.

"Thank you. Where can I park?"

"Follow the driveway down into the garage. Use any space marked 'visitor.' Take the elevator up to the third floor and turn left."

He pressed a button and the gates swung open.

As I drove past the front of the building, I didn't see any "Gorgons" at the door. Nor did I see any as I steered the Jeep into the dim, subterranean parking garage. I'm not fond of poorly lighted garages. It would have been comforting to see a couple of those big guardians playing cards down here. Maybe they were on a break.

I found an empty "visitor" space near the elevator and

parked. With the bowl of pudding cradled against my chest, I got out and locked the Jeep.

It took only a few seconds for the elevator to arrive at the garage level. As I was whisked upward, I was pleased that I didn't feel any protest from my stomach. I didn't really expect one because it was empty, except for a spoonful of pudding. The fact that I was hungry again was testimony that my distress of the morning was over.

The third floor hallway was well lighted and painted a soft shade of blue. Plexiglas-enclosed prints of beautiful birds in flight decorated the walls. Without traditional framing, it looked as though the birds were soaring through the sky.

At the door to apartment 312 I reached into my bag and turned on the recorder.

I'd no sooner touched my finger to the bell outside apartment 312 when the door opened.

Roland Gray, a welcoming expression on his face, greeted me warmly and stepped aside for me to come in. He was wearing a soft blue open-neck shirt, and a red cashmere cardigan. The only sign that he'd been shot four nights ago was the narrow strip of tape almost the color of his skin that ran across his forehead, just below his hairline.

I saw his nostrils twitch. Gesturing at the bowl I carried, he said, "I'm getting the scent of a heavenly something. What have you brought?"

"It's a new kind of chocolate nut butter pudding I made this afternoon. My partner and I are considering selling containers of it in our retail store. You're the one who got me interested in pudding, so I would appreciate your expert opinion."

"It will be my pleasure."

We were in a large, comfortable, no-particular-style living room with a dining area on one side. The room opened up onto a balcony enclosed by a waist-high ornamental iron railing. Several big terra-cotta tubs filled with bright red geraniums provided wonderful splashes of color against a sky that today was gray with smog.

Roland took the bowl of pudding from me and smiled with pleasure.

"Ahhhh, slightly tepid. Exactly how I like it, from a little warm to room temperature. Cold pudding I regard as a beastly perversion."

Roland gestured toward the dining room table, which was already arranged with two sets of cups, saucers, and dessert plates, silverware, a teapot in a cozy, a platter of little pastries, and a basket of scones. The scones were surrounded by tiny pots of jam and a dish of whipped cream.

Still holding the bowl of pudding, Gray used one hand to pull out a chair in front of one of the two sets of cups and saucers and dessert plates. "Sit here," he said.

My chair faced out onto the patio; behind me was a swinging door that I presumed led into the kitchen. I put my bag down casually on the chair beside me.

"You have a lovely view," I said. "No tall buildings around."

Roland removed a metal trivet from the nearby sideboard, placed it on the table next to me, and put the bowl of pudding on it. "The flat agent said that on a clear day one can see the ocean, but I've yet to spot it. I suppose one must take that statement on faith."

He took the seat opposite me and smiled. Indicating the teapot, he said, "Would you like to be Mum?"

I knew that the phrase "to be Mum" meant that he wanted me to pour the tea.

He placed a silver tea strainer over his cup as I removed the cozy from the pot and put it to one side. As I poured the dark amber-colored liquid into his cup, a very pleasant aroma was released.

After serving Roland, and depositing the wet leaves into the little saucer next to the strainer, I strained a cup for myself, and took a sip. Although I'm essentially a coffee person, I had to admit that this was very good.

"What kind of tea is it?" I asked.

"A special blend I get at Harrods in London. I haven't found it anywhere else. If you like it, I'll ring Will tonight and have him bring some back for you."

"Thank you; I'd like that. And when you speak to him, please tell him that I hope his mother is all right."

Roland indicated the scones and the pastries. I took a frosted pink petit four.

"He'll appreciate that."

"I was rereading the first of your Roger Wilde books and I noticed your acknowledgment to Will. You said he helped your hero out of a tight spot?"

"Ahhh, yes. I was doing research on the British Commandos when I met Will. It was at a point in the book where I'd written myself into a corner, so to speak."

I frowned in sympathy. "That must have been an awful feeling."

"It was more painful than I can describe." He sipped his tea. "There's an old story in publishing circles—I've used it several times when I've lectured to rooms full of poor sots who think they want to write. It's about a writer of magazine adventure serials—long ago, when periodicals serialized such things. The late, great Sidney Sheldon told me the story. He said he didn't know where it came from because he'd have loved to give proper credit. But here it is. Each month the serial writer plunged his hero into worse and worse trouble—just as I was trying to do to poor Roger Wilde. The readers loved those stories and the magazine's sales went up. Partway through the adventure, the writer asked his editor for a raise. He was denied. That was disappointing, but like a good soldier, the writer turned in the next episode on schedule. The end of that chapter was especially exciting. He had plunged his hero into a deep pit filled with poisonous snakes. Up above was a ring of hungry tigers, and beyond them there was a raging forest fire. The sides of the pit were so hard and slick it was impossible to make handholds. The snakes at his feet were coiling to strike.

"After that issue went to press, the writer went back to his editor and said that he wasn't going to write the next episode unless he was paid more money. The editor refused, and ordered his other serial writers to come up with a way to get the hero out of that pit.

"Time went by. The publication clock was ticking. No one could figure out how the hero was going to survive. Finally, just before the next issue absolutely had to go to press, the editor surrendered. The writer got a fatter pay packet and he handed in the next chapter. The first line began, 'Once out of the pit . . .' "

I laughed. Roland's smile was wry.

"You may find that amusing. So would I have—if I hadn't been in a similar spot, and unable to take the easy way out. My publisher would have rejected that solution in a novel, cancelled my contract, and blackened my name in the industry. Publishers regard lack of imagination in a thriller writer as a worse failing than heavy drinking."

"There are eight or nine Roger Wilde books, so you must have solved the problem."

"I didn't," Roland said. "Will was the one. We were drinking in a pub in London and I was crying in my cups, telling him my problem. He wasn't sympathetic. He said he'd been in a military unit dubbed 'Thatcher's Butchers' by other commandos and that he'd faced a lot worse than—as he described Roger—'that silly *ponce*.' Then he proceeded to tell me some things . . . If my hair hadn't already begun to go gray it would have started on the spot that night. We went back to my flat in Cadogan Gardens and I showed him my troublesome pages. He suggested a few changes to the situation, and then he showed me how

Roger could rescue himself. It turned out to be a great scene. Many of the reviewers mentioned it favorably, even the ones who look down on the espionage genre."

"That was a lucky meeting," I said. "Will has the most interesting business card—he gave it to me the night you were in St. Clare's Hospital. 'NID question mark, space, and then WCD.' I figured out the WCD pretty quickly: 'Will Can Do.' But what does the NID question mark stand for?"

"That's one of his old cards. Those first three letters stand for 'Need It Done?' and then you were right, the rest is: 'Will Can Do.'"

"What does it mean?" I made my tone light to sound innocently curious. "Is he a kind of handyman?"

"Not in the usual sense of the phrase, as you might understand it," Roland said. "Will likes complex challenges. But he can also fix anything mechanical. I haven't needed to hire a plumber or an electrician in ten years."

Roland finished his first cup of tea and asked for another.

Since he was already talking about Will, as I poured, I took a chance and probed deeper. "I met Yvette Dupree the night of the gala. She's delightful. Have she and Will known each other a long time?"

"Oh, at least a decade or so, but Will likes to stay out of her limelight. He never goes around with her to social engagements, but they're quite devoted to each other. I call them—jokingly, of course—Beauty and the Beast."

At that moment, I heard a slight squeak, and felt a whoosh of air from the swinging door opening behind me.

"You bloody dim-witted sod!" Will Parker said. "Why don't you tell 'er the lot? I warned you this bird knew too much already."

Turning, I saw that he'd leveled the barrel of a pistol at my head. Screwed onto the end was a sound suppressor.

45

Terror held me frozen for a moment, but then the powerful instinct for self-preservation took over. I dropped my teacup, letting it break on the top of the table, grabbed the full bowl of pudding beside me, and heaved it at Parker's head.

His reflexes were too good. He ducked, but my white Wedgwood missile struck him on the shoulder and split with a *crack*. Great globs of chocolate fudge pudding splashed all over the front of his shirt.

Enraged, Parker screamed, "Bloody 'ell!"

I jumped out of the chair, but he caught my arm, spun me around, and hit me a sharp, terrible blow on the side of the head. I went down . . .

■ ■ ■

When I woke up, I sensed that it was dark, but I kept my eyes closed and lay still. I heard Roland Gray and Will Parker talking and hoped they'd think I was still unconscious. Moving my limbs just fractions of an inch at a time I realized that I was bound at the ankles and that my wrists were tied behind my back with some soft material.

I was lying on my side, one cheek and my nose pressed down against the carpet. There were particles of dust caught in the fibers. I had an urge to sneeze, but forced myself to hold it in while I listened and tried to learn what my fate was going to be.

"Compare me to a bloomin' plumber! Weren't fer me, you'd be teachin' in some low-class boarding school, licking the 'ead master's arse."

"Will, don't say things like that. We're a team."

Parker's voice was bitter. "Some bloody team. You get all the credit," Parker said.

Roland sounded close to tears. "We split all the money. I told you it has to be this way because the publisher pays more with just my name on a book."

"You wouldn't get a freakin' Euro without me. An' we wouldn't be in this fix if you 'adn't started everything by messin' with that girl's speech. Bloody stupid prank you pulled. Nobody with the brains in a donkey's arse deliberately makes an enemy—especially not one that rich."

"Eugene Long humiliated me. I had to get back at him. He said my books were dreadful, and he said it in print where people could read it!"

"So the bloody 'ell what? They sell in the millions! And they're *our* books, not yours. Don't you forget that."

"Look, Will, why don't we talk about this when we get to Rio?"

"We got something to do first—an' this time *you* be the one to do it."

"What are you talking about?" I heard sudden panic in Roland's voice.

"'Er," Parker said. He kicked me in the stomach. It hurt, but I willed myself to stay nonreactive. "I've been doing every bloody thing! I tried to scare 'er off the scent by letting myself be seen watching 'er at the library. Then when I figured she'd gone to see old man Long, I slashed 'er tires. I took care of Ingram for you before he could expose you as a fraud and spill the beans about me doin' most of the work on the books."

"Now wait. You killed him for Yvette, too. He was blackmailing her—"

"Leave 'er out of this. Not a word out of yer 'ole about

'er or I swear to God I'll shoot you for real, not like that
trick we pulled at the coffee'ouse."

I heard Roland gasp. Or maybe it was a choked-back
sob. When he spoke again it was in a defeated tone.

"The plane for Rio leaves at nine o'clock. If we're going
to get there in time to go through all the security . . . What
do you want me to do?"

I felt rough, strong hands pulling at the cloth around
my wrists.

"Untie 'er ankles," Parker said.

I heard Roland kneel down—his knees actually creaked.
He began to fumble with the binding around my ankles,
pulled the fabric off, and stood again.

My hands and feet were free now, but I lay limp and
kept my eyes closed.

There was a tremor in Roland's voice. "She's so still.
Maybe you killed her."

"She's got a pulse. Maybe she's faking. We'll see."

I braced for another blow—

"No!" Roland cried. "Don't do that. Here, this will tell
us."

I felt liquid splash against my face, but I didn't flinch. A
drop went between my lips. It was tea.

"'Elp me get 'er on 'er feet," Parker said.

The two men, each grabbing an arm, pulled me upright.
I let my head fall forward toward my chest and remained
a dead weight.

"This way," Parker said.

I felt myself being dragged . . . dragged toward fresh air.
Out onto the balcony.

Oh, God! They're going to throw me over!

I felt the men prop me up against the waist-high iron
railing.

Suddenly Roland began to sob. He dropped my arm. I
heard him shuffle backward. "I can't!"

Cursing, Parker leaned forward, his head against my

chest. One of his hands held my arm and the other reached down behind me toward the back of my knee—

Now!

I let out a blood-curdling scream, twisted around, scratching at his eyes as I thrust my knee as hard as I could toward his groin. I only caught him on the thigh, but I was close enough to the sensitive area that he let out a yelp.

Cursing again, he threw his arms around my torso in a grip so hard I cried out in pain. He was squeezing the life out of me!

Desperate, I threw my body side to side, forward and back, twisting. Putting most of my weight behind it, I stomped on his foot with the high heel of my shoe. He grunted and slapped me. But to slap, he had to loosen his grip.

I was pushing at him—he was shoving at me, ramming my body against the railing. Each smash against the small of my back was agonizing. I spiked him again with my heel, simultaneously twisting enough to open a few inches between us, but suddenly—

The balcony's railing gave way.

Clasped together, we went tumbling out into empty space.

A voice inside me cried, "It's too soon!"

Somebody screamed.

And then there was silence.

46

My eyes began to open.

The room was dark, but there was light spilling in from somewhere. As my eyes adjusted to the dimness, I could see just enough to know that I was in unfamiliar surroundings, hearing an unfamiliar sound. A soft *beep . . . beep . . . beep*.

With growing consciousness came the awareness of pain. My head throbbed. My whole body hurt. I couldn't move my left arm.

Where am I?

As my vision sharpened, and objects near me came into focus, I realized I was in a hospital bed. I couldn't move my left arm because it was in a cast.

Trying to ease the pain, I shifted my body and moved my right hand—and felt another hand.

A third hand?

I groaned.

And the extra hand closed over mine.

"Hey . . . you're awake." A man's voice broke through my haze. A familiar voice.

"Nicholas?"

He leaned toward me and I saw his face. Nicholas was in the chair next to my bed.

I'm alive.

"You gave us one hell of a scare," he said. "How do you feel?"

"Everything hurts. What time is it?"

"A few minutes after three o'clock in the morning. You had a big crowd here until midnight: me, O'Hara and his wife and daughter, Liddy and her husband, and Phil Logan acting like General Patton, demanding the best care for you, threatening to sue the hospital if your broken arm didn't mend perfectly. The attending doctor finally threw us all out. As we were going down in the elevator, Phil Logan was grinning. He said that your solving a murder was going to be great for your ratings."

"If everyone had to leave, how come you're here?"

"I waited downstairs for a little while, then I came back up and used my charm on the floor nurse." He moved his face closer to mine. "Do your lips hurt?"

"That's about the only part of me that doesn't."

His mouth descended on mine for the lightest, most gentle kiss I've ever felt. "Hello, Sleeping Beauty," he said.

"Not such a 'beauty,' I'll bet."

"You are to me," Nicholas said.

"What happened—how did I get here?"

"You fell off a third-floor balcony."

"No." My memory came back in a rush. "No, I didn't fall. He tried to push me over, but I fought—oh, my God. We went off the balcony together. Is he . . . ?"

"The bastard's alive," Nicholas said. "But that's only because the paramedics and the police got to him before I did. Thank God you fell into a garden and not onto some cement patio." He shuddered and took a breath before he went on.

"Parker has two broken legs and a broken wrist," Nicholas said. "Maybe some internal injuries. You two may have gone over together, but he hit the ground first. You landed on him. That's why you've only got a broken arm. They're letting you go home tomorrow."

"Home . . . Tuffy and Emma! Who's taking care of them?"

"Shhhh. Don't try to sit up. There's nothing to worry

about. Eileen's at your house. Everybody's fine—except you and Parker. Roland Gray is in custody. It was Gray who called 911 and told them you'd fallen from the third floor. He was on his way to the airport—"

"He was going to Rio. Both of them were."

I saw Nicholas nod. "Brazil—where there's no extradition to America. But after he called 911 he went back to his building and gave himself up to Detectives Hatch and Weaver. He said he couldn't live with the guilt anymore."

"And without Will Parker, he doesn't think he can write. Parker murdered Ingram, and he killed Yvette's husband in London."

"I know. The police found your purse with the tape recorder in it. Their own words are going to convict them."

"I feel sorry for Roland."

Nicholas looked shocked. "Why?"

"He's a weak man," I said. "Parker controlled him."

"I don't think that's much of an excuse, but because he came back to try to help you, I'm willing to cut him some slack. In fact, I recommended an attorney for him to call."

I smiled. "Olivia—your favorite criminal lawyer."

"That's the one. She said to tell you that because she's going to soak Gray for everything he's got, she's decided not to send you a bill after all."

"That's nice . . . What's going to happen to Yvette?"

"Parker claims she had nothing to do with the murder of Ingram, and he's claiming that he killed Talib years ago in London because he caught Talib beating her after she told him she was leaving him. Parker said he wanted to protect her, so he staged Talib's death to look like she hit him in self-defense."

"Parker really loves her," I said.

"Let's not talk about them. Can I get you anything?"

"You," I said.

"You've got me," he said. "You've had me ever since you came to my house and started ripping my clothes off.

Stupid me, it took a while before I realized you'd taken me off the market."

I yawned. "I'm so sleepy. Would you lie down here next to me?"

"Are you sure that's a good idea?"

"Umm humm."

"All right." I saw his lips curve into a teasing smile. "Promise you won't get frisky."

"I won't . . . At least not until tomorrow."

"I think we'll wait a little longer than that."

He gave me another gentle little kiss before he eased his weight onto the far edge of the hospital bed. "I can't even begin to tell you how happy I am that you're alive," he whispered.

"Me, too," I said. Then my eyes began to close.

47

The following afternoon, while Phil Logan was completing the insurance paperwork for my release, Liddy Marshall came into my hospital room carrying a shopping bag.

"New clothes," she said,

"That's a sweet thought, but I don't need new clothes."

"Yes, you do," she said. "Think about it. Your arm's in a cast. How are you going to zip and button yourself?"

I admitted that I hadn't thought of that.

Liddy opened the shopping bag and pulled out a pair of black knit slacks. "Elastic waistband," she said. "You can pull them up with one hand."

"That is a good idea."

"I'm not finished." She removed a garment in a soft shade of blue and held it up. "A tunic. This morning I had a seamstress open up the left side to accommodate the cast on your arm, and sew on strips of Velcro that you can stick together with your right hand."

"That's really clever," I said. "Thank you."

"I'm glad you like it, because right now she's making up six more for you, in different colors. Also, you have six more pair of these pull-up pants at your house, so you'll have a separate outfit for each day of the week. This top looks and feels like silk, but it's one of those great new fakes. You can toss everything in the washing machine."

"You are amazing."

Liddy grinned. "With twin sons and a husband whose dental practice consists mostly of gorgeous actresses, I've had to be amazing. There's one problem I couldn't solve for you: a bra."

"How about a strapless that fastens in front?"

"No. I was with Julie, the Neiman Marcus lingerie buyer, this morning. We experimented like a pair of contortionists, but even with that style, you wouldn't be able to get it on and off by yourself while your arm's in a cast. You'll have to go braless for a while. Luckily, you don't droop."

■ ■ ■

Liddy had just finished helping me dress when Phil Logan arrived, brandishing a manila envelope. "I've sprung you, Del."

Liddy picked up the bag with the clothes I'd worn when I fell from Roland Gray's balcony. "We're ready."

Right behind Phil was a nurse steering a wheelchair. She stopped in front of me and opened up the footrest.

"Here we are," she said cheerfully.

"Thank you, but I don't need that. I broke my arm, not my leg. "

"Hospital rules." She pronounced those two words in a tone that discouraged argument.

I sat.

She pushed.

Phil talked.

"I've organized everything for you while you're plastered up." He ticked off items on his fingers. "One: You'll have celebrity guest cookers helping you on your next eight shows. Two: I've arranged to have catered meals delivered to your house every day so you don't have to cook at home. Three: Eileen will be running Della's Sweet Dreams full-time. Four: Mickey authorized me to hire a dog walker to come to your house three times a day to take Tuffy out. She starts this afternoon. Her name is Helen. Five: Shannon and Liddy are going to come over every day to see what you need. I wanted to hire a private nurse to stay with

you, but Liddy said you'd never go for that. Actually, she
expressed it in surprisingly strong language."

"Thank you, Liddy," I said

Phil ran out of fingers and started on his other hand.
"Six: I'm assigning the intern in my office to take you
wherever you need to go. While I made my rounds this
morning I had him drive me, as a test. He passed."

"Once again, you've thought of everything."

Phil beamed. "That's my job."

When we got to the hospital's entrance and the nurse
wheeled the chair back inside, Phil said, "Liddy's taking
you home. I'd come with, but I've got places to go and
problems to solve."

With that, Phil took off at his usual warp speed toward
the hospital's parking lot.

■ ■ ■

As soon as Liddy opened my front door, Tuffy bounded
out to greet me. He leaned against my thigh and looked at
my cast with curiosity. I gave him an ear scratch. Then I
stepped inside and found several of my favorite people in
the living room.

Shannon called out, "Surprise!"

"I am surprised." Mostly I was surprised to see Nicholas talking to John and Weaver, with none of the three of
them scowling.

"We're celebrating your return," Bill Marshall said. He
was standing behind one of the two card tables someone
had set up and covered with tablecloths, passing out beer
and soft drinks. Behind the other card table, Shannon and
Eileen were arranging deli platters and a basket of bagels.

"I smell Junior's," I said, looking at Nicholas. He smiled
at me.

"Welcome home," John said quietly.

"We've got terrific news, Aunt Del!" Eileen said.

"John's back on the force," Weaver said.

"I've got more good news," Nicholas said. "After what Detective Hatch put you all through, I wanted to tell you before you saw it in the paper tomorrow morning."

Shannon grimaced. "I hope somebody shot him."

"Mother! You don't mean that."

"Not *fatally*," Shannon said. "Just in some place that really hurts."

"He's taken early retirement. And he's leaving the state."

"I feel safer already," I said.

John looked skeptical. "It's hard to believe he quit. Where did he go?"

"Not where I'd like to see him," Nicholas said. "He was offered a job in Washington—at Homeland Security."

"Now I feel less safe," Liddy said.

Weaver grunted. "At least he's no longer a pimple on our ass."

"Elegantly put," I said with a smile. "Now let's have some celebration bagels."

■ ■ ■

John and Weaver left together because they were on the four-to-midnight shift. Liddy and Bill went home to change because they had theater tickets. Eileen had gone to her parents' house for the night, to keep her mother company.

Nicholas and I were alone on the couch in the living room. Tuffy lay on the floor near my feet, and Emma was curled up on the cushion of the club chair to the left of the couch.

"This looks pretty domestic," Nicholas said.

I glanced around the room. "I never thought I'd get things put back together after Hatch turned the house upside down."

"I wasn't talking about the furniture. I meant us."

I shifted my left arm into a more comfortable position.

"I know I'm not very exciting with my arm in a cast and pain pills making me sleepy. You don't need to stay, really. I'm fine."

Nicholas sat up straighter. "I know you're fine—and independent—and can take care of yourself." I was surprised that he sounded angry.

"Don't be testy," I said.

"You make it very hard for me to—I'm trying to say something."

"We don't play games with each other. You can say anything you want to me."

Nicholas took my right hand in both of his. "I'm trying to tell you that I've fallen in love with you."

"I know."

"You *know*?"

"Of course I know. You've done everything except say the words."

"How do you feel about it?"

"I'm glad."

Nicholas let go of my hands and drew back. "What do you mean, you're glad? Is that all you're going to say?"

"What do you want me to say?"

"I want you to tell me in one simple, declarative sentence how you feel about me."

"I love you, too."

Nicholas expelled an exasperated sigh. "In journalism we call that burying the lead!"

Then he kissed me. Deeply, at first, then, as I responded, he was tender. After a few moments, he brushed my mouth with his lips and whispered, "Marry me."

"Louder, please. I didn't hear you."

"You make me crazy." He kissed me again. Pulling away, he fixed me with a hard look and said, "Marry me. This is a onetime offer."

I stroked his face with my good hand and ran the tip of my index finger around the outline of his full lips. The sight of him, the scent of him, the taste of him, his touch, all made me melt. "How long do I have to think about the onetime offer?"

"As long as you need . . ."

He kissed me again, and I lost track of time.

Recipes

▪ Carole's Quick and Easy Chocolate ▪ Nut Butter Fudge Pudding

*¼ cup honey (first, lightly coat inside of
measuring cup with butter to make it slide
out after measuring)*
*2 tablespoons sweet butter (¼ of a quarter-
pound stick, unsalted)*
½ cup dark or semisweet chocolate chips
*½ cup smooth or crunchy nut butter (any kind:
almond, cashew, macadamia, walnut,
pecan, or peanut butter)*
2 cups whole milk
*3 tablespoons cornstarch (or ⅓ cup Kuzu starch
chunks if allergic to corn products)*
1 teaspoon good vanilla extract

Use a double boiler set (or a heat-safe bowl and a slightly
larger pot to simulate a double boiler). Add about 1 inch
of water to bottom pot, set it on stove burner, and turn
burner on. While water is coming to a boil, put all the
ingredients *except* starch and about a half cup of the milk
into the top part. Add the starch to the reserved milk, stir
until dissolved, and then add that mixture to the other
ingredients. Place top container over—not in—bottom

container of boiling water and constantly stir the lumpy mixture until ingredients are melted, thoroughly combined, and thickened into a pudding with a glossy sheen. Turn off burner.

Remove top container from stove and pour pudding into 4 to 6 small bowls, pot-of-crème dishes, or heavy dessert glasses. Chill in refrigerator about one hour, or serve warm. This is delicious served plain or topped with pieces of the same kind of nut as in the pudding, or with whipped cream—or both.

Enjoy!

■   ■   ■

▪ Linda Dano's Italian Meatballs ▪

The world knows Linda Dano as an Emmy-winning actress, talk show host, and designer, but she's very much at home in the kitchen. Even during her busiest times, she loved preparing a nightly meal for her husband, Frank Attardi . . . although sometimes that meant starting the meal with her coat still on, on the many days they ran late at the TV studio.

> ½ lb. ground veal
> ½ lb. ground pork
> 1 lb. ground beef
> ½ to ¾ cup unflavored breadcrumbs
> ⅛ cup chopped fresh parsley (I like to use
>   Italian flat leaf parsley)
> ½ cup grated cheese

Salt to' taste
Pepper, if desired (Linda doesn't use pepper,
 but I do)
5 eggs
About half a cup of marsala wine, poured into
 a bowl
Marinara sauce

Mix together all ingredients *except* wine. When rolling
meat mixture into meatballs, moisten hands frequently with
the marsala wine. Fry gently in olive oil until browned.
Serve with your favorite marinara sauce (heated), with or
without pasta.

■ ■ ■

■ Pasta Caruso ■

This recipe came from my friend Fred Caruso, who produced *The Rat Pack* and *Blue Velvet* for HBO, and was
production manager on the first *Godfather* movie.

3 slices Italian pancetta, chopped (American
 bacon may be substituted)
1 small onion, diced (use Vidalia or Maui for a
 sweeter flavor)
3 cloves garlic, diced
½ medium red bell pepper, seeded and diced
A "splash" of olive oil (about 1 tablespoon)
12 green olives, pitted and chopped (if stuffed
 with pimentos, discard the pimentos)
12 large black olives, chopped

3 tablespoons capers, drained
3 tablespoons sun-dried tomatoes, chopped
1 6 oz. can tomato paste (save this can for
    measuring)
1 6 oz. can red wine
1 6 oz. can water
½ can (not tightly packed) Italian parsley,
    chopped
½ can (not tightly packed) basil leaves, chopped
1 tablespoon Italian seasoning (available in
    spice section of supermarket)
1 tablespoon dried oregano
1 pinch cayenne pepper
Salt and fresh ground black pepper to taste
Grated Romano cheese (any brand)
1 lb. spaghetti (Fred suggests the De Cecco
    brand as best for this dish)

Have all your ingredients prepared and lined up in order of
use prior to beginning to make the sauce. Use small bowls
or water glasses.

In a large hot skillet, over medium heat, render the chopped
pancetta until crispy. Add the onions and a splash (about 1
tablespoon) of olive oil. Cook over medium/low heat until the onions are transparent. Add garlic and red pepper.
Cook 5 minutes.

At this point: Bring a large pot of water to boil for the spaghetti. Add salt to water just before tossing the pasta into
the boiling water. Cook per directions for al dente, usually
12 minutes.

Back to the sauce: Add the chopped olives, capers, and
sun-dried tomatoes. Cook for another minute. Add the to-

mato paste and stir well. Cook for 3 minutes, then add the wine, water, and seasonings. Simmer a few minutes. Now: Remove a cup of the hot pasta water. If sauce is too thick, add a few tablespoons of the pasta water.

As soon as the pasta has reached al dente, drain the pasta and toss it with the sauce. Serve with the grated cheese. Serve (and cook) with a good sangiovese or chianti wine. Serves 4. (Leftover Pasta Caruso is delicious the next day, when reheated in microwave.)

■ ■ ■

■ Della's Italian Chicken Stew ■

3 skinless, boneless chicken breasts (or 6 half
   breasts) cut into big nugget-size pieces
½ cup olive oil
Salt and (fresh ground) pepper for seasoning
   chicken breasts
6 bell peppers: red, yellow, orange, sliced in
   1-inch strips (don't use green peppers)
3 oz. prosciutto ham, chopped (packaged, in
   deli section of market)
4 cloves garlic, peeled and chopped
1 28 oz. can of diced tomatoes
1 cup white wine
1 cup chicken stock
1 tablespoon fresh thyme leaves
1 tablespoon fresh oregano leaves
Only if needed: a little more salt and pepper, to
   your taste

NOTE: If serving immediately, include the following two ingredients, but if making for next day only add them when reheating the dish:

> 2 tablespoons capers
> ¼ to ½ cup Italian parsley (fresh and cut up
>   with kitchen shears)

Heat olive oil in a Dutch oven over medium heat. While heating, season the chicken breasts with the salt and pepper. Brown the chicken breasts on both sides. Remove from Dutch oven and set aside.

Into the Dutch oven, put strips of pepper and prosciutto and sauté over medium heat until peppers are tender and prosciutto is browned, about 9 or 10 minutes. Add garlic and cook for no more than 1 minute. Add tomatoes, wine, fresh thyme, and oregano leaves. Stir thoroughly to combine, including the browned bits from bottom of the Dutch oven.

Add the chicken back into the Dutch oven. Add chicken stock and bring to a boil. Reduce heat, cover the Dutch oven, and simmer for about 15 minutes, until chicken is thoroughly cooked. (If you prefer chicken with the bone in, cooking to doneness will take longer, 20 to 25 minutes.) Taste to see if you need to add salt and pepper. (You probably won't. Remember that the capers will add a bit of salt.)

This dish is best if "rested" for a day. (Cooled to room temperature, and then stored covered in refrigerator overnight.) When getting ready to reheat to serve next day, add 2 tablespoons of capers (drained), and ¼ to ½ cup of chopped or cut up Italian parsley.

Reheat in the Dutch oven over medium flame. When ready, serve with rice, or with boiled baby gold or red potatoes (skin on), or with mashed potatoes. I like to make mashed potatoes that are half potatoes and half cooked spinach, chopped.

■ ■ ■

■ Penni Crenna's ■
Mexican-Style Chicken Kiev

Penni Crenna, wife of actor Richard Crenna, always loved making meals for her family and doing the cooking when they gave parties. Her Mexican-Style Chicken Kiev was a great favorite with their guests. When I made it I understood why.

Don't preheat oven, because this needs time in the refrigerator before baking.

> 4 whole skinless, boneless chicken breasts,
>   halved
> 1 large can (approximately 16 oz.) whole green
>   chilies
> ¼ lb. Jack cheese
> 1 cup fresh breadcrumbs (but you can also use
>   prepared dry crumbs, unseasoned)
> ¼ cup grated Parmesan cheese
> 1 teaspoon chili powder
> ½ teaspoon garlic salt
> ¼ teaspoon ground cumin
> ¼ teaspoon ground pepper
> 6 tablespoons butter or margarine, melted

Pound the chicken breasts between two pieces of wax paper until each is about ¼ inch thick.

Slit the green chilies into halves lengthwise and remove seeds (unless you want this dish hotter), then cut into 8 equal pieces.

Cut the Jack cheese into 8 fingers about ½ inch thick and 1½ inches long.

Combine the breadcrumbs with Parmesan cheese, chili powder, garlic salt, ground cumin, and ground pepper. (Penni makes her own breadcrumbs: instructions below.)

Lay a piece of green chili and a finger of Jack cheese on each of the chicken pieces. Roll them up to enclose the filling. Tuck ends under. Dip the bundles into melted butter, drain briefly, and then roll in the crumb mixture to coat evenly. Place bundles seam-side down without sides touching in a 9 x 13-inch baking dish. Drizzle remaining melted butter over all. Cover and chill at least 4 hours, or overnight.

When ready to bake, heat the oven to 400 degrees F.

Bake uncovered in a 400-degree oven for 20 minutes or until chicken is no longer pink when slashed. Remove to a serving platter. Serves 8.

NOTE FROM DELLA: Penni served this with black beans, rice, and tortillas. I like to add salsa and guacamole.

FOR PENNI'S HOMEMADE BREADCRUMBS: She takes the crusts off slices of white bread and chops the slices in the food processor. Then she mixes these crumbs with the spices listed in the recipe above.

▪ Seana Crenna's Quiche ▪

Seana, actor Richard Crenna's daughter, grew up in Hollywood, but instead of going into show business, she earned a Masters in Psychology and went to work with troubled adolescents in residential facilities. When I asked her how she handled them, she said, "Bring homemade Goody Bars and the kids will do anything."

This quiche is an easy main course for a luncheon or for a light dinner. Seana says she usually serves it with mini muffins and Caesar salad.

> *1 single piecrust: refrigerated, frozen or*
> *   homemade (see note below)*
> *2 cups cottage cheese (low-fat and small curd)*
> *3 eggs (room temperature and beaten)*
> *½ cup shredded Swiss cheese*
> *½ cup shredded Gruyere cheese*
> *2 or 3 green onions (white and green parts)*
> *   finely chopped*
> *1 cup French-fried onion rings in a can*
> *   (crushed with your fingers)*
> *Salt & pepper to taste (I use about ¼ teaspoon*
> *   salt and ⅛ teaspoon ground pepper)*

Prick the bottom and sides of the unbaked piecrust and bake according to the package directions. (Or the directions in your cookbook if you make the crust from scratch.) When the crust is light brown, remove from oven and cool on a wire rack.

Preheat the oven to 350 degrees.

In a large mixing bowl, combine cottage cheese, eggs, cheeses, green onions, salt, and pepper. Hand mix until thoroughly combined.

Pour mixture over cooled piecrust and bake for 30 to 40 minutes until the quiche has puffed (about ½ inch).

Pull out the oven rack beneath the quiche and cover the quiche with the crushed onions. Then continue to bake until the onions appear lightly toasted—about 5 more minutes.

Remove from oven and cool for 5 or 10 minutes before serving.

NOTE FROM DELLA: For homemade crust, I recommend the standard pastry recipe for an 8- or 9-inch one-crust pie in Betty Crocker's Cookbook.

■ ■ ■

■ Penrose Anderson's ■
Tomato Soup

This recipe is from British author Penrose (Penny) Anderson. She wrote for Thames Television in London, is a published poet, and is also a voice-over actress. She said her favorite voice job was in *Warhammer*, a fantasy video game in which she got to play both the High Elf and the Dark Elf, contrasting characters she described as the "video game's version of *Jekyll and Hyde*." When Penny's not providing the voice for various animated characters, she's working on a novel.

2 tablespoons butter
1 large white onion, finely chopped
1 clove garlic, crushed
5 red ripe tomatoes
1 tablespoon tomato paste
4 cups chicken broth
1 bay leaf
1 teaspoon basil (or 1 teaspoon herbes de
  Provence, if you have them)
Juice of ½ lemon
Salt and freshly ground black pepper (to taste)
2 tablespoons parsley, finely chopped, to
  garnish

Sauté onion and garlic is hot butter for 3 minutes, until softened. Add quartered tomatoes, tomato paste, chicken broth, bay leaf, and basil (or *herbes de Provence*). Put into a blender. Pulse *briefly* so as not to liquefy, but to have bits of tomato visible. Pour into saucepan. Add lemon juice, salt, and pepper. Return soup to simmering point. Garnish with chopped parsley. (*Della's note:* I like Italian flat leaf parsley.) Serves 6.

■ ■ ■

■ Charlotte's Irish Soda Bread ■
(Irish Scone/Pan Bread)

Richard Fredricks is a former Principal Baritone of the Metropolitan Opera, television, and musical theater. Before show business, he was a sonar man, in the Submarine Service. Richard was kind enough to share this recipe from his mother, Charlotte, who was born in Londonderry, Ireland.

> 3 teaspoons baking powder
> 1½ teaspoons baking soda
> 1½ teaspoons salt
> 4½ cups unbleached flour
> 1½ teaspoons nutmeg (to taste)
> ½ cup currants (some cranberries are nice for variety)
> ½ cup raisins (or just a wee bit more)
> 2 handfuls of chopped walnuts
> 2¼ cups 2% buttermilk

Lightly flour a dry, cured 10-inch iron skillet and set over a low flame to preheat.

In a large mixing bowl, sift together all dry ingredients four times. Add currants, raisins, and chopped walnuts and fold them until coated with dry mix.

Make a well (hole) in the center and add all the buttermilk at once. Fold together (with two large, strong spoons) until thoroughly mixed, adding buttermilk as necessary to make it moist, but not overly wet.

Make a big ball of the dough (pushed away from the sides of the bowl with the spoons) and lightly flour the top and sides, lifting and working the flour under the ball as you rotate the bowl. Lightly flour as needed to be able to transfer the moist mix to the hot skillet.

When the entire surface of the ball is lightly floured, place it in the center of the heated pan and gently flatten it out until the entire pan is filled to the edges.

Cook approximately 20 minutes on the first side. With a large pancake turner or spatula, gently left the scone to see that it is sufficiently well browned, then turn it over by tilting the pan to meet it as it is gently "flipped." The second side takes approximately 18 to 20 minutes.

Pierce the center with a knife to determine when the soda bread is done: dry to slightly moist, nice light to moderate brown crusting.

Remove from heat, wrap in terry-cloth towel, and place on a rack for cooling (the oven rack is fine with the door open) until just warm. In half an hour or so, you can slice off a piece or three and begin to enjoy one of the simple but elegant pleasures of Ireland, complemented by a lovely cup of tea, with milk and honey. Refrigerate the scone in a large Ziploc bag with as much air removed from it as possible. To reheat, slice off pieces in ½ inch slices and warm in the toaster or toaster oven.

Richard says, "Oh, such a delight, delicious—plain or with butter, jam, or both, or a smidgen of marmalade."

■ ■ ■

▪ Betty Pfouts's ▪ English Plum Pudding

½ cup brown sugar
1 egg, well beaten
½ cup softened butter
½ cup milk
½ cup currants
½ cup raisins
1 cup flour
1 teaspoon baking powder

 1½ teaspoons allspice
 1½ teaspoons cinnamon
 1½ teaspoons nutmeg
 1¼ teaspoons cloves
 1½ teaspoons salt
 ⅓ cup dark molasses
 ½ cup walnuts, coarsely chopped

Put 5 cups of water into pressure cooker with rack in the bottom.

Combine sugar, egg, and butter, mix until smooth. Add milk, currants, and raisins. Sift together all dry ingredients and add gradually. Mix batter well. Add nuts.

Turn into a buttered bowl or mold that may be set loosely in cooker. Cover the bowl with wax paper, securely tied. Place the bowl on the rack with water in the cooker. Close the cover on the pressure cooker securely. Allow steam to flow from the vent pipe for 20 minutes. Place pressure regulator on the vent pipe and cook for another 40 minutes. Let pressure drip on its own accord. Serve warm with Brandy Hard Sauce. (Recipe follows.) Serves 6.

BRANDY HARD SAUCE

 ½ cup butter
 2 cups powdered sugar
 ⅓ cup (about) brandy

Cream butter with sugar, add brandy, and blend to taste and form. It should be firm, not stiff, at room temperature. It softens on warm plum pudding.

NOTE: If a Lemon Sauce is preferred, substitute the juice of a lemon and a pinch of salt for the brandy.

▪ Della's Italian Pot Roast ▪
(in a Crock-Pot)

4 medium potatoes, peeled and cut into 6 pieces
     each
1 package fresh baby carrots (approximately 4
     cups)
1 stalk celery, cut into 1-inch pieces, including
     the leafy tops
2 diced Roma plum tomatoes, with seeds
     removed
2½ lbs. boneless beef chuck roast
½ teaspoon freshly ground black pepper
2 cans tomato soup (10¾-ounce can—I prefer
     plain Campbell's tomato soup)
¾ cup water
1 bulb of roasted garlic (see method below)
1 teaspoon dried basil
1 teaspoon dried oregano
1 teaspoon dried parsley flakes
1 teaspoon white distilled vinegar (ONLY white
     distilled)

TO ROAST GARLIC: place a whole garlic bulb on a piece
of aluminum foil and drizzle over it a little extra virgin
olive oil and wrap it up. (Twist top of foil to make it look
like the garlic bulb is in a little sack.) Roast in a 350 degree oven for 45 minutes. When it's soft, open the garlic
bulb enough so that you squeeze the roasted garlic out
onto a little dish or piece of wax paper or foil. Discard
the casing.

Place the potatoes, carrots, celery, and diced Roma tomatoes into the bottom of a Crock-Pot slow cooker. Season the

roast with the fresh ground black pepper and place roast on top of vegetables.

In bowl, mix together the tomato soup, water, garlic (squeezed out of the roasted bulb), basil, oregano, parsley flakes, and distilled white vinegar. Pour over the meat and vegetables in the Crock-Pot.

Cover and cook on LOW for 12 hours.

After 12 hours, remove the roast from the Crock-Pot and let it rest for at least 20 minutes before carving. It should be pink inside. I pour the vegetables and the juice (sauce) into a saucepan and reheat just before serving. I ladle some of the hot liquid over the slices of pot roast and vegetables. Serves 6.

NOTE #1: There are likely to still be vegetables and sauce left over after the meat has been consumed. I heat this up in a saucepan and serve in wide-brimmed bowls, like pasta bowls, as a hot vegetable soup lunch, with thick slices of bread for sopping.

NOTE #2: There is, intentionally, no salt in this recipe. There is some salt in the tomato soup, but I don't salt the roast. When the pot roast slices and vegetables are served, if you feel you want a little salt you can add it then, but taste it first to be sure.

WITHDRAWN

continued . . .

Praise for
Killer Mousse

"A delectable novel full of delicious moments and charming characters . . . An appetizing debut!"
—Earlene Fowler, national bestselling author of *Love Mercy*

"Melinda Wells provides an exciting, tightly plotted culinary thriller that will keep you on the edge of your seat."
—Nancy Fairbanks, bestselling author of the Culinary Mysteries

"A treat—a classic culinary mystery . . . blending an artful plot with engaging characters in a fast-paced whodunit."
—Harley Jane Kozak, Agatha, Anthony, and Macavity award–winning author of *Dead Ex*

"[A] wonderful combination of mystery, romance, redemption, and girl power."
—Linda Dano, Emmy Award–winning actress and author of *Living Great* and *Looking Great . . . It Doesn't Have to Hurt*

"A scrumptious morsel of mystery and mayhem. Take a pinch of murder, a dash of danger, stir it all together . . . An amateur sleuth to savor!"
—Linda O. Johnston, author of the Kendra Ballantine, Pet-Sitter Mysteries

"With verve (and recipes) Wells cooks up a tasty puzzle with a likable protagonist." —*Richmond (VA) Times-Dispatch*

"How nice to discover a story that breaks that mold."
—*San Jose Mercury News*

"It will be a winner for readers who like a well-written book with a deftly plotted mystery . . . Not one to miss. [Wells's] future as a writer is a bright one." —*Front Street Reviews*